CHASING THE BANGKOK DRAGON

ALSO BY K. E. KARL

Our Man in Mbabane: A Novel Based on a True Story
The Red Door and Other Stories

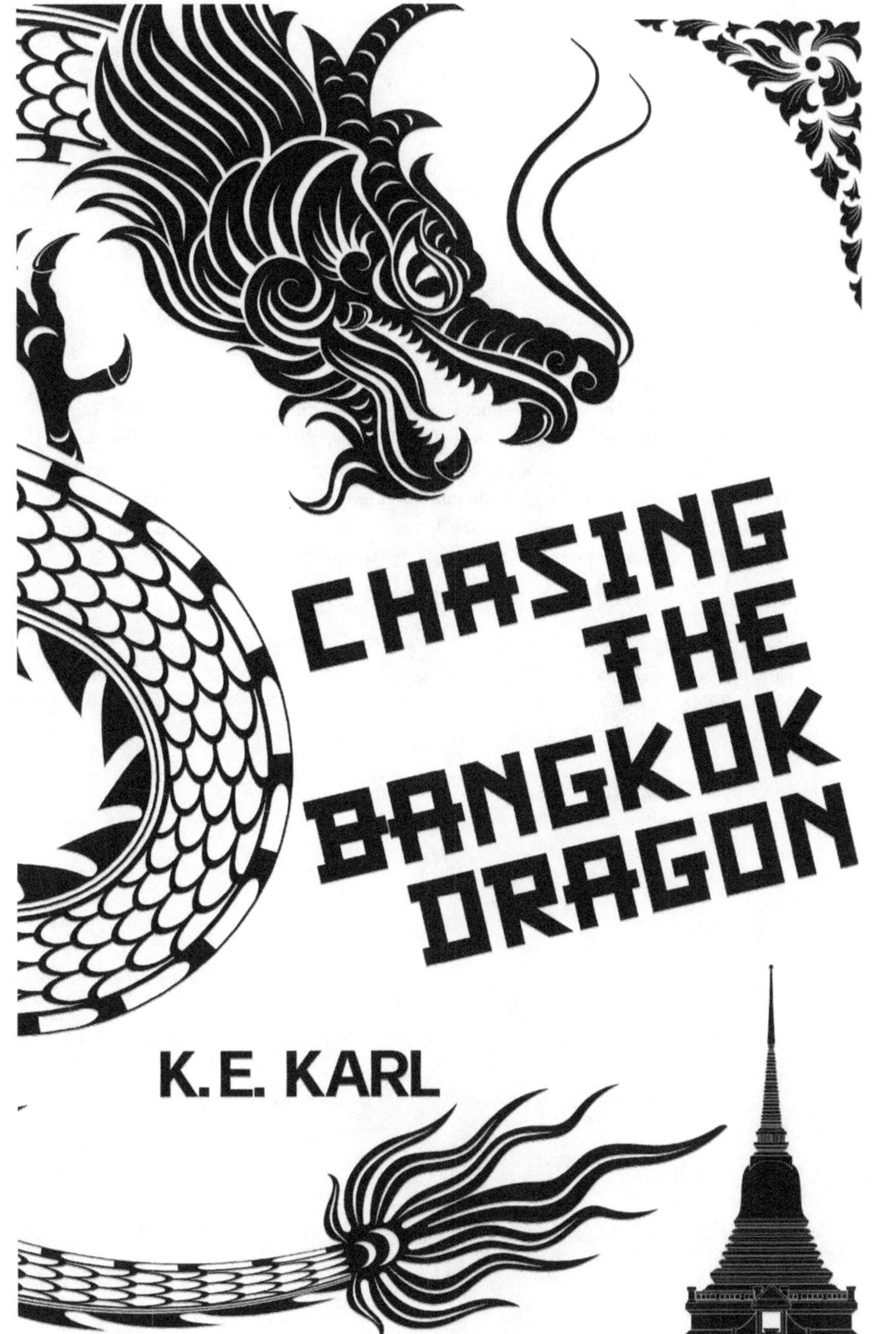

CHASING THE BANGKOK DRAGON

K. E. KARL

Hardback ISBN 979-8-9870141-5-8
eBook ISBN 979-8-9870141-6-5
Softback ISBN 979-8-9870141-7-2

Book and design by Matthew Revert

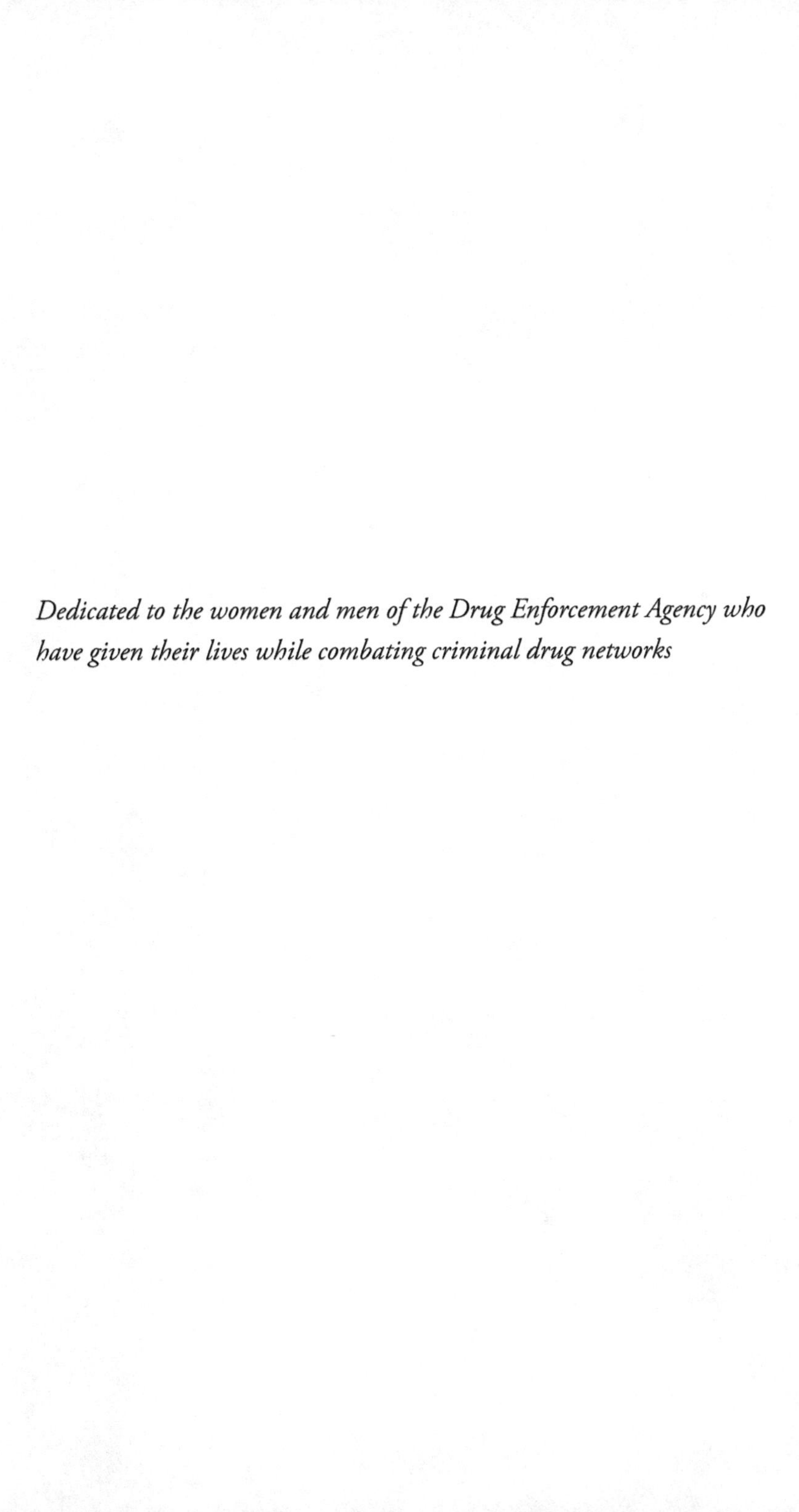

Dedicated to the women and men of the Drug Enforcement Agency who have given their lives while combating criminal drug networks

CHAPTER 1

June 1984

"You mean I'd have to carry a gun?" Thomas asked, his voice cracking.

He stared in disbelief at Stan, who sat on the other side of a table in an interview room. They were buried deep in the Drug Enforcement Agency building, where they both worked—Thomas in a research unit and Stan in human resources. The bleached-out room was unadorned save for a large one-way mirror. Its furniture consisted of the tired-looking brown table, dented with marks from dropped staplers, that separated the two men and classic oak high-school teacher's chairs, with slats at the back and a groove for your butt on the seat. A single fluorescent light glared from the ceiling, casting an intense light into the chamber, which smelled vaguely of Mr. Clean.

Stan had invited Thomas to the meeting to discuss an interesting "opportunity." After more than ten years with the DEA, Thomas was eager for a promotion. And at thirty-five, he knew he needed to kick it up a notch if he wanted to advance his career. However, an advancement with a gun in his hand? He'd had a corner office with a window in mind.

"Sometimes. Yes," Stan Stephens said. "But an experienced agent will always accompany you. The main reason we want you in Bangkok is your language skills. No one, except your partners and your station chief, should know that you speak Thai."

Thomas resisted the urge to turn around to find the spot behind him that Stan was staring at.

"We're finding that we are at a tremendous disadvantage when we negotiate with our Thai partners and when we use interpreters for interrogations," Stan continued.

Thomas had never met Stan before this meeting, but he remembered seeing him at his recent Thai language class. After the class had ended, he'd glanced back and seen Stan speaking to his teacher. He'd gotten an email from Stan the next day inviting him to this Monday morning meeting.

Stan was in the DEA's local HR department, but he apparently also handled agents assigned to overseas missions. He had the personality of a brick—no emotions affected him, nor did he emote. When Thomas had greeted him warmly upon entering the room, Stan had shaken his hand but hadn't reacted other than to look at his forehead. Thomas had then placed his resumé on the table, facing Stan, who had ignored it. Thomas squirmed, thinking Stan had already sized him up for an assignment and judged him unfit for the task.

Stan had read the memo on "How to Dress Like a Bureaucrat." He wore a gray suit, a white shirt, and a black pencil tie. His gray fedora rested on the table to his right. He was dark in complexion with jet-black hair slicked back on his round head. Medium height with wide shoulders, he was straight out of central casting for a government official.

In contrast, Thomas wore a brown wool sports coat, cotton slacks, and a blue tie. Thomas stood a couple of inches over six feet tall, had a crooked nose, unruly brown hair, and looked like a back-office researcher. Which he was.

"Interrogations?" Thomas asked, picking up where Stan had left off.

"Sometimes you will need to support our other staff when they are questioning Thais."

"So, it's my language skills that qualify me for this job?" Thomas couldn't understand why Stan was speaking to him now as if he had offered him a job already. He fidgeted in his chair, shifting from one hip to the other.

"That and your high level of security clearance."

"But I've never fired a handgun." He recalled his skills with a .22 rifle. He'd won a shooting contest when he was in the Boy Scouts, but he had never used a revolver. The trick his dad had taught him before he died was to aim with the sights and squeeze the trigger gently.

"You will get a standard field-agent training course. You will pass."

"How do you know?" *I'm guaranteed a job and a passing grade for the training? This is too bizarre.*

"We'll make sure you have sufficient support and enough chances to get through the program."

"OK," Thomas said, unconvinced. "And what is it exactly I'll be doing in Bangkok?" Thomas liked the idea of returning to work in Thailand; he had fond memories of the country from his Peace Corps days. He'd lived for two years in a village outside of Surat Thani, teaching mathematics and English to high school students. To communicate better, he became fluent in spoken and written Thai. Now, ten years after leaving Thailand, he took Thai language classes to maintain his language skills and to spend time with his buddy, Jermaine.

"This is a special undercover unit of the DEA. Ostensibly, you'll be an employee of a charity organization, The Orson Group, which provides support for drug rehabilitation centers. You'll be working at its Bangkok office, reporting to the local head, Alex Butler. You'll do some government liaison work, visit our rehab facilities, and attend charity events. Surreptitiously, you'll be working with one of our best field agents to thwart a drug syndicate that keeps eluding us. We have information that they are behind the new drug that is increasing overdose deaths.

"For you, this will be a short-term assignment. They're short on staff, but we're short on funds. So, we're looking for a current DEA employee to fill this role, and you fit the bill perfectly."

Thomas found the discussion of guns and interrogations troubling. He enjoyed playing *Mario Bros*, not *Battlezone*. How much training would he need to be a real field agent, maybe even using a gun on a drug bust?

"Sounds serious."

"It is. We'll give you a new identity and alter your looks slightly, so no one you met while you were living in Thailand will know for sure it's you."

"Alter my looks?" Thomas imagined himself clothed in bandages like the Invisible Man. His face turned pink.

"Yes. Slightly."

"Not a whole new face?" Thomas asked, his eyes darting back and forth, moisture beading on his upper lip.

"No, that's not necessary. How long have you had the broken nose?"

"Since I was fourteen."

"Good. Before you leave for Thailand, we'll fix that."

Thomas touched his nose reflexively and realized he'd like to have a straight nose.

"Assuming you get back after a successful mission, you'll return to your old identity. It will make it hard for these drug people to trace you."

Assuming I get back? Thomas broke into a sweat, and he felt his cheeks flush.

"But you can keep the new nose."

"Gee. Thanks. And, uh, you said 'assuming I get back,' which means what?"

"It doesn't always happen that way."

"Excuse me?"

"Our last fluent Thai language agent didn't make it out alive."

Thomas struggled to find a comfortable position in the unforgiving chair as his mind raced to absorb what he had just heard.

Did Stan think that this was a selling point? Or did he think Thomas was crazy?

"Thanks for that, Mr. Stephens. Very useful and informative." Thomas, though he could barely speak the words, couldn't resist a deadpan joke that he knew Stan wouldn't grasp.

"Call me Stan."

"Would I get a pay raise or something, Stan?" Thomas didn't want this job, but neither did he want to antagonize someone in HR; maybe Stan would have a safer option in the future.

"Yes, thanks for asking. You get fifteen percent extra for an international assignment. The Bangkok office will pay your rent, and you'll have a food stipend. Upon successfully completing your assignment, we would promote you one pay grade."

"Thanks, Stan, that sounds generous." Doing some quick calculations, Thomas estimated the amount of money he could save with those remunerations. But then there was the minor detail of survival.

"This would be a big change for me, so I'll have to think about it and perhaps consult with a friend." Thomas was thinking of Jermaine, his longtime buddy. Mostly, he wanted to get out of the room and was relieved he'd come up with this stalling device.

"You can discuss going to Thailand on a short-term assignment and the specific benefits, but you cannot mention the undercover work you'll be doing. No one must know. You'll need to keep your new identity and passport hidden from your friends and family."

"I understand," Thomas said, wondering if talking with Jermaine was a good idea. But he couldn't disappear without saying something.

"You'll need a legend."

"A legend?" asked Thomas, crinkling his forehead in puzzlement.

"Yes, a legend. You'll tell your friends that you're going to Thailand on a short-term research project. While there, you'll use your language skills to learn more about Thailand's role in the international drug trade. Sound good?"

"Oh, my cover story. Yes, that's fine."

Stan focused his eyes on Thomas's face, looking through him as if seeing the door behind him. Then he stood and launched into a sales pitch as he marched back and forth within the confines of the small room, never glancing at his interviewee. He told Thomas he would do great work for his country and its citizens, protecting them from a deadly new drug. Mom, Pop, the flag, and even apple pie figured in his spiel. The odd part was he delivered it as if he were reading from the back of a cereal box.

When Stan was done with his speech, he charged around the table and stuck out his hand. Thomas leapt to his feet, nearly knocking over his chair. While Stan crushed his hand, squeezing the blood out, the room collapsed in on him.

"I know you'll do the right thing," Stan said, pumping Thomas's arm while staring at his brow. "And don't worry about the field-agent aspects of the work. You're unlikely to be needed for any drug raids. Also, we'll train you so well at our facility in Georgia, I'm sure you won't have any problems. And you'll be working with excellent agents. You'll be fine. I'll give you a week to decide."

I'll be fine? The last guy died!

That evening, after a day of futilely trying not to think about the interview, Thomas stuffed his papers into his backpack, jammed his baseball cap onto his curly mop, and headed out. His hair pushed out from under the hat on both sides, creating a comical look. Exiting, he shoved thoughts of the morning's meeting to the back of his mind.

On his way to the Metro, he checked the headlines at a sidewalk newsstand. Not only was Mondale behind Reagan in the polls, but Geraldine Ferraro—his VP pick and the first female candidate on a presidential ticket—was getting hammered by the press. Expectations for the Redskins were high, despite their blowout January loss to the Raiders in the Super Bowl.

When he emerged from the Capitol South station, he had to maneuver around a couple of homeless people. One muttered to himself, his eyes glassy, his hands twitching. Crack. Thomas had joined the DEA because his dad had died young from an alcohol-related disease and his brother, also an alcoholic, occasionally used drugs. He hoped to reduce addiction in the US, but sometimes the latest epidemic seemed overwhelming.

As he approached his building, a tabby cat jumped out of the shrubs in front of a house and raced across the sidewalk in front of Thomas, chasing a mouse. The rodent disappeared into a hole near a tree planted in the pavement, frustrating the predator. The cat pulled up abruptly and stared at the entrance of its prey's burrow. Thomas shook his head; if he took the job Stan offered, he'd be like that cat pursuing an elusive prey. More likely, he'd be a dead cat. What was he thinking? He was no secret agent. However, the money intrigued him, and his career needed a boost. On the brink of middle age, he wanted a brighter future.

Thomas brooded as he mounted the stairs to his apartment, the top floor of a row house. Cocaine wasn't the only problem; heroin devastated some cities. The drugs streamed in from around the world. Stan got one thing right—fighting the drug epidemic would help people in the US. Could he be more useful in hindering heroin production in Thailand? Could anything stop the cartels? More pertinently, could he survive packing a gun in the alleys of Bangkok?

While he cooked, Thomas thought about how to broach the job offer with Jermaine, whom he'd invited to dinner. His friend sat at his glass kitchen table on one of its clear plastic chairs, nursing a beer and reading the *Washington Post*.

"I got an offer today for a short-term assignment in Bangkok," Thomas said after deciding on a direct approach. He shook two haddock filets in a paper bag filled with flour, salt, and pepper, then placed the dusted products on a paper towel.

His flat had a simple décor: white modern minimalism. The cabinets and even the appliances were white—stove, fridge, dishwasher. He'd covered the refrigerator with colorful magnets to cut down on the glare.

Sitting at the table, Jermaine stretched his long legs in front of him as he read. He was also tall, about six feet, but much broader than Thomas, with hulking shoulders and biceps almost as large as Thomas's thighs. As big as he was, he walked with a languid ease Thomas envied. No one would guess by looking at him that he was a nerd, but Thomas knew his friend loved everything technical.

Jermaine didn't look up from his paper. "Huh?"

"The DEA wants to send me to Thailand for a short period."

"How long?" Jermaine's head popped up, but he gazed at the wall, not Thomas.

"Six months if everything goes well." He put the filets into the skillet, while the potatoes fried and the string beans steamed.

"How long if it doesn't go well?" He turned to Thomas, eyes wide, mouth open.

Thomas realized he would have to improve his lying techniques. "It could be shorter, but probably not longer. Either the assignment works, or it doesn't." He neglected to mention the brief tour might mean he would return in a body bag. He loathed being deceitful, but what else could he do?

"What *is* the assignment?"

Thomas reiterated the cover story that Stan had provided.

"Might be interesting. Is it more pay? A chance for a promotion?"

"Yeah, both."

"Cool. You should do it." Jermaine returned to his newspaper. Then his head rose, and he focused on the calendar tacked on the wall. "But then you'd be away for six months. Who will I hang out with?"

"Yeah, I'd miss you too."

"Never mind. I'll be fine. You should take the job. It sounds like a great gig." Jermaine turned to Thomas, nodding his approval.

"Maybe I'll phone my sister and talk to her. She always provides good advice. I need to phone my brother too—his birthday is coming up. But he's no help on these things." Thomas dished the fish, potatoes, and beans onto two plates and set them on the table, along with two fresh beers.

"Sure, it can't hurt to discuss it with others. It's a big decision."

Yes. So big, I can't even talk about it. Why am I even considering it?

CHAPTER 2

Arriving at work the next day, Thomas slung his backpack onto the L-shaped desk in his cubicle. His office had one defining characteristic: it was gray. Dark gray fabric covered the modular walls of the cubes, while the desktops had a lighter shade of gray. The carpet? Gray. The rectangular drop-down ceiling tiles housing the too-widely spaced fluorescent lights had originally been cream colored but had since faded to an indescribable shade of soot. Downsizing had left many of the square workspaces empty. Thomas had chosen his space out of eight in their windowless area. The arrangement of the cubicles in blocks of two created a "cross" that separated them. He had picked the middle of the X, across the aisle to the right of Bryce, the only other employee in this zone. After making coffee in the kitchen, he sat at his desk.

"Thomas, how are you?" Wade asked from right behind him.

Thomas lurched forward, splashing the coffee he was sipping onto his desktop. Wade liked to take him by surprise when he asked for help with his projects, which he did frequently. He covered Eastern Europe because he could read all the languages except Hungarian, at least according to him. He spoke fluent Czech because his mother was born in Prague and his maternal grandparents lived with him when he was growing up. Wade had a PhD in languages from Yale and never let you forget it. He dressed impeccably in Canali suits and Ferragamo ties and always had one of those fake hankies in his breast pocket.

Does he think he works at Goldman Sachs? Thomas shook his head.

"I'm fine. You?" Thomas asked, irritated by the sneak attack and immediately suspicious. He wiped the coffee from his desktop and rubbed his wet hand on his sock.

"Sorry, I didn't mean to startle you, but I have a question for you."

"OK. What?"

"I'm writing a paper about Poland's economy and its drug usage. As usual, there's not much information, but I read an article about young, working-class people using more drugs. Have you done any research on the connection between drug use and income?"

"Sure. I discuss it in several reports," Thomas sighed. Wade would know he had—if he bothered to read any of Thomas's papers.

"I've written this article, but I'm unsure if my line of argument is clear." Wade plodded on, intent on his own agenda. "Could you look it over for me and make suggestions and change anything you think might be out of line? You do this so well for someone who didn't go to an Ivy League college. I really appreciated your help on my last paper about Romania."

"OK. Yeah. Sure. I'll look it over," Thomas groaned, ignoring the backhanded compliment.

"Thank you, Thomas. You are a *real* sport and a *terrific* analyst."

"Yeah, you're welcome." Thomas dropped his head and let out a deep breath. He'd been helping Wade for months, and there was no end in sight. No amount of coaching on how to improve his writing helped. But if he didn't fix Wade's reports, they could lower the reputation of their unit, which was perennially under threat of elimination.

Wade walked over to Bryce's cubicle across from Thomas. Bryce Flowers was nearly blind and wore coke-bottle glasses. As usual, he was hunched over reading something, his face about six inches from his computer screen.

"What're you seeing today, Bryce? Maybe if you get closer, it'll become clear," Wade said, putting his hand on Bryce's desktop and leaning over to view the screen.

"It's a p-p-paper on Colombia abou-bout a d-d-drug kingpin," Bryce said.

"Is tha-that r-r-right?" Wade mocked with a huge grin on his face.

Thomas walked over and confronted Wade. "Leave him alone."

"We were just having a pleasant conversation. Weren't we, Bryce?"

Bryce ducked his head but said nothing.

"I said leave him be, Wade."

"Just having a little fun, Thomas. No harm in that."

"If you want me to help you with your paper, I suggest you stop bothering Bryce."

Wade looked at Thomas, grinned mischievously, bowed his head, flourished his arm, and said, "As you wish, sire." Then he sashayed away.

Thomas returned to his seat.

"Th-thanks, Thomas."

"Oh, no problem, Bryce. If he ever bothers you again, let me know."

"Su-sure."

Thomas returned to his cubicle and looked over Wade's report. Though Wade spoke and read many languages, he lacked analytical capabilities, and his writing style bordered on stream-of-consciousness chaos. Frustrated, Thomas walked to their editor's office. Their boss, Theo, had assigned Jane Fleming a converted closet because of her smoking habit. No one else on their team had an office, not even Theo, though he had an extra-large cube and a window. They were lucky to have Jane—she was extremely talented. She made their output sing with clarity and conciseness. *If* it was reasonably intelligible to begin with. Unfortunately, this disqualified Wade's work.

Braving the smell of burning tobacco, Thomas knocked, then entered Jane's office and sat down. She looked up from across her desk, her head barely breaching the height of it. Her eyes narrowed to slits behind her bifocal, rimless eyeglasses. She ruffled her mop of blond hair, an attempt to tame it in the face of company that only increased its disarray.

"This is totally incoherent," Thomas said, waving Wade's report at Jane.

"Another stellar work of art from Wade?" Jane asked, arching her right eyebrow. Her eyes squinted as she took a drag on her cigarette and blew out a cloud of smoke.

"How did you guess?"

"Why do you agree to review his papers? You never say 'no,' and you let him push you around."

"I don't know. It would be embarrassing for our department to circulate his raw work."

"Well, I can tell you, I can't work on it until you—or someone—fixes it. I think I'm a capable editor, but I need semi-literate English before I can improve it. Wade's writing doesn't meet that standard. So, thanks for helping me. We're a team, and I need support sometimes."

"I know. But what's the solution? He's the only person with the language skills to read this Eastern European stuff."

She shrugged. "I gave him a copy of Strunk and White's *The Elements of Style,* and he's taken a composition course. Even so, his writing stinks. He must have paid someone to ghostwrite his Yale dissertation."

"I wouldn't put it past him. Yet he thinks he's the cat's meow."

"More like the cat's hairball."

"That's good. I like it." Thomas paused to reflect, then added, "What are we going to do?"

"You beat up his paper, bash it into something comprehensible, and I'll take it from there."

"OK. Another day, another dollar. Ugh."

Back at his desk, Thomas put his head in his hands, releasing his breath in a long blast. Then he drew in some oxygen, lifted his head, grabbed the paper, and began looking it over. He'd need to rewrite it from scratch. He could understand what Wade meant to say but needed to put it into a logical, clear thesis. Fixing his colleague's gibberish frustrated Thomas. How could he ever get ahead at work if Wade's rubbish took up so much of his time? Maybe he should consider the Thai job after all?

Several hours later, just before 5 p.m., he finished Wade's piece and turned it over to Jane. It was time for his Thai language class. He packed up his things and headed out, pushing Wade's paper from his mind. He skipped out of the building, smiling at the prospect of speaking Thai. Also, Jermaine was in the class, and they always went for a drink afterward.

Stepping into the late afternoon of a sunny, warm, humid DC day, Thomas joined the other civil servants who were pouring out of their buildings and clogging the wide sidewalks, then standing in clusters at corners, waiting for the stoplights. A faint breeze eased the heat and carried the scent of the cedar trees from Franklin Park. He walked several blocks to the classroom, enjoying the perfect day. Cars flooded the streets, but at the crosswalks everyone waited as the more-established workers drove to the suburbs. Thomas wove his way through the streams of young people on the street and ducked into a small building. Eschewing the ancient elevator, he took the stairway two steps at a time.

Thomas and Jermaine settled into their usual booth in the far corner of O'Malley's after picking up their beers at the bar. A typical Irish pub, O'Malley's had a long wooden counter lined with stools and a row of booths opposite. Irish paraphernalia decorated the wood-paneled walls—flags, Guinness and Harp signs, adverts for Irish whiskey, and shamrocks.

The class had gone well. Thomas made sure he didn't dominate the session, and Jermaine had chipped in with a couple of amusingly mangled Thai phrases, getting a chuckle from the other students. Their native Thai instructor was always patient and supportive, simply correcting the students' errors. Thomas, at the teacher's request, often wrote Thai script on the board, even though she didn't expect the other students to learn it.

"That weird guy didn't show up this week," Jermaine said. "Who was he, do you think? He never said a word and sat there with his trench coat on and a dark look on his face."

"Oh. He's the HR guy recruiting me for the Thailand job." Thomas's voice was devoid of emotion, but his hands were clammy, and his temples ached. He had the urgent desire to tell Jermaine the details of the work. Could he trust him? Of course he could! Thomas remembered the first time he had met Jermaine at a Boy Scout camp.

The Scout Masters had randomly assigned Thomas and Jermaine to the same bunkhouse, but they had barely spoken because, coming from different middle schools, they were in separate troops.

At the end of one day, as Thomas approached their cabin, he saw three scouts shoving Jermaine and shouting at him.

"Hey, leave him alone!" Thomas yelled at the trio.

"Fuck off! This is between us and the monkey," the leader of the pack snarled. Thomas recognized him as Vern, a bully from his school. The other two were Micky and Jack, who often hung out with Vern.

Thomas stepped in between them, putting his hands up to separate them. "I said, 'Stop!'"

Vern swung a right cross into Thomas's nose, sending him to the ground. "Get out of the way!"

Jermaine hit Vern in the eye, rocking him backward. Micky and Jack jumped at Jermaine, then grabbed his arms to restrain him. While they held him, Vern punched Jermaine in the stomach, making him keel over. Thomas leapt up and slammed an elbow into Jack's head, allowing Jermaine to free his right arm, which he used to whack Micky in the face. Vern dove into Jermaine's midriff, hoping to take him down. But Jermaine stepped back and slammed him hard in his lowered head, and Vern went to his knees. Meanwhile, Jack, infuriated at Thomas's attack, had knocked Thomas down to straddle and pummel him. Thomas covered his head with both arms to ward off the blows. His nose seared with pain, but he kept Jack occupied—his role in this inequitable fight.

With Vern on his knees, Jermaine turned his attention to Micky. He grabbed the smaller opponent, lifted him, and rammed his head into a nearby tree, knocking him out. Vern sprang onto his back, taking him into the dirt. Between Vern and Jermaine, it was a fair match; both were about the same size and build. They rolled in the dust until Vern got on top of Jermaine and raised his right fist, but Jermaine grabbed his arm, then twisted and lifted his hips to slide Vern forward on his chest as he smashed his knee into the middle of Vern's back, sending him over his head. A left punch to the stomach and a right jab to his face bloodied Vern but didn't slow him down.

They jumped up, and Vern hit Jermaine in the face. Jermaine then ducked out of the way of a one-two combination and smacked Vern in the gut. He followed up with an elbow to Vern's skull, stunning him. Jermaine seized his advantage and tripped Vern, knocking him down. Jermaine hurtled himself on top of Vern and thrashed him until he conceded by throwing up his hands to surrender.

"OK, Jack. We're done here." Vern coughed out the words. "Let's get Micky back to our bunkhouse."

Jack hit Thomas one last time and stood up. When he turned, Jermaine sent him reeling with a wallop to his jaw. Jack moved to attack Jermaine but then looked at Vern, still crumpled on the ground, and backed away.

Jack and Vern picked up Micky, who was now conscious enough to shake his head. The three of them staggered away.

"Thanks," Thomas said from his prone position on the ground.

"You're a lousy fighter. You need to work on that."

Thomas laughed, "You got that right. But I kept Jack busy."

"You did. Thanks for that. Three would have been too much for me," Jermaine said, his hands on his hips. Flecks of blood covered his face, and he panted heavily.

Thomas struggled to his feet and checked his nose to see if it was broken. It was. Over the rest of the camp outing, the pain eased, and the bone set into a crooked gnarl.

After that, Thomas and Jermaine were friends, watching each other's backs through high school and taking fighting lessons together. Jermaine excelled while Thomas improved. Later, they went to the same college and then joined the Peace Corps, Jermaine in Swaziland, while Thomas went to Thailand.

Part of their connection was an enthusiasm for electronics. As teens, they used their Cap'n Crunch whistles to phone their long-distance pen pals. At university, they both took computer programming courses, learning FORTRAN and BASIC, which enabled them to create silly games. After they finished their foreign assignments, they both landed jobs in DC. Jermaine worked at the Bureau of Economic Analysis, a big government statistical office. Aside from drinks after studying Thai and taking boxing lessons, they also enjoyed trying to hack into computers—especially government departments—just to see if they could do it. Their success was moderate and always benign; the fun came from the challenge of getting into the systems.

Thomas leaned over the tavern table and said, "I'll need you to keep this to yourself."

"What? Sounds serious," Jermaine said, his head jerking back, eyes widening.

Thomas explained what he knew of Stan's proposal to Jermaine, who listened with his temple nearly touching his pal's forehead, his eyes studying Thomas's face as if he were electronically scanning it.

"Are you nuts?" Jermaine hissed. "What do you know about cloak and dagger stuff? I'll tell you—nothing!"

"I don't know. It's definitely intriguing. It might help my career. The pay is good. But, yeah, it could be dangerous." Thomas leaned back, flustered.

"Could be dangerous?" Jermaine gasped, with a panic Thomas had never seen before. "You said the last translator died! You'd be crazy to do it. Say no, flat out. Turn. It. Down."

"You're right. I don't know what I'm thinking. I had another lousy day at work improving one of Wade's moronic reports. Thanks for listening and advising me." His headache eased.

Jermaine leaned back in the booth and breathed a sigh of relief. "No problem. That's what friends are for. I'm glad that's settled."

Jermaine surveyed his friend to assure himself it *was* settled. Then he grinned, and his eyes twinkled. "On a completely different subject, have you thought about meeting Chloe, the woman I told you about? I think the two of you would really hit it off."

"Thanks, Jermaine, but I don't think I'm ready yet. It went so badly with my last girlfriend. Her lies exhausted me. I need some more time."

"Suit yourself, and let me know when you change your mind."

"I will. Thanks, man. You're a good friend."

By the time they left O'Malley's, dusk had descended on the warm early summer evening. His burden lightened, Thomas asked his friend to dinner at a nearby Greek restaurant. While there, Thomas drank most of the bottle of Assyrtiko they shared; Jermaine sipped on one glass of wine. After the meal, Thomas lurched home and collapsed into bed.

In the night, he had a weird dream. He watched his brother, Russ, on a merry-go-round that was spinning out of control. Thomas chased Russ as he spiraled around on the accelerating carousel. Every time Thomas grasped at Russ to get him off the horse he rode, the carousel lifted Russ out of reach. His sister, Maddie, shouted at them from across the playground, "Don't take any drugs!" Thomas whirled around and shook his head at her. Was she talking to him, Russ, or both of them? He turned back to grab Russ, but the ride had slowed down, and his brother was nowhere to be seen. He awoke.

After he shook off the nightmare, Thomas couldn't get back to sleep. His skin itched, as if he'd fallen into a patch of poison ivy. His head pounded like kettledrums, so he treated himself to some individually wrapped chocolates he kept in the fridge. He tucked his pajama top into his bottoms and dropped five of them down his shirt, cradling them; they tasted better after warming up on his belly. He made coffee and ate the softened sweets. His body felt like he'd been sleeping on a stone beach, and his head was an inflated balloon about to burst, but the black brew and the chocolates eased the aching and prickliness.

Over breakfast, Thomas remembered it was his brother's birthday, which gave him the idea to stay home from work and phone Russ. He called in sick, hoping his coughing would dispel thoughts of the real reason: his hangover. Russ lived in New Orleans, so Thomas dialed his number at ten o'clock in DC, nine in NOLA, which would be before Russ started drinking.

They'd been close when they were young, at least until Thomas turned seven. He'd looked up to Russ, six years his senior. But as Thomas aged, he understood his brother differed from him and his sister. Their mom had always said it was because Russ had fallen off his bicycle and cracked his head on the curb when he was thirteen. He'd gone to the hospital and had never been the same after that. Years later, Thomas read that head injuries in young people could change their conduct, causing angry outbursts and impulsive behavior.

One time, when the family was picnicking near a stream on a hot summer day, Thomas dived into the water, thinking he could cross the stream, but the current was too strong for him and the water was deeper than it looked. He bobbed up and down, gasping for air as the water swept him away. Russ jumped in after him and caught him a moment before he crashed into a boulder. Thomas was angry that he hadn't made it to the other side and pushed his brother away. But Russ persisted and dragged him to safety on a small, sandy beach. Russ stood over him, hands on his hips, panting from exhaustion and exasperation. Thomas, eight at the time, burst into tears. After a few minutes, he looked at his brother and said, "Thanks. Sorry I shoved you."

The cloud on Russ's face cleared. He took a deep breath and said, "The rapids are dangerous here. I'm glad I caught you in time."

That was one of the last fond memories Thomas had of his brother. The six years didn't help; the gap grew wider when Russ entered high school. He always got into trouble. There were fights, detentions when teachers caught him smoking, beer parties with his peers, and a car crash. Thomas was a straight-A student, never in trouble—or at least too clever to be caught. Over the years, they'd kept in touch but were never close again. Now, Thomas called or visited Russ. Russ sent a card for his birthday each year and a box of pears or maybe a voodoo doll at Christmas, but he never phoned or came to DC.

"Hey, Russ. Happy birthday! How're you doing?"

"Hay-lo. I'm good, I'm good. Tanks. Be celebrating at my local today. They usually spot me a drink on my big day." During his years in New Orleans, Russ had picked up his own unique good-old-boy accent.

"Cool. Good to hear. You'll be with friends." Thomas could hear Russ moving around his kitchen and pictured him, phone in hand, long yellow cord stretching from the wall. It sounded like he was preparing breakfast—eggs, bacon, and toast, most likely.

"Yeah. Unless they throw me out."

"Nah. Not on your birthday."

"I gotta bottle of the good stuff at home if'n they do."

"Are you making a cake?"

"Nah, I hate cake. I'll bake some of my fresh sourdough for dessert."

"I envy you that—best sourdough in New Orleans."

"Yup."

"No other plans?"

"No golf today. My buddy Mike will join me for lunch at the bar. We'll stumble back to his place."

"OK. Well, don't overdo it."

"When have I not?"

Thomas and Russ talked about old times, their last visits—separate—with their mom before she died and what was happening with their sister, Maddie, now on her second husband. Thomas enjoyed catching Russ when he was sober. Later in the day, his brother's rambling thoughts would cascade freely from his addled mind, producing an interesting, but incoherent, jabber. Thomas worried about him; his smoking and drinking weren't good for his health. He knew, too, that Russ sometimes experimented with drugs—whatever was cheap on the streets. An extremely risky activity. Still, he was getting by on his pension from the navy and the occasional construction job.

Thomas and Maddie understood that the head injury was only part of the problem. The rest of it came from their mom and dad. Ellen and Richard Sebastian were functioning alcoholics. As an adult, Thomas had learned that growing up in such an environment often pushes the children into stereotypical roles; he had seen it in his siblings. Russ was the bête noire and Maddie was the caregiver, while he was the peacemaker. Adopting a character part allowed them a modicum of control over the chaos that blasted from their parents. It was a coping mechanism; everyone knew their task.

Their dad, Richard, died shortly after Thomas turned fifteen—cirrhosis of the liver. The alcohol and his smoking habit took him early. His untimely death created financial problems, stressing the family further. But Thomas and Maddie were soon in college with scholarships, and Russ was already in the navy. As for their mom, Ellen continued working as a bookkeeper until her health failed her. Cancer. She died after Thomas turned thirty. After their tumultuous home life, the three children found careers in stable environments.

While Thomas and Russ chose government jobs, Maddie worked in hospitals as a social worker, helping patients and families cope with death and disease.

When their mom was dying in the hospital, she spoke to him about Russ. She had a tube in one arm, and her voice quavered. The words had rattled out of her, barely audible. "Take care of your brother, Thomas. Russ needs help and love." She died a few days later. When Thomas told Russ, he replied, "I'm older. I be takin' care of you, bro." The logistics of minding his brother when he lived a thousand miles away troubled Thomas.

Shortly after Thomas got to work on Thursday, Stan called and made an appointment for the afternoon. Thomas knew he would make another pitch to convince him to take the job, but he agreed to meet because he didn't want to antagonize anyone in HR. After the phone call, he tried to work on his latest paper about Thailand but had difficulty focusing and made little headway.

They met in the same room. Stan asked Thomas whether he had any concerns about taking the position. So Thomas pressed Stan about the risks of the work in Thailand. Stan reassured him that nothing dangerous was likely to happen but that he would need training because it was protocol. Training would include physical drills, coaching in hand-to-hand combat, and practice with weapons. It would last twelve weeks, and he'd be in great physical condition afterward. Stan concluded their discussion by repeating that he did not expect Thomas ever to face a perilous situation. The more Stan said it wouldn't be risky, the more Thomas worried it *would* be. Not knowing what else to say, Thomas said he would think about it and let Stan know by Monday. He couldn't bring himself to disappoint

Stan; the guy was so eager to have him take the job.

Thomas slogged through the rest of Thursday and stayed late, exhausting himself. At home, right before he fell asleep, the phone rang, and he rose to answer it.

"Thomas, I have some bad news. Are you sitting down?" his sister, Maddie, asked, her voice thick with anguish.

Thomas's throat constricted, and a ball of pain formed in the middle of his forehead. "Yes," he said, though he stood where the phone hung on the wall.

"Russ is dead."

"What?" The news hit Thomas like a sledgehammer to the heart, and suddenly he was sitting on the floor.

"His friend Mike got in touch with me today. Apparently, he and Russ were on a bender yesterday. I could hardly understand Mike; he bawled so much. But I gather Russ wanted to experience a new street drug. Mike stuck to whiskey, but Russ took some and never woke up."

Thomas saw his brother's smiling face morph into the photos he'd seen of OD victims, their faces contorted with rigor mortis. They'd spoken just yesterday! The memory of Russ's happiness about his birthday plans crashed into the reality of his death. A wave of guilt flowed through his body as he recalled his mother asking him to care for his brother. He worked at the DEA to stop these overdoses, and now narcotics had taken his brother? This wasn't fair! His stomach bucking with grief, he rolled onto his side. Then he grabbed the counter and pulled himself upright and willed his brain to stop swirling.

"Shit. Do we know what it was?" he asked, panting.

"Something called the Bangkok Dragon."

CHAPTER 3

Thomas's body teetered. His apartment looked the same, but the white walls and cabinets glared at him. The decorative magnets on the fridge shrieked, hurting his eyes and ears.

Though he and his brother had been distant for years, he still clung to fond memories from when they were young. Russ wasn't that old; he'd turned forty-one the day before. He had always been careful when doing drugs, making sure he didn't take too much. Russ told him once that he knew he had not developed a tolerance to heroin or cocaine, so he was always careful. Though he sometimes experimented, alcohol and cigarettes were his vices of choice. He'd never OD'd before, so this narcotic must have taken him by surprise—even a small dose must be deadly.

At the office the next day, he couldn't stop thinking about Russ and this new drug. Before settling into work, he visited the DEA's library to scan the back issues of the *Times-Picayune* to learn more about narco-trafficking in New Orleans. He learned that, though crack was more popular, opioids were also available. Small neighborhood gangs, or "cliques," distributed the drugs. Hoping for more information, Thomas phoned the DEA number in New Orleans and left a message. It was a two-person regional office, so he wasn't sure he would get a response, even after stressing the urgency of his request. But a couple of hours later, an exhausted-sounding young man, the analyst of the team, returned his call. Thomas explained his situation, and the agent expressed his regrets and condolences, but mildly chided him about calling this "urgent." When Thomas asked about the Bangkok Dragon, his colleague explained it was heroin with some kind of additive. They'd had many overdoses lately from this particularly lethal blend. Their informants believed that the heroin and the supplement came premixed from Thailand, hence the name.

After the call, Thomas slumped and laid his head in the crook of his elbow on his desk. After about half an hour of that, he shook himself. He needed to find out more about this deadly additive. How could he not go to Thailand now? From there, he could learn about it and its role in the drug trade and then stop it from coming into the US. He couldn't do that while working at his desk in DC.

He told his boss about his brother's death and that he couldn't continue working today. Then he went home.

Thomas stood in his empty apartment, doubting the floor beneath him, thinking he might slip through it into the flat below. He needed a friend to console him and be sympathetic, so he met Jermaine for dinner after telling him the news. His spirits weakened by his grief, Thomas left early, having finished a bottle of wine. Over the weekend, he filled the hours with busywork to avoid thinking too much: he shopped for food, dusted and vacuumed the apartment, cleaned the bathrooms, and got the grease and grime off the stove and its overhead fan. He went for a run each day and cooked his favorite recipes for dinner—steak Diane on Saturday and mussel linguine on Sunday—and washed the meal down with Sangiovese and Gavi. But the food and wine tasted bland. He couldn't stop thinking about his brother Russ.

Soon after he arrived at his desk Monday morning, Thomas phoned Stan to let him know he would take the assignment, saying his brother's recent death tipped him toward accepting. Stan spoke for ten minutes. Not a word of sympathy. Was that enthusiasm Thomas heard? He had clearly made Stan's day, if not his week. Stan repeatedly expressed his happiness at Thomas taking the job. How many ways did he say it? Several. Stan said he could get the nose job next Monday, recuperate for a week, then go to training. Why wait? He'd clear everything with Thomas's current boss.

Thomas shook his head throughout the entire conversation. At least someone was happy, but Thomas just felt numb. Stan's excitement in response to his decision, made because his brother had died, jarred him.

After he hung up the phone, he stared at it for half an hour, wondering if he was looking forward to this career shift, if one could call it that. He couldn't tell. Mostly, he felt empty. No more birthday calls with his brother. No more drunken weekends in New Orleans. No more voodoo dolls for Christmas. But he had a reason to go to Thailand, an important mission to accomplish. A purpose. He also knew he'd enjoy returning there but couldn't feel that right now. It was an ephemeral thought and remote—like smoke he couldn't grasp.

Other than stepping out quickly at lunchtime, Thomas spent the rest of the day racing to finish a report due by the end of the week. He told Bryce he'd be out next week, then most likely leave for training, followed by an assignment in Thailand.

"Wh-what'll I do about W-wade?" Bryce asked.

"Just ignore him. But I got you this, which should help. Put on the earphones if he bothers you and play some music." Thomas handed Bryce the Sony Walkman he'd picked up on his lunch break.

"Wow. Th-thanks, T-thomas. I…I d-don't kn-know what to say. Th-that's s-so kind of you."

"Hey. It's nothing. You'd do the same for me."

"Yeah. I'll h-have a g-gift for you wh-when you come home."

"Thanks, Bryce. You're a good man. I look forward to that."

A week later, after his surgery, Thomas stayed at home, resting, his nose swathed in a giant bandage. He took a couple of days to travel to New Orleans, where he, his sister, and Russ's buddy Mike attended a service for Russ at the VA cemetery. A sad, short affair. While he recuperated, he read, relaxed, and walked in The Mall or along the C&O Canal. Having worked at a desk for a decade, he wasn't in top physical condition. The training he'd done had been sporadic, depending on when he and Jermaine had time to work out or take a martial arts class. His walks served more to clear his mind than to get in shape before his training began next week. But the training assessment wouldn't be a problem; Stan had assured him he would eventually pass it.

At the end of the week, he took his bandage off and saw his red and swollen nose in the mirror. It would require a month to fully heal, but it was no longer bent.

On his last evening in DC, while Thomas washed the dishes after another elaborate meal he had prepared, the phone rang.

"This is Instructor Jim Westhoff, your drill master for the training you start tomorrow."

Thomas straightened his spine and pulled back his head. "What can I do for you, sir?"

"I want to make a few things perfectly clear. I spoke to Stan Stephens, and he said you *had* to pass this training course. This is a rigorous course. You will get *no special treatment* from me for any reason, certainly not because of Stan. You'll have to pass this course on *your merits*. Finally, if you do any drugs or alcohol while in training, you will be out the door so fast your head will spin for a month. Yes, I know about your brother—he was an alky and a druggy. That was my son you spoke to in our New Orleans office. Now, do you understand what I'm saying?"

"Yes, sir. It's perfectly clear."

CHAPTER 4

Thomas woke up late on Monday morning and hurried through his breakfast and coffee. He needed to pick up a rental car and get to the DEA training center in Glynco, Georgia, by six that evening, and it was about a ten-hour drive.

When he got to the rental agency, he couldn't believe the length of the line. He should have thought that Monday morning would be peak time. The drive was long and uneventful, but he had the same problem in returning the keys—a long wait. And the cab arrived after a half-hour delay.

The person at the front desk of the training center directed him to a classroom where everyone was being briefed; he'd need to check into his assigned quarters afterward. Lugging his suitcase, he finally walked into the classroom at 6:03 p.m. The other trainees sat in rows facing Jim Westhoff, who was briefing them.

"Thomas Sebastian, so good of you to join us," Jim said. "I hope we haven't inconvenienced you too much."

"Sorry to be late," Thomas said.

"Sorry to be late, *what*?"

"Sorry to be late, sir!"

"In the future, you will always be on time, or you will do fifty push-ups. Are we clear?"

"Yes, sir!"

Thomas found a chair at the back of the room and sat down. Apparently, everyone had already checked in and had their rooms assigned because no one else had luggage with them.

Jim summarized the course and stated the rules, emphasizing three: no phone calls during training, no fighting, and no drugs or alcohol. Then he handed out a leaflet with the physical requirements for the program. One requirement caught Thomas's eye: he'd need to finish a one-and-a-half-mile run in ten minutes. Thomas knew from high school gym classes that he wasn't great at running distances. After about half a mile, he slowed down considerably.

He looked around the room. Most of the men and the two women were young. Certainly under thirty years old. Only one other person, a male, was about his age of thirty-five years.

After the briefing, Thomas returned to the front desk and got his room assignment. He crossed the yard to the barracks and discovered that his roommate was the person closest in age to him. Or should he say "cellmate"? The room was about the size of a prison lockup with two single beds, two four-drawer dressers, and a small wardrobe. Its bleak severity reminded him of his college dorm room. But at least the room smelled like clean sheets, and there were no bars on the window.

"Dinner's at seven thirty," Thomas's roommate said when he entered the room. He sat on his bed, his hands patting his knees as if to comfort himself.

"Thanks for the dining tip," Thomas replied, extending his hand. "I'm Thomas, by the way."

"Sorry. I'm Howie. Howie Fowler." He stood, and they shook hands. Howie's hand was moist, limp, and flaccid in Thomas's firm grip. "What happened to your nose?"

"I got it straightened. Its deformity blocked my breathing," Thomas said, making up the last part. His nose was still swollen and a little red.

Thomas reviewed his surroundings and wondered what was agitating his roommate. Howie had chosen his bed and staked out his dresser by placing a picture of a woman on it. The wardrobe was already nearly full of his things. Howie had a doughy soft face, thinning dirty-blond hair, and a thirty-pound paunch. He had remained standing, pulling things out of his suitcase, his back turned to Thomas. His hands trembled while he folded his underwear to put in his open bureau drawer.

"Your wife?" Thomas asked, tilting his head toward the photo. Howie's head snapped toward Thomas as if he had forgotten his roommate was there.

"Yes. Amy. We've been married three years." Howie sighed and placed his hands on his hips, took a deep breath, and looked up at Thomas. "I'm sorry. I'm *really* nervous about this course. Everyone is so young and fit-looking! I'll have to lose weight to keep up, but you may have guessed that I enjoy eating."

"You'll do fine. At least you're not the *bête noire* of the class—I seem to have gained that distinction."

"He was very sarcastic when you got in late." Howie's eyes formed a question.

"Last night, he phoned me and read me the riot act because he took offense at someone in HR saying I had to pass this program." Thomas accepted the battle that lay ahead. It gave him more determination to succeed.

"Yes, I don't think he's going to cut us any slack."

"How long have you worked for the DEA?" Thomas asked, changing the subject.

"Five years—all in accounting. You?"

"Ten years in the research department." Thomas knew what was coming next.

"Oh, yeah, I've heard of that group. What do you do exactly?"

"We do country reports, which cover the economic, social, political, and drug issues in various countries." Thomas's response was firm and confident. He'd dealt with criticism of his unit frequently in the past, and he would not apologize for it; he took pride in his work even if others didn't find it so valuable.

"I guess that makes sense…" Howie said.

"The articles are useful for clarifying the status of our work around the world, and we estimate drug production and assess country interdiction programs."

"Huh."

"Yeah. That's what most people say. But the senior management finds it beneficial." Thomas had found this last comment to be the deal clincher; if the brass wanted it, then it must be worthwhile.

Howie nodded in acknowledgment, but his eyes said his mind was elsewhere. His face brightened when he suggested they go get their evening meal.

At dinner, they found an empty table, sat down opposite each other, and soon realized that no one was going to join them. However, as they were finishing their desserts, one of their fellow students sat down next to Howie.

"Hi. I'm Cole." They introduced themselves and exchanged pleasantries. Then Cole said, "I wanted to give you guys a heads up. You need to watch out for Fletch. He's that muscular guy with blond hair and no neck sitting behind Thomas."

"I see him," Howie said, his fork in midair.

"Don't turn around," Cole said when he saw Thomas shifting in his seat.

"What's he got against us?" Thomas asked.

"He's a hard ass and likes to pick on people who are vulnerable."

"I guess we qualify because we're older?" Thomas frowned.

"Yep. Older and probably slower."

"Thanks," Thomas said, his expression turning sour.

Cole looked at Thomas, blinked, and said in a near whisper, "Look. I'm only trying to be helpful."

"You're right," Thomas said. "And we appreciate it. Thanks for the information."

"Yeah, thanks," Howie said, staring at his empty plate like he'd lost a friend.

As they walked to their quarters after dinner, they encountered Fletch walking toward them. Just as they were about to pass each other, Fletch shoved Howie and said, "Out of my way, butterball."

Thomas and Howie pulled up and glowered at him. Fletch pushed Thomas in the chest and asked, "What are you looking at, big nose?" Then he walked away.

"Cole was right," Howie said. "But it doesn't make any sense. Why bother us?"

They both shook their heads and continued to their room.

The next day, Jim wanted to evaluate them on the key physical components of the course: running, hand-to-hand combat, physical strength, and accuracy at firing a pistol and a rifle. After breakfast and a warm-up, Jim separated them into groups of six for the 440-yard dash. Thomas's time of under one-and-half minutes pleased him, even though it was the slowest allowed. Cole ran it in fifty seconds; Thomas and Howie had learned the 440-yard dash was his race on his college track team. Though Fletch excelled at wrestling at his university, he could run—he qualified as well. Many of the others didn't finish under the time limit, but everyone came close, except for Howie, who had the slowest time in just under two minutes.

For the hand-to-hand combat, they worked out on punching bags and speed bags and lifted weights. In addition, there were instructions on defending yourself and attacking an opponent and some light sparring. But there were no fighting bouts. That would come later and be part of the final test. They needed, at a minimum, to bench press a barbell weighing their own weight less fifty pounds. Thomas could do 110 pounds, so he practiced on that, figuring he could work his way up to 125 pounds by the end of twelve weeks. Howie couldn't lift his 150 pounds but hoped he could lower his target by losing weight and gain strength to pass the test.

At the firing range, Thomas delighted in discovering he was one of the best with the rifle and even the pistol, a weapon he had never used before. Only Cole shot better.

The coach had saved the one-and-a-half-mile run for the last test of the day. Thomas started out well, but after finishing half of it, he slowed to a crawl and finished in just over ten minutes. From his high school running days, Thomas knew two things. First, he could not run two races in one day. Somehow, he would exhaust himself on the first race, and it'd take him twenty-four hours to recover. Next, something was not quite right with his blood sugar or endurance *or something*; he could not sustain any speed after running a half mile. He hoped his hard work would improve his distance running.

Cole, of course, had the fastest time, under seven minutes. He starred in their group, achieving the best at everything physical. His agility in hand-to-hand combat even surprised the instructor. A great all-around athlete, he shone in each of the activities. It was disgusting. Worse—he was a nice guy. Sometimes, Thomas wanted to hit him with a stick.

Each day followed the same schedule. The mornings began with physical activity, which was followed by target practice with various firearms. In the afternoons, they attended classes and delved into relevant topics, including drug trafficking, traffickers, and prosecution. They learned about highway interdiction, and—last but not least—they studied the legal and ethical aspects of their work.

Both Thomas and Howie found the classes and the shooting practice easy, but they struggled with the physical activity, especially Howie. However, his beer-belly continued to shrink.

On the third morning, when they were about to start the 440-yard dash, Thomas noticed Jim nodding at someone. Following his instructor's gaze, he saw Fletch give a quick nod, a shadow of a smile on his face. Fletch looked at Thomas, pointed his two fingers at his eyes and then directed them at Thomas. Thomas shook his head. *What's with this guy?*

As usual, Jim split them into five groups of six each for the run. When Thomas spotted Fletch in his group, he grew wary but put him out of his mind to concentrate on the run.

Their group began well from a staggered start and flowed into a single file on the far side of the track. Thomas could hear Fletch breathing heavily behind him, so he stepped up his pace. Thomas passed a couple of runners who typically slowed at the midpoint of the run, but Fletch kept up with him.

Then it happened.

As they reached the last curve to come down the home stretch, Fletch's foot came down hard on Thomas's heel, sending him sprawling. He hit the rubber/asphalt surface hard and rolled into the grass of the inner track. Without taking time to check for injuries, he pushed himself up as rapidly as he could and ran onto the track.

"What are you doing, Sebastian?" Jim shouted when Thomas came in last in his heat. "You're supposed to run, not take a break on the grass!"

"I got clipped from behind," Thomas replied, keeping his voice even as he took in great gasps of air. He'd given the run everything he had.

"That's the thing with you desk people—always an excuse," Jim retorted.

Later that morning, as usual, Thomas ran the one and a half miles too slowly. His sore knee and scraped thigh didn't help. He would have to step up his game if Jim and Fletch continued to play theirs.

A couple of days passed before Fletch was again in Thomas's group. Thomas kept ahead of his foe as best as he could and even tried slowing down, but Fletch stayed behind him until the last bend and again tripped Thomas.

The third time Thomas and Fletch ran in the same group, Thomas was ready for him. He knew the inevitable stepping on his heel would occur on the last turn, where Jim couldn't see what was happening. Instead of running smoothly, Thomas suddenly stuttered his step, slowing down, so when Fletch stomped on his foot, Thomas went down but flipped over swiftly and kicked Fletch's leg, sending him crashing onto the track face down. Thomas leaped up and ran, finishing in just under one and a half minutes. But Fletch was so shocked by Thomas's maneuver that he picked himself up slowly and finished over the minimum time.

"What the hell do you think you are doing?" Fletch demanded, confronting Thomas after the run.

Thomas looked at him, panting, his hands on his hips. Fletch shoved him hard, but Thomas didn't react; he just stepped back. Fletch moved closer to him and pushed him again on both shoulders. Thomas had planted a foot behind himself, so he only swayed with the shove, daring Fletch to do it again. A crowd formed around them.

"Why'd you trip me?" Fletch asked, spit flying from his mouth.

"You know why," Thomas replied calmly. He refused to escalate the confrontation, but he would not back down either.

"Hit him!" someone said from the surrounding pack.

Jim pushed his way through the group of trainees and jumped between Fletch and Thomas. "Back off!" he yelled, thrusting his hands into their chests, rocking them back. "You know the rule: no fighting!"

After Jim chewed them out, making sure he thumped both their chests with his stubby index finger, he told them to get back to work. The rest of the morning passed uneventfully.

"Fletch really has it in for you," Howie said to Thomas when they were back in their room, getting ready for dinner. Howie always ran behind the two of them, watching everything.

"Yeah, but the rule on fighting is strict, and I don't think Fletch will clip me again when we're running. I made him look bad." Thomas hoped his maneuver would stop the nonsense.

"Everyone sees what Fletch is doing."

"Yep, and nobody says anything. I feel like we're in high school; it's so childish. I'll deal with it. But, hey, you're getting better and losing weight. What do you think about how you're doing in the program?"

There's no point whining about Fletch. I need to focus on meeting the program's requirements and making sure I get to Thailand.

"I'm not sure I'll make it," Howie said. "I can't seem to improve on the one and a half miles."

"We need to stay focused and keep working hard," Thomas said, slapping Howie on the shoulder.

"Sounds plausible," Howie said. "You're doing OK. Your time keeps improving."

"Barely."

After failing to stymie Thomas at running, Jim harassed him on the shooting range. The coach would hover behind his scapegoat, then lower himself and give unneeded advice, suggesting adjustments to Thomas's position, critiquing the way he handled his weapon, and offering unnecessary instructions on aiming. But it didn't work; the DEA researcher was an excellent shot and kept his ear protection firmly in place, paying no attention to Jim. After a few days, Jim gave up.

The last week of training arrived, and it was time to qualify on the metrics for physical activity—running, hand-to-hand combat, physical strength, and accuracy on the firing range. In addition, they would take tests on the course material. Before handing out the awards, the school would provide one last chance on Friday to anyone who failed a physical requirement. On the first day, they all passed the coursework exam. On the second day, they tested everyone in the fitness part. The thirty recruits passed the tests for the straightforward exercises—sit-ups, push-ups, pull-ups, and weight presses. Everyone qualified on the running times, except Howie, who failed to finish the one-and-a-half-mile run in under ten minutes; Thomas passed, but with only a few seconds to spare.

For the hand-to-hand combat evaluation, the participants needed three minutes of contact with an opponent on a wrestling mat.

Jim paired Thomas with Fletch.

Thomas was glad he had spent years training to fight with Jermaine. He would need it to face off against Fletch, a stronger, heavier combatant.

Cole coached Thomas on Fletch's weaknesses. "Fletch is a wrestler," he said. "Don't go to the mat with him; stay upright. Fletch is shorter than you—use your height and reach. Remember that he's heavy and not so quick on his feet." It almost sounded easy.

It wasn't.

Fletch immediately went on the attack, racing across the mat to engage Thomas, so he dodged to his right, making Fletch work to catch him. After twenty seconds, Jim shouted at Thomas to stop running and start fighting. Thomas evaded Fletch one more time, but on his rival's next charge, he sidestepped to the left abruptly and tripped Fletch, sending him to the mat. Thomas waited for him to get up. As soon as he was on his feet, a furious Fletch ran straight at Thomas, who darted to the right and used Fletch's momentum to propel him down again. Fletch leaped up, and Thomas could see he would be more cautious for the rest of the fight. Fletch started to box with him. Thomas landed some blows, using his longer arms for the punches. But Fletch succeeded with many counterpunches and body strikes. He even got Thomas on the mat once, but before Fletch could leap on top of him, Thomas rolled over and sprang to his feet. The match proceeded for the full three-minute round. Although Fletch won the fight, Thomas had often held his own, giving many hits, but taking more.

When Thomas went to shake Fletch's hand, he got a good grip so Fletch couldn't crush his knuckles, but it wasn't necessary. To Thomas's surprise, Fletch looked him square in the eye as they shook hands. Was that grudging respect he detected?

"You fought well," Fletch said. "Good job."

"Thanks. You were better."

"Yes, but you hung in there."

Thomas's eyes widened, and he lifted his chin, appraising Fletch in this new light.

"He did a good job!" Fletch shouted to Jim, pointing his finger at him as he walked off the mat. Jim gave one brief dip of his head.

They both passed.

For Friday morning, Jim had scheduled Howie to run the longer race, his second and last chance to pass. The entire class showed up to watch, curious to see the outcome.

Jim stood at the start/finish line with his stopwatch. A mile and a half, six laps around the track.

"Ready, set, go!" Jim shouted.

Howie sprang out of his crouching position. Thomas encouraged him each time he came around the track, clapping and yelling, "Keep going! You can do it!"

On the last lap, Thomas knew it would be close, so he raced to the last bend to run alongside Howie to the finish.

But he had clocked in at seven seconds over ten minutes. Jim shook Howie's hand while he gave him the bad news.

When Thomas returned to their room before lunch, Howie was already packing.

"Sorry you didn't make it," Thomas said.

"Ah, hell, I lost some weight, and I'm in better shape than I've been for a decade. I'm heading home to Amy. I won't stay for the awards ceremony. Congratulations, Thomas. I knew you could do it." They shook hands.

"Thanks, Howie. I wish you could have passed with me."

Howie turned back to his packing, removing his things from the wardrobe, folding them, and placing them in his two large suitcases. Thomas's face drooped. He always thought they'd both make it through the program. Howie and Cole were the only two people he had connected with over the past twelve weeks.

"Nah. It's better this way," Howie said, talking to one of his bags, now overflowing with clothes. "Amy was never keen on my being a field agent. She married an accountant, not someone who puts his life at risk. Nothing's dangerous about spreadsheets. At worst, I might get a paper cut."

"I'm glad you're cool with how it turned out." Thomas stood in the middle of their room, shifting his weight from one foot to the other and tapping his hands against his thighs. He'd miss Howie, but even if he'd passed, they wouldn't see each other again. And they couldn't write to each other; Thomas was going undercover.

"Yeah, I'm good. You. You be careful and take care of yourself. Congratulate everyone for me," Howie said, turning and putting his hands on his hips. Then he grabbed his cases and strode out the door.

"I will. Bye, Howie," Thomas said to his colleague's retreating back, his voice choking.

The awards ceremony was anticlimactic. Everyone knew who had passed and who hadn't. Some people asked after Howie, and Thomas relayed his buddy's congratulations to them. When Cole took his award, the crowd bellowed a deafening roar. He held up his certificate and shook it a few times, beaming. Thomas received his award after all the others.

As Jim shook Thomas's hand, he said, "You're lucky I pushed you so hard during this course; otherwise you wouldn't have made it."

To which Thomas could only reply, "Yes, sir!" He lifted his certificate in the air and waved it. The crowd applauded politely, then turned away. The program was over.

While Thomas packed his kit to leave, Stan came into his room without knocking and walked right up to his recruit.

Thomas looked up. "What are you doing here?"

Stan stopped less than a foot from Thomas and said, "There's been a change of plan. You leave immediately for Bangkok." For the first time, Stan's stare penetrated Thomas's eyes, not his forehead. "The office needs you as soon as possible."

"I don't understand. Why the urgency?" Thomas rasped as he pulled his head away from Stan's face. He'd never seen Stan so intense.

"Thugs killed another one of our agents."

CHAPTER 5

"Umm…well, can I at least make a phone call?" Thomas asked, regaining some composure.

"Sure. Phone your mom."

"I meant Jermaine, my friend. I told him I'd see him when I got back. My mom's been dead for a while." Thomas noted that his mother's death made no impression on Stan.

"Sure, phone Jermaine, but don't tell him anything about what you'll be doing." Stan leaned into Thomas, eyes wide, looking for a response.

"Of course not."

They went to the guard at the front desk, who directed them to a room with a phone.

"If there are things at your apartment you want shipped over, maybe you can ask Jermaine to pack them for you. We can send someone to collect the stuff, then ship the things to you."

Thomas picked up the phone and got an operator to dial Jermaine's number. He told his buddy he'd passed the training program, relayed some of the more annoying experiences, and expressed his sadness about Howie not passing. Then, he gave his friend a list of things to pack for Thailand; his landlord knew Jermaine, so he'd have no problem entering the apartment.

Stan had stood staring at the wall while Thomas talked on the phone, but the moment the call ended, he pulled two booklets out of his briefcase and said, "Here's your ticket to Bangkok—you leave tomorrow from Atlanta. And here's your new passport and identity. Our document guy is a fan of Hemingway." Stan returned his gaze to the wall.

Thomas opened the passport to read his new name—Robert Jordan.

"Robert Jordan? But he dies at the end of the novel."

Stan looked at Thomas, his face vacant as always. "So?"

"Well, couldn't I have the name of a hero who lives and saves the day?"

"No, this is what you get. The hero dies?"

"Yes, Jordan is the hero in *For Whom the Bell Tolls*."

Stan bobbed his head, taking in this new information. "Like Davy Crockett?"

"Yes, like Davy Crockett!"

Stan kept nodding. "Like I said, our document guy likes Hemingway. He has a sense of humor too. He knew you had two first names. So does this Jordan guy."

"Thanks, Stan. That's reassuring."

Stan and Thomas shared a hotel room in Atlanta—government regulations. Early the next morning, Stan drove him to the airport, parked, walked into the terminal with Thomas, and stuck with him all the way to the gate. He evidently wanted to make sure Thomas got on the flight.

When they called his row, Thomas rose and shook Stan's hand, looking him in the eye. Stan focused, as usual, on the wall behind him.

"Safe travels and best of luck in Thailand," Stan said, his gaze in the distance. "I'll see you when you return." Thomas's head rocked back; this was the first time Stan had delivered an honest, optimistic message.

Even so, Thomas rushed to grab his hand luggage, relieved to leave his babysitter behind. Stan's total lack of emotion sapped Thomas's energy.

The flight was a cheap one, with layovers in Los Angeles and Taiwan. Thomas didn't exactly feel pampered. But he watched movies and read Le Carré's *The Spy Who Came In from the Cold*. That protagonist also died at the end of the novel. Not exactly what he had hoped.

During the journey, he had time to reflect on his upcoming assignment. Stan's news about the agent in Bangkok unsettled him. Was this assignment going to be more dangerous than he expected? Thomas knew he could handle translation work and all types of research, but he'd had only twelve weeks of training to be a field agent. Would he need to use those skills on this mission? And if so, how much? He felt like the unanswered questions were birds snatching tufts of hair from his scalp, leaving painful bald patches. The cramped seats exacerbated his uneasiness and made sleeping almost impossible. Throughout the thirty-hour journey, he considered himself lucky to doze a few times, his chin on his chest.

Thomas landed at about midnight, stepped out of the air-conditioned jet, and descended the stairs into a wall of heat and humidity. It hit him like a smothering feather pillow, stealing his breath as the gritty air clawed the back of his throat. He found a grimy taxi, whose driver grinned over his shoulder at him, revealing six teeth and many gaps. Thomas showed him the address of a hotel near the Orson Group office written in large type on an index card. His apartment wouldn't be ready until Monday afternoon. When he arrived at the hotel—a bare-bones affair but at least clean—he went straight to bed, awakening just in time to get breakfast at a nearby street stall. The *jok*—rice porridge with eggs and pork meatballs topped with chopped ginger and scallions—brought back fond memories of his

Peace Corps days in Thailand. He showed the address of the Orson Group to the hotel manager. Ignoring the gentleman's incomprehensible arm-waving directions, Thomas nodded politely and listened to his spoken Thai. Even with this verbal guidance, he still needed help from pedestrians as he wound his way through the confusion of Bangkok's alleys. Cars honked, the three-wheeled taxis—*tuk-tuks*—beeped, and the motorcycles revved. The throngs of pedestrians jostling Thomas reminded him of a time he visited New York City. However, the smell was all Bangkok—fumes from the vehicles and the scent of smashed mangos from the stalls he walked past.

Thomas entered the building carrying his luggage. He climbed three flights of stairs and arrived in a long hallway. At the opposite end of it, a woman, framed by the window behind her, sat at a desk, typing. She jumped up and glided toward him, her feet barely touching the floor. As she approached, she looked up at Thomas… way up. Slim and neat, she wore the standard female Thai business attire of blue skirt, white blouse, and black low-heeled pumps. She introduced herself as Lamai, Mr. Butler's assistant, then grabbed his bag and placed it inside a room before leading him to his boss's office.

Stepping into the wood-paneled space, Thomas saw a man sitting at an expansive desk with two chairs placed in front of it.

"Welcome to Bangkok, Mr. Jordan." Alex Butler, the head of the local DEA office, rose and walked around his desk to greet Thomas, now Robert. Alex was rotund and bald, with twinkling eyes and a grin that made his greeting superfluous. They shook hands. Hearing his new name startled but soothed Robert; his jet lag made everything surreal but reassuring. Still, he'd need to embrace it. *Robert Jordan, Robert Jordan,* he repeated to himself.

"Thanks," Robert said. "I'm glad to be here." In reality, he felt an overpowering fuzziness and exhaustion from the twelve-hour difference in time zones after more than thirty hours in planes and airports.

Alex returned to his seat behind the desk and waved both arms at a chair for Robert to sit facing him. Then he leaned forward, still beaming, hands spread wide on his blotter. Alex would have no trouble making friends at a party, but he was also resilient; he still oozed optimism, even though he'd lost at least two agents from his team.

While Alex beamed at him, Robert surveyed his surroundings. Behind the desk, a set of three double-hung windows framed the Bangkok skyline. An air conditioner in the far-right window whirred and blasted a pleasant breeze into the room. A globe lay on top of a two-door cabinet to the left of the desk. In the opposite corner, a six-chair conference table filled a good chunk of the square footage. Across from the entry, two enormous filing cabinets and a standing safe completed the décor.

"This is how our operation works here." Smile gone, Alex was all business now. "We are employees of the Orson Group, a charity that funds drug rehabilitation centers. We're Thai government approved, and we do a decent job of it. Lamai does the paperwork for that, distributes the money, and oversees our three Bangkok facilities. So, to the general world of Thailand, you work for an NGO. This means we must always be careful when we interact with outsiders, so we never reveal our secret mission. Clear so far?"

"Yes," Robert said, although his brain was firing on one cylinder.

"Good. But because we are DEA agents working to suppress and apprehend drug dealers, the police and government know what we really do. We work with them—helping on raids, trading information, etcetera. This worked well for a couple of years, but then we learned that the confiscated drugs were returning to the market within a few months. By using tracking devices, we established that contraband held by the police left their warehouses and showed up in the storage facilities of the local drug kingpins. Hence, our tactics needed to change. Are you following me?"

"Got it." The police are corrupt. Not exactly news to Robert.

"We have recently obtained permission from headquarters in DC to confiscate and destroy drugs. So, we work with the police, but we locate where the drugs are, and now we will steal them from the cops or the gangs, then burn the dope. We'll try to do this without letting the authorities know it was us. Make sense?"

"No," Robert said, more bluntly than he intended. "If we're working with the police, how can we steal drugs from them?"

"We exchange intel with the police and assist them on raids if asked. But once we know where the drugs are located, our actual mission is to destroy them, preferably before but even after the police have confiscated them. And do it without being detected or identified. We don't want the police excluding us from raids or actively working against us on the next bust."

"What's stopping the drug squad from figuring that out, fingering us to a drug gang, and having us eliminated?"

"Good question. It's international politics!" Alex exclaimed, leaning far back in his chair and grinning like the Cheshire cat, his arms thrown wide open, then he wrapped his hands behind his head and rocked in his chair. "The Thai government doesn't want the embarrassment of having the DEA lose its entire force in Thailand. They'd lose face with the US government, which has been very supportive of Thailand's progress. Through USAID, we've trained Thais in agriculture, science, health, and infrastructure development. We also buy Thai goods—rice and manufactured products. Through diplomatic channels, our president threatens economic sanctions and cutting off aid to countries that aren't sufficiently cooperative with our drug policies. So, the police haven't told the drug lords we help them. At least, so far as we can tell. The tricky part will be making sure no one knows it's us torching the narcotics."

"Sounds precarious," Robert said, his head swimming from the new information. He felt the jet lag pulling him underwater and took a deep breath.

"I'm sure it will work."

"Cloak and dagger," Robert said, all he could think to say, lame as it was.

"Yes!" Alex grinned at the comment. "It's also why we have undercover identities. When we return to the US, we can disappear into our real lives."

"Cool." Robert began repeating his name to himself again, hoping the mantra would make him look alert.

Alex hit a button on his desk, and—within seconds and without a sound—Lamai opened the door and entered the room.

"Lamai, could you bring Agent Cannon into my office?"

Lamai disappeared, and shortly thereafter a tall woman arrived.

"I'd like you to meet your partner, Senior Agent Andrea Cannon," Alex said, waving to her as she stood to the right of his desk. Robert rose to his feet in slow motion, the ache of fatigue weighing down his body. They shook hands, and Robert looked at her. She was his height, six-foot-two, and her pale gray eyes showed nothing but scorn. She had disheveled cropped blond hair, wide shoulders, and a grip that made him wince. Her short-sleeved shirt revealed arm muscles that put his to shame. His training had helped, but he would need to work out regularly to catch up. He could smell her sweat, and assumed she must have been in a gym most of the morning. Drips on her neck provided corroboration. Besides the shirt, her uniform included casual cotton slacks and sneakers. She wore no makeup but sported one adornment—a pair of silver-ball stud earrings.

"Agent Cannon," Robert said, shaking her hand and thinking about the aptness of her name; he thought of the phrase "if looks could kill." Then he remembered it was her cover name, given to her by the DEA. Her eyes burned into his like laser beams. "The Look" is how he came to think of it.

"Jordan," she replied with a hint of disdain.

"Now, Robert, have a seat, and I'll briefly explain our situation," Alex began.

As Andrea and Robert sat down, he said, "As you know, we lost Agent Colson recently. Colson was an excellent agent—"

"Way better than you," Andrea interjected with icy derision, turning her head toward Robert.

Robert's head jerked back, suddenly awake. Alex ignored the comment.

"—with many years of experience in the field. You will be his replacement, working with agent Cannon. You'll follow her instructions without question. She's one of the best field agents in the DEA. She can hold her own against any of our top US colleagues.

"I won't sugarcoat your assignment—it will be dangerous. I'm glad to hear you're good with weapons; you'll need that expertise here."

"Stan Stephens said the assignment wouldn't be dangerous. I'd be doing translation work. Surreptitiously." Robert's thoughts spun wildly and he let his shoulders slump forward. Recovering, he raised his chin, straightened his back, and returned Alex's gaze. In front of his new partner, whose contempt was palpable, he wanted to look strong. But he yearned for a bed and a solid night's sleep.

"Hah! Stan told you that. That's a riot. Gotta love Stan," Alex said, chuckling. Then he turned quiet and cajoling. "It's simple, Robert. Here, you report to me, and you'll do what I say. And exactly as Andrea says. Is that clear?"

"Yes."

"Good. It's true we want your expertise in the local language. Only Andrea, Sakchai—our other field agent—and I are to know that you're fluent in Thai. Not even Lamai. That is also important. However, we're short of staff because of the budget cuts in Washington, and I need you to step into some big shoes. It will take months, if not a full year, to find a full-time replacement for Colson, especially since this is the second agent we've lost in three years. I see nothing in your training report that says you can't make this level of commitment, and we need you to do it. You will do it."

"Yes." Sweat trickled down Robert's forehead, his armpits were like leaky faucets, and his face felt flushed. Two agents in three years; no wonder Stan was so eager to recruit him. He wiped his brow with his hand and dried it on his pant leg.

"You'll need to get up to speed fast," Andrea said, tossing the words at him like small grenades. "We never know when we'll need to leap into action."

Alex rose, walked to a tall filing cabinet, and opened the top drawer. Turning, he said, "Here's your gun, Robert."

Robert took the bundle of leather and pulled the pistol from its sheath: a Beretta 92SB. He'd practiced with one at training and enjoyed its ease of firing. Though it had a longer nose than the compact version, it still came out of the holster in a quick, simple motion.

Alex hit the button on his desk again, and Lamai materialized.

"Yes, Mr. Butler?" she asked.

"Lamai, could you show Mr. Jordan to his office?" Alex said.

"Of course, Mr. Butler. This way, Mr. Jordan."

"Let us know if you need anything, Robert," Alex said as he shook Robert's hand.

Lamai took Robert down the hallway, opened the door where she had placed his bag, and waved Robert into his office. Following him, she then walked to the window and turned on the air conditioner, swiveled around, and left. Robert first noticed the single desk with a terminal on it. One desk. He wouldn't be sharing this room, which was about half the size of Alex's expanse. His window displayed a view of a typical back alley of Bangkok, with chaotic trash cans, bicycles, chairs, and tables. Not a great view, but better than no window at all. Maybe he would replace the Thai tourist posters on the walls, but the rest seemed luxurious compared to his DC cubicle. He could get used to this. If he stayed alive long enough.

After Robert left Alex's office, closing the door behind him, Andrea approached her boss. She leaned her tall frame forward, put both her hands, knuckles down, on his desk and said, "I want to go on record that I object to being assigned a rank amateur as a partner. Even Colson, good as he was, couldn't cut it here. It's a jungle out there, and this Jordan character is so wet behind the ears he's leaving puddles of sweat wherever he sits down." She glanced in disgust at the chair where Robert had sat. Alex stretched himself to look and noted that the seat had a bit of moisture on it.

"I understand your concerns, Cannon. But this is the best we're going to get. Besides, his language skills will come in handy. He'll be able to listen in on the private conversations that our Thai colleagues are having—in front of our faces—and maybe even with our adversaries. Give him a chance. Train him. But remember, you don't have a lot of time. We need to be making a move on Hao Wang and his crew in a few months. Our international sources tell us he's sending a big shipment of drugs to the US in February."

Andrea took her hands off the desk and reared up to her full height, glaring at Alex. She turned and walked out of the room without saying a word.

"Good talking to you, too, Andrea!" Alex called after her.

Andrea made a beeline for Robert's office, then walked inside without knocking. She found him unpacking a couple of things and searching drawers to find out what supplies he had.

"Get dressed for a workout. Alex told me to train you. I want to see what you can do."

"My training record wasn't good enough?"

Andrea scowled at Robert as she shook her head—once to the left, then to the right.

"OK, Agent Cannon. Give me five minutes, and I'll be ready. But just to give you a heads up—I'm not much good at running over a mile."

"Is there anything you *can* do?" Andrea sneered at him, turned, and walked out, leaving the door open behind her.

Once he was ready, Robert wandered out into the passageway. They had a full floor in a drab commercial building. Five people worked in the Bangkok DEA office: Alex, Andrea, Lamai, the Thai agent—Sakchai Sangthong—and himself. They had offices for eight people, but it had been a long time since that many people had served in Thailand for the DEA.

The hallway was all wood, with only a few dim overhead lights. The floor had an elaborate dark inlay with light-oak accents along the edges and in front of each door. Dark paneling covered the walls in a series of squares. The ceiling molding echoed that pattern with miniature cubes. Robert smelled the muskiness of sandalwood. At the end of the hallway, Lamai typed furiously on a report, the clacking of the typewriter echoing down the corridor. Her work area also had an air conditioner.

"Excuse me, Lamai, which office is Andrea's?"

Without a word, Lamai rose and floated to an office, softly knocked three times, and cocked her ear to the door.

"Who is it?" Andrea's muffled voice came from within the office.

"Mr. Jordan, to see you, Ms. Cannon."

"Send him in."

Lamai opened the door, and Robert stepped into the office. He half expected to see the heads of wild game on the walls—tigers and lions that Andrea would have shot in Africa. But the office was stark—nothing on the walls, nothing on her desk but her terminal, and the simplest of lamps in the corner. The wood paneling everywhere had a few nails sticking out where previous occupants must have hung paintings, photos, or maps. A barren room. Aside from her desk, empty bookshelf, and filing cabinet, the only other feature was a table that seated four.

"Before we go, Alex wanted me to show you who we are up against," Andrea said, slapping two photos onto her desk.

"This is Hao Wang, the drug kingpin. Here's Tianhao Zheng, his lieutenant and top enforcer."

Robert looked at the photos. Wang was small compared to his deputy, but the photo gave the impression of a coiled cobra ready to strike. Tianhao looked like a cement block with a head.

"Wang's a cold-blooded killer. To work his way to the top, he eliminated at least seven rivals, some in hand-to-hand combat. He's an expert in kung fu. Tianhao prefers to use a knife, but he's much stronger than Wang, so could kill with his bare hands. Oddly, he seems to avoid guns, but Wang has no such qualms." Andrea paused.

Robert committed the photos to memory and looked up at Andrea.

"Right. Let's go. I'll drive. Take your luggage; I'll drop you at your apartment after our workout," Andrea said, grabbing a set of keys from a drawer. Robert soon learned that Andrea mainly drove the DEA office's red, right-hand drive Toyota Corolla. He also understood that they had access, through the US Embassy, to a sports club, which included a horse track for running, a gym, tennis courts, indoor racket facilities, a pool, and a golf course. Not to mention a restaurant and a cigar room with a whiskey bar. At the insistence of the embassy, Andrea was one of the first women to be admitted into the club.

Andrea drove like a local maniac, honking and swerving through the traffic and swarms of people. When Robert put on his seat belt, she looked down at his waist and scoffed, shaking her head. She guided the car with supreme confidence. They arrived without incident at the front of the club. Andrea gave the keys to the valet and marched through the front door, waving to the two attendants who welcomed her by bowing their heads in a respectful *wai*. Seeing the Thais' formal greeting and Andrea's casual response embarrassed Robert. *Wai*, a traditional Thai greeting, showed respect with a bow and palms pressed together in a prayer-like fashion. Local etiquette required both parties to perform a *wai*. But he could only nod his head at them and return a vague bow since he wasn't yet supposed to know Thai manners. He followed Andrea into the sumptuous entryway, which looked like a luxury hotel lobby. She walked at an easy, relaxed pace, greeting a few of the members they passed. Robert trailed behind, craning his neck to look at the art on the walls.

On the horse track, Robert kept up with Andrea's running on the first trip around, about five-eighths of a mile, but flagged halfway through the second lap. She forced him to do a third, shouting at him the entire time, but he couldn't move any faster. The jet lag didn't help, but that wasn't it. He suffered from an innate inability to sustain any speed for two miles. So, he shuffled along at a glacial pace.

They went into the gym, a simple room. Equipment lined one side, mirrors the other. A large mat covered the floor, for exercising or sparring. Aside from the wooden benches, everything was white—the walls, the ceiling, and the mat.

"I want to see how good you are at hand-to-hand combat," Andrea said. "First, we'll do boxing."

Robert had a flashback to his match against Fletch in training camp. He sighed and said, "But you're a…"

"Right, so it should be easy, huh? Don't worry about hitting my breasts; I'm wearing protective cups. And let's get this straight: I don't like you," she snarled, baring her perfect white teeth.

"Should I be wearing a crotch cup?"

"I never do low blows."

"Good."

"Unless it's for real, then it's my first punch."

I hope I never run into you in a dark alley.

"OK. Right. Sure." A sense of doom crept over Robert. This didn't seem right to him. A male versus female fight? He looked around the gym and sighed, relieved to see there were no witnesses.

They put on their protective headgear and faced each other in the center of the room. Robert held his own for a minute or two, dodging blows and landing a few on Andrea's head, shoulders, and midriff, using his long arms to reach her body. But then she picked up her attack and thrashed Robert with punches that landed faster than he could repel them. They rained down on his stomach, chest, and head. The few times he punched out from his defensive stance—usually hitting thin air but sometimes landing a strike or two—it was nothing compared to her volley of blows. Then, as he ducked a series of thumps, she landed an uppercut, which sent him to the mat.

He counted himself out and stayed prone.

Andrea bounced around him, waiting for him to get up. She took a deep breath, exhaled, and offered him a glove. He took it and stood up, cringing in dread of another punch.

"That was good," Andrea said. "You did well. Not as good as Colson, but better than I expected."

Robert briefly wondered if Colson had met his demise in the ring with Andrea but dismissed the idea.

"How did Colson die?"

"We were preparing to enter a warehouse to confiscate some drugs when three of Hao Wang's goons jumped on us. They stabbed Colson. I dispatched two of the thugs, but the third one, Tianhao, ran away after I wrestled his knife out of his hand. I had a choice of chasing him or saving my colleague. Colson's guts were hanging out. I took him to the hospital, but he died on the way there. He was an excellent agent."

"Dispatched them…?"

"Yes, Jordan, I killed them. It's a tough world. Wang does not value human life. His wealth and his business are all-important to him. He has a son, but his wife died. He has cats."

"Cats…?"

"Yes. Cats. What's with you, Jordan? Brain fog?"

"Well, I just took a beating in boxing, and I'm jet-lagged. So maybe."

Andrea looked at him, her brow knitted with consternation. She sighed, shook her head, and punched him in the shoulder.

Robert staggered back from the blow.

A Thai entered the room. He had broad shoulders and moved like a cheetah, all muscles and speed.

"Ah, here's Chakan, your trainer. He'll be teaching you Muay Thai—Thai boxing. While you two work out, I'll be in the weight room. I'll meet you at the front entrance in an hour and a half."

Andrea departed, and Chakan began Robert's training. Much to Robert's relief, his instructor first taught him the levels of *wai*, how and when to bow—to monks, to teachers and elders, to peers and younger people—and the general, casual *wai*. Now, he could react appropriately and not have to pretend he didn't know the rules he'd learned when he first came to Thailand.

With that out of the way, they performed a *wai* to each other, and Robert learned the basic Muay Thai kicks. Rather than take on anything more on the first day, they went over these moves for the entire session. Chakan wielded a large pad for Robert to kick, so he could build up his speed and power to strike his opponents. At the end of the session, they sparred briefly so Robert could experience some actual combat. Afterward, he crawled to the shower room.

Back in the Toyota, Andrea said, "You'll need to train every weekday for two hours. We'll get here after I pick you up at 6 a.m., run twice around the track as fast as we can, recover, and then you'll learn the local fighting technique. Chakan will train you each day—but no head punches. We need to keep your brain functioning and translating. Also, you'll do weights for leg and upper body strength. The usual stuff."

Andrea drove Robert to his new apartment and left him to fend for himself. Robert surveyed his new digs—bare yellowed walls with a few nail holes, a basic kitchen, and through the door to the bathroom, a white toilet and curtained shower. His bedroom held a double-size bed. The furnishings in the living room were sparse—a couch with a coffee table on a threadbare rug, a lamp, and a side table with cigarette burns. That was it.

He went shopping, nursing his aching body through each step, and found a market nearby and a store with plenty of canned goods, spices, and bottled water. As he ordered what he wanted at the various stalls, he listened to the Thais' banter about Americans. When he bought a whole chicken, they compared him to it—pale with bumpy skin. He ignored the comment, his face vacant. In the bazaar, he spotted two artworks he liked, so he made a second trip to pick them up. One piece, a hand-carved teak panel with a lotus blossom at its center, calmed him. The other, a shadow puppet of a dancing devil, amused him.

When he got home, the phone rang.

"Change of plans. No workout tomorrow. Alex wants us in the office at 4 a.m." Andrea's flat voice issued just the facts.

Standing near the kitchen table, where the phone hung on the wall, Robert absorbed this unexpected news.

"Are you still there?" Andrea asked, irritated.

"Yeah." Robert couldn't hide the tiredness in his voice. "What's the meeting about?"

"Can't say over the phone. I'll pick you up at 3:30 a.m. Be ready." *Click.*

Robert shook his head as he looked at the buzzing handset he still held. This assignment wasn't what he had expected. Meet at the office at four in the morning? He shook his head and resolved to prepare as best he could. He set his alarm, threw a meal together, ate it, and hit the sack. Whatever he needed to face tomorrow, the more sleep he got, the better he could deal with it. Or so he hoped.

CHAPTER 6

Andrea strode into Alex's office at 4 a.m. with Robert trailing behind her, rubbing his eyes. Alex sat at his desk, drumming his fingers against its surface—rump, rump, rump. A Thai gentleman faced Alex, his hands folded in front of him. To show respect for his boss, he stood six feet back from the desk. A slight, short man with warm brown skin, he had the air of a devout Buddhist, even though he was wearing a business suit.

"Robert, this is Sakchai Sangthong, the other member of our team," Alex said, straightening his shoulders and pushing his chest out with pride. "His informants have told us about a large cache of drugs at one of Wang's warehouses near Bangkok Port. Given this information, the police will stage a raid this morning, and we're allowed to tag along. Your mission will be to figure out the type and quantity of drugs that are being confiscated and then to keep track of where they go after the police seize them."

"OK. Sounds good," Robert said, nodding his head to gain some mental alertness while wondering how he was going to accomplish this assignment.

Alex stopped drumming his fingers, leaned back in his chair, looked at his new recruit, grinned, and said, "Great! I love this team!" He paused, taking a relaxed breath. "And Robert..."

"Yes?"

"Here's where your special skill comes in. Stick close to Colonel Pravat, the police drug chief, to find out what is happening with the drugs. Got that?"

"Sure. Piece of cake," Robert said without a trace of irony, though he wasn't sure this would be easy at all.

"That's the spirit!"

They left the building and piled into the Toyota, Andrea and Robert in front and Sakchai squeezed into the back. Their heads had enough room, but both Andrea and Robert needed the front bucket seats slid back for their long legs.

"Do you have enough room back there, Sakchai?" Robert asked.

"I am sufficiently comfortable, Mr. Jordan."

"Call me, Robert."

"Yes, Robert."

"Cut the chitchat!" Andrea ordered. "This is what we're going to do. Sakchai and I will leave you with Colonel Pravat. Learn everything you can about where they are taking the shipment after they confiscate it. We'll regroup at the car, then follow the police van, but it will have to be at some distance, so they don't spot us."

She pulled into the light, early morning traffic, swerving among the cars, motorbikes, and *tuk-tuks* as if she were driving an ambulance with a dying patient in the back. Robert fastened his seat belt. Andrea glared and leaned on the horn to warn a motorcycle to make way. Soon, they arrived near the warehouse in the Phra Khanong neighborhood, parked at a distance so no one would know the vehicle they were driving, and walked several blocks to the edge of a police cordon.

A man with a megaphone at his side stood in the middle of the street, surveying the police officers who sourrounded the warehouse. The building was situated several streets away from the main port storage area.

"Colonel Pravat?" Andrea asked.

Pravat turned quickly. "Yes? Ah, Agent Cannon, I'm glad you could join us. We have them encircled, and I will soon tell them to surrender. We'll see if they're smart enough to do that."

"Colonel Pravat, you know Sakchai, of course, but I'd like to introduce you to our new agent, Robert Jordan."

"*Sawasdee khrap. Sabai dee mai?*" Colonel Pravat asked, making an awkward *wai* with the megaphone tucked under his arm.

Robert looked panicked, shook his head, and turned to Sakchai. "What did he say?"

"He said 'Hello. How are you?'"

Andrea and Sakchai exchanged quizzical glances, and Robert knew his acting had hit the mark. Even they questioned how well he spoke Thai.

"Oh, sorry, Colonel Pravat. I'm new here. I will try to learn a little Thai, but right now… Anyway, I'm well. Thank you. How are you?"

"I'm well, thank you," Pravat said, giving another *wai*.

Robert put his hands together in front of his face and bowed his head slightly, making sure his *wai* crudely imitated the colonel's greeting. He didn't want the officer to think he knew much about Thailand.

"We're going to leave you two to get to know each other," Andrea said. "Right now, I need a cup of coffee."

"You'll find some tea in the truck behind you," Colonel Pravat said.

"Yeah, it will have to do," Andrea grumbled. She and Sakchai turned and made their way to the tea van.

Robert had little to do while he waited beside the Colonel. Pravat soon used his megaphone to tell the gang members in the warehouse to come out with their hands up. After several minutes, three forlorn-looking Thais came out of the building, their hands in the air, their heads bowed. Several police officers grabbed and handcuffed them, then put them into a police van. Another officer approached the colonel, and the two of them had a brief conversation. Three officers began loading the drugs, stored in cheap carryalls, into a separate van. Robert carefully counted the number of parcels and estimated how many kilograms of drugs were in them, given their size and the effort of the couriers.

"Excellent work, Colonel Pravat," Robert said. "What did we secure?"

"It's about one hundred kilos of heroin," Colonel Pravat replied.

Robert estimated the haul to be double that. After the crew secured the cargo in the van, the man Pravat had spoken to earlier climbed into the driver's seat and closed the door.

"Congratulations, Colonel Pravat. That went smoothly."

"Thank you, Agent Jordan. It was a pleasure to meet you."

"Likewise. Well, I'd best join my colleagues now. Good day," Robert said, sloppily returning the colonel's bow.

Robert strolled over to the tea van, and the three of them began walking toward their car. As soon as they were around the corner, they ran to get into it.

"The dope is in a police van. I estimated it to be about two hundred kilograms. Colonel Pravat said it was heroin and only half that amount."

"What was the license plate number of the van?"

"Uh…" Robert wracked his brain for an image of the plates. "I think it was 8191?"

"You think! Details, Robert. Details! Get them next time. Observe. Absorb." Andrea spat out the words.

"Yes, Agent Cannon," Robert said, deflated. He thought he'd done a good job in calculating the quantity of drugs. He hesitated to say his next observation, also a shaky one. "I heard Pravat tell the driver to take the drugs to a warehouse at…it sounded like the address was 37 King Kaeo Road."

"Sounded like? You can't be sure?"

"I'm not sure," Robert said, convinced nothing was worse than pretending to be certain when you knew you weren't.

"Shit! We'll have to follow it in case you heard wrong," Andrea said.

They climbed into the Toyota and waited. Less than a minute later, the van passed them and Andrea, giving it a wide berth, pulled into the road to follow it.

"See that—8161," Andrea said, pointing at the plate of the vehicle. "You were close, but not accurate! Accuracy is what we do. It's police work."

They zigzagged across Bangkok, keeping a cautious distance behind the truck. The roads were still relatively quiet at 6:30 a.m. but filling fast. When it came, the extra traffic helped hide their pursuit of the van.

After traveling along Udom Suk Road, the van pulled into a narrow one-way street. Andrea growled, then said, "Fuck!" A large lorry in front of them had abruptly stopped to unload goods from the back, trapping them. Cars behind them began honking, and Andrea leaned on her horn as well and then pounded on the steering wheel in frustration. "Shit. Well, I hope you got that address right because we've lost them."

Robert got out and looked down the street. The van turned a corner and moved out of sight.

"Worth a try," Robert said. Andrea glowered at him when he sat back down and, fearing what would come next, he leaned away from her.

She hit him anyway. A sharp jab into the muscle of his upper arm.

The truck finished its delivery and got out of their way. Andrea's insane driving carried them across to the other side of Bangkok. They parked at a safe distance from 37 King Kaeo Road, and there was the van! Robert breathed a sigh of relief, and Andrea gave a grudging nod of approval.

The driver emerged from the warehouse, unlocked the back of the van, took out two carryalls, relocked it, and walked into the building. He continued this routine until all the drugs were secured inside.

They couldn't know where he went in the storeroom, so they counted the seconds it took for the driver to enter and return. Forty seconds, twenty in and twenty out.

"Sakchai, go around to the back and see if there is any security and maybe find out where he is putting the dope."

Sakchai got out of the Toyota and walked to the back of the building.

Robert and Andrea watched as the driver finished the transfer, hopped into the van, and drove away. Soon, Sakchai rejoined them.

"There were no windows, so I couldn't tell if there was any security," Sakchai said after he squished himself into the back seat. "There was no one behind the building but me."

"Now what?" Robert asked.

"We'll have to check in with Alex to see what he wants us to do. Sakchai, you stay here and monitor the building to make sure the drugs don't get transported elsewhere. We'll drop you at the café across from the warehouse. Contact us with the café's phone if anything changes."

Andrea and Robert got back to their headquarters at about 10 a.m., and Alex was waiting for them in his office.

"How'd it go?" he asked as soon as they entered.

"We followed the drugs to a building near the airport," Andrea said. "Sakchai's watching it and will phone if someone moves the heroin."

"Good work!"

"Robert even proved to be useful," Andrea continued, giving Robert another thump to the right shoulder. Robert winced. The gentle blow had landed on the sore spot left by the previous punch.

"Oh?"

"Tell him, Robert." Another punch.

"I eavesdropped on Pravat when he spoke to the van driver and… uh…overheard the address where he was to take the drugs," Robert said, stumbling over his words because of his fatigue.

"He wasn't certain of the address, so we followed the van, but we lost it. He's also good at faking he doesn't know Thai. Even Sakchai wasn't sure he could speak the language after Pravat greeted Robert in the local lingo."

"But he speaks Thai well?" Alex asked, his voice strained.

"He must. He got the address right."

"That's great. Mission accomplished…so far." Alex breathed a sigh of relief. "We'll have to retrieve the drugs this evening and destroy them. They might ship them somewhere or move them again, and we might not be so lucky to find them next time."

"Tonight?" Robert asked, his shoulders sagging under the weight of his jet lag.

"Yes, you have a problem with that?" Alex asked.

"No, sir. Tonight, it is." Robert straightened up and lifted his chin.

"You can call me Alex. 'Sir' makes me feel old. Andrea, take our new agent home to get some rest. He looks tired."

"Thanks, Alex," Robert said, and he and Andrea turned to leave.

"And Andrea, Robert?" The two swiveled their heads to look at their boss. "Good job so far. Let's finish it tonight."

"Absolutely," Andrea said as she cuffed Robert, pushing him toward the exit.

Robert heard a sharp rap on his door. He thought he'd been asleep about ten minutes, but when he looked at his watch, he realized he'd been slumbering for twelve hours. It was midnight.

More tapping and a whisper, "Robert!"

He lifted himself out of bed. He hadn't changed clothes. "Coming," he said to his apartment's entrance. The moment he opened the door, Andrea burst into the room, taking in his apartment with a sweep of her head.

When Andrea finished surveying Robert's digs, she asked, "Ready?"

"Let me wash up first."

"Yeah, do your duty." Andrea waited in the living room, whistling. When Robert came out of the bathroom, she asked, "OK now?"

"Ready to rock and roll."

"Did you forget something?"

Robert looked down to make sure his pants were on and his fly zipped. "No, I don't think so."

"Maybe your gun and backpack?"

"Oh, yeah. Thanks," Robert said, too sleepy to feel chagrined. He put on the shoulder holster and a jacket to hide the weapon and snatched up his rucksack, then they left his apartment.

They drove toward the warehouse and picked up Sakchai at the café, which was still open for the late-night airport workers. Then they parked near the building so they could easily fill the Toyota with the drugs. They put on their balaclavas, grabbed their flashlights, and checked their guns to make sure they were loaded.

The front door was locked. Andrea listened intently and, hearing nothing, picked the lock with a tool she produced from her jacket pocket. She opened the door.

Andrea went in first, gun drawn. The silence reassured her, so she motioned Robert inside while Sakchai stayed outside as a lookout.

Andrea turned on her flashlight and paced into the cavernous building. Tables, crates, and traffic control barriers cast ghostly shadows as her torch shone on them. She counted twenty steps, which placed her near an office on the left side of the floor plan, also with a locked door. She flashed her light in its window and spotted the bags on the floor. After picking the lock, she entered and turned on the light. Robert stood outside the office, keeping watch. Andrea unzipped one bag, drew out a white brick, cut it open and tasted the powder. Heroin. She gave a thumbs-up to Robert and picked up two carryalls.

Suddenly, a man jumped from behind the traffic barriers on the other side of the warehouse. He waved a gun in his hand and shouted Thai obscenities. Robert's DEA training kicked in, and he automatically dove behind a crate, dropped his right knee to the ground, pulled out his gun, and pointed it with both hands at his assailant.

Then he froze.

The man lifted his gun toward Robert, screeched and fired—once, twice, three times. Still screaming, he ran toward Robert, waving his gun in the air, and discharging more rounds. He dodged between tables and crates, zigzagging closer to Robert. He was shooting the gun as if he were throwing the bullets from it, cowboy-style, pulling it back behind his head, then flinging it forward, his shots missing wildly. They sprayed throughout the warehouse, hitting tables, chairs, boxes, and the back window. He closed in on Robert, his mouth ejecting growls, hisses, and squawks. Robert crouched lower, his pistol held in front of him, the man in his sights, but he couldn't pull the trigger. The Thai was only twenty feet away, arms spinning in a whirlwind, firearm still blasting.

Andrea stepped out of the office and shot him dead.

"What the fuck's wrong with you? Why didn't you shoot him?"

Sakchai had entered the warehouse but didn't fire his gun because Robert blocked his view of the shooter.

"You mean kill him?" Robert asked, still stunned.

"Yes. That's the idea, ugly as it is. He was going to kill you. You are so fucking lucky he was a terrible shot."

"I don't know. I couldn't."

"You owe me, Jordan," Andrea hissed. "Next time, I might not be there to help you. Let's get this shit and get out of here."

Robert approached the dying Thai, now prone on the floor, his arms spread out and his gun well out of reach. He was panting, a raspy, grainy gasp every half second, as if struggling to pull air in from the large wound in his chest. Robert took his hand and looked the man in the eye. He was old, perhaps sixty, with white hair and a weathered face. Robert saw the panic in his eyes and then…nothing. He closed them gently and said, "Go peacefully, old man."

Andrea spoke with derision. "Would you get up from there and help me with these bags?" Robert rose, walked over, picked up two carryalls of dope, and headed toward the exit.

While Andrea and Robert carried the drugs to the car, Sakchai knelt by the fallen man. He touched his neck and held his wrist. He began murmuring a prayer, which sounded peaceful and consoling.

Once Sakchai emerged from the warehouse, he stayed with the car, making sure no one bothered it while Andrea and Robert transferred the drugs. Andrea and Robert placed some bags on the front passenger seat floor, some on the back seat, and the rest in the trunk. Four hundred forty pounds of dope doesn't ride easily in a compact car with three passengers. Sakchai locked the warehouse's front door when they had finished.

They drove south to the waterfront and found a secluded spot to dispose of the heroin. Andrea slashed open the plastic-wrapped bricks, and Sakchai and Robert sprinkled them into the water.

"What about the fish?" Robert asked. "This can't be good for them."

"What about the fish?" Andrea mocked. "You're worried about the fucking fish after you nearly got shot? Of all the agents in the world, I get the one who is brain dead. What's wrong with you, Robert?"

"I need some sleep."

"And a brain transplant," Andrea said.

Two hundred bricks and an hour later, they were done. Sakchai took a deep breath and gave a *wai* to Andrea and to Robert. Then he strode into the night.

CHAPTER 7

Sakchai walked two miles to his home. He could have asked Andrea to drop him off in front of his house, but he needed time to think. They'd destroyed drugs. A successful mission. They'd removed them from the streets, here and in the rest of the world. A small victory. However, they had killed a man, and that did not bode well. A potential danger. The man's family and employer would want revenge. Fortunately, no one knew who had done the killing. But the death troubled Sakchai; the police employed the guard, and Orson Group needed to stay on good terms with their Thai counterparts.

He enjoyed working for the Americans. The Bangkok police were problematic and too often uninterested in stopping the drug lords; instead, they were eager to share in the gains from the trade in the toxic substances. They viewed ten percent of the profits to be their rightful share. Sakchai doubted that Colonel Pravat intended to keep the drugs in this shipment; most likely, he would have returned the goods to Hao Wang for a fee. Having now lost the drugs, he would be in trouble, and that couldn't be good for the Orson team. Colonel Pravat had probably only invited them along on this raid so that he could show off his drug-busting skills to the Americans. What hornets' nest had they stirred up?

It saddened Sakchai that he had never seen Andrea show respect for those she killed; they were workers for drug lords, and she despised them. No remorse, no regret. What darkness led her into this life of fighting drug gangs? Sakchai didn't believe, as some Thais did, that someone who died violently became an evil spirit or could be reborn and take revenge. But still. Showing respect and aiding the soul to a more peaceful afterlife was the right thing to do. His mood lifted when he remembered how Robert knelt by the fallen Thai and paid his respects.

These thoughts swiveled his mind to his sister, Kalaya. His family hailed from Chiang Mai, but he and his sister had moved to Bangkok to get technical qualifications, leaving behind their brother, Tao, to mind their parents. Sakchai got a certificate in law enforcement and became a police officer, while his sister learned the skills to provide beauty parlor services—hairstyling, manicures, pedicures, waxing, and facials. Since they both lived in Bangkok and had always been close, they often did things together.

On one Songkran, the Thai New Year, they were not able to return to Chiang Mai for the celebration, so they went for a walk in their neighborhood. One street was having a traditional water fight—one side of the street against the other. They joined opposite sides and used plastic bowls to shower each other and the locals with water from nearby coolers. By the time they escaped, their clothes were soaking wet. They sloshed into a market to buy their dinner ingredients. Later, at Kalaya's flat, they dried off, and she cooked the customary *khao chae*—a multi-dish meal with fragrant rice, fried meat, and carved fresh vegetables. As always with her cooking, the aromatic spices and the savory meat and fish flavors exploded in his mouth, delighting his senses.

But he had failed to help Kalaya when she needed him.

Sakchai walked down a crowded alley in Samut Prakan until he came to his small house. The alley he lived on had some apartment blocks and many single homes packed in next to each other. Some were well kept, but many had structural problems. He felt lucky with his home. To him, it was a palace compared to his family's wooden hut with a corrugated metal roof. He maintained it at a high standard. It had running water, a toilet, a crude shower, and a stove fed by a gas tank. The Americans paid well, and he reveled in his good fortune to be employed by them.

When Sakchai opened his front door, he awakened his wife, Sirikit, who sat in a chair in their tiny parlor. His heart danced when he saw her, a great blessing in his life. She leapt to her feet and greeted him with a deep *wai*. He returned the gesture, and she turned and trotted into the kitchen to make him a cup of tea. It was 3 a.m., and the burden of the night's activities made his bones ache.

While she brewed tea, he went into his son's room. Niran lay sleeping on his back, his head turned away from his dad, his small breaths even and relaxed. Sakchai bent over him and smelled his sweet scent, like apple blossoms. Then he put his fingers on Niran's chest, feeling the quiet movement of his breathing. Sakchai's breast burst with pride as he recalled the week before when Niran took his first tentative steps without help. The third miracle in his life—his job, his wife, his child.

"May you suffer no calamity and be healthy in mind and body," Sakchai prayed over his son.

Sirikit appeared behind him with a cup of tea. He turned, and the two of them walked into the kitchen, where she had laid out his dinner. The table and four chairs filled the small space, leaving just enough room to cook at the stove and prepare food on the short counter. He wasn't hungry but knew he would need to appreciate her prepared meal.

He didn't like talking about his work. Its ugliness disturbed him, and he didn't want to bring sordidness into his wife's life. "Did you have a pleasant day, my love?" Sakchai asked. They were across from each other, holding hands as he ate.

"In the morning, I took Niran, and we went shopping," Sirikit said, with joy in her lilting voice. "He's heavy; I'll be glad when he can walk with me. At home, we played with a marble, and I sang to him. I'd hide the marble in my hands, and he'd have to pick the one holding it. He's good at that, hard to fool.

"But I worried about you," Sirikit whispered with anguish. "You didn't come home for dinner." Seeing her distress, Sakchai's gut plunged.

"I'm sorry, sweetheart," Sakchai said, looking up from his plate, his brow knitted. "Andrea assigned me to watch a warehouse from a café, and I couldn't contact you."

"I wish we had a phone."

"I know. But they are difficult to get." Sakchai struggled for a reassuring response. "This is my job. It's important work; we support rehabilitation centers, which help people stay off drugs. We also work with the police to reduce the quantity of opiates on the street. It's an excellent organization, and I'm proud to work with my American colleagues."

"Yes. They are good people. I see that when we dine with them on that eating holiday of theirs, Thanksgiving." At this, Sakchai smiled; he was happy his wife could see the decency of his colleagues.

They held hands, drank their tea, and Sakchai finished his meal of *tom kha kai*, coconut chicken soup. She made it the way he liked it, with extra chilis, which inflamed his nose and mouth. Delicious.

In bed, Sirikit fell asleep as soon as she lay down in their narrow bed, her head turned to Sakchai. While listening to her soft purring, Sakchai gazed at the ceiling, unable to sleep. At first, his thoughts raced back to his sister.

The proprietor where she worked recognized the value of her beauty and befriended her. He invited her to lavish parties with many glamorous people, delicate food, and plentiful alcohol. Kalaya, coming from a provincial town outside Chiang Mai, had never seen anything like it. The opulence dazzled her. But one evening, an altercation occurred between two guests, a fight ensued, and one person died.

As it happened, the incident occurred in Detective Sakchai's district, so he investigated the death. None of the attendees were allowed to leave, and Sakchai spotted Kalaya in the crowd hiding behind two tall Thais. He said nothing. She had not been involved in the dispute, but his research on the case brought him face to face with Hao Wang, the notorious drug lord. It turned out that Wang owned Kalaya's workplace and these elaborate parties were a way of thanking his wealthy clients. When Sakchai's inquiry led him to Wang's office, and he pressed the kingpin on his reasons for funding the festivities, Wang offered Sakchai a bribe to drop his investigation. He refused, but the next day, his boss assigned him to another case.

This, the first time he learned Kalaya could be in trouble, darkened his spirit.

He pushed the memory aside, but as he drifted to sleep, an image of Andrea shooting the Thai guard in the police warehouse appeared. A giant mask loomed behind him. It looked like a photomontage of Pravat's boss, Amonsak Suwannarat, and Wang.

CHAPTER 8

Alex was at his desk at noon when Andrea, Robert, and Sakchai filed into his office. Andrea had phoned him in the middle of the night after they had disposed of the drugs, so he was in a festive mood.

"This calls for a celebration!" Alex proclaimed when they had gathered in his office. Alex stood up and walked to his liquor cabinet. "Whiskey, anyone?"

"Yes, thanks," Andrea said.

"Sure," Robert said, lifting his left eyebrow, surprised at the early afternoon offer.

Sakchai was silent.

"I know you don't drink, Sakchai," Alex said. "How about water with a slice of lime?"

"Thank you, Mr. Butler."

Alex passed out the glasses and resumed his seat at his desk. "A job well done. Congratulations!" he said, lifting his glass in a toast. Then he took a sip, breathed a long, satisfied sigh, and leaned back in his chair, his eyes on the ceiling, lost in reflection. This would be good for his standing within the DEA, a little nudge toward a promotion.

Remembering himself, Alex sat upright again. "The three of you did a fabulous job. Our first success at destroying narcotics. I am very proud of you. Everything went smoothly; no issues, right?" Alex asked. Observing Sakchai looking worried, he continued, "Yes, Sakchai? You have something to say?"

"We must be careful. We have killed a man and disrupted a deal, which involves the Thai police and Hao Wang. Both sides would be unhappy with us if they knew we had interfered with their transaction. They will initially accuse each other, and perhaps the rival gang, the Scorpions, but may also become suspicious of other parties. And we were the only group to witness the raid."

"Hmm. Doesn't sound like too bad a situation. You don't think they know it was us, do you?"

"No, but both organizations are formidable and may come to suspect us. We need to be cautious."

"Agreed. We're careful, but you're right. I'm always surprised at how much the police know about the drug trade and what we are planning. Could you spread some rumors through your contacts that the Scorpions hijacked the drugs? Maybe we can take the suspicion off us."

"Of course, Mr. Bulter," Sakchai replied.

Alex paused, finished his drink, and said, "Well, on that note, thank you again for your stellar work. I need to speak with Robert now."

Andrea and Sakchai withdrew from the room.

"Have a seat, Robert," Alex said, gesturing to a chair across from his desk.

Alex looked into Robert's eyes, seeking to bore into his mind.

"Tell me what happened with the watchman at the warehouse," Alex said.

Robert looked down at his hands in his lap, exhaled, and said, "We didn't know he was there. Perhaps we awakened him. Anyway, he jumped up from behind a heap of barricades and began shouting and shooting at me. He was running toward me when Andrea shot him dead."

"And what were you doing?"

"I had him covered with my Beretta…but…I…uh…couldn't shoot him." Robert was still gazing at his knees, and his ears were bright red. He took a deep breath.

"Why not?"

"I don't know. If I had shot him, I would have killed him."

"Yes?" Alex said, with a hard voice. He watched Robert squirm in his seat but couldn't ease up; Robert's life depended on his response to these dangers.

"I don't know. I froze and couldn't pull the trigger."

"Robert, you need to protect yourself. You need to shoot next time this type of situation arises. That guy could have killed you, Andrea, or Sakchai. I can't afford to lose another agent. God knows when they would send me a replacement. I know this isn't what you expected, but you need to react differently next time. You'll do that for me? For you and the team?"

"Yes, I'll work on it." Robert raised his head and looked at Alex, his eyes desperate with despair. But Alex didn't know if his behavior would change.

"Andrea can arrange for you to have some shooting practice with torso silhouette targets. Maybe that will help." Alex scrutinized Robert, his eyes darting back and forth across his agent's face. They sat like that for a long while: Alex searching the agent's visage, Robert looking back at him. Alex hoped the protracted stare would impress his new employee with the gravity of the matter.

Finally, Alex said, "Good. You did well on your first mission. A commendable job, with that small but significant hiccup of failing to fire. I expect you to become even more effective."

"Thank you. Will that be all?"

"Yes. But make sure you reflect on what I said," Alex said, still wondering if he'd been successful at making his point.

"I will, thanks."

Robert rose and left the office.

After he exited, Alex locked the door. From his desk, he took out a large bottle of Tums, shook five out into his hand, popped them into his mouth, and crunched them between his teeth. Then he poured himself another whiskey and stared out the window at a cloudy, muggy day, much like any other in October, hot with a chance of rain. From his window, he could see into the street and hear the muffled sound of traffic. People were bustling along the sidewalks and skating between vehicles to cross the busy alley, which was jammed as usual with only the motorbikes making any headway weaving through the cars that were inching forward.

Alex turned to gaze at his closed door and thought, *What a fuckup. I'm short an agent, so I have to put a Thai language specialist into a role he may be incapable of doing. That sucks.* And then, after a moment's reflection, *I hope the kid survives.*

Later that day, when Robert had settled into his office with a cup of tea, Andrea walked in. No knock. Just barged in.

"Welcome, come right in," Robert said, shaking his head. "Please have a seat." He pointed to the chair opposite his desk.

Andrea closed the door in a slow, dramatic fashion, making no sound. She marched to his desk and put her knuckles on it, leaning her head forward until her face almost touched Robert's nose.

"Have you been thinking about what Alex said to you?"

"Yes. Lunch improved my insights enormously."

"Don't get cute with me, Jordan."

"It's not something one can simply think about, and it goes away. But, yes, I reflected on how I reacted and envisioned myself acting more aggressively next time."

"You pulled the trigger in your visualization?" Andrea gave him The Look, and the inimitable glare burned into his eyes.

"Yes," Robert lied. How could he say anything else? The heat from her stare made him sweat. A damp spot formed in the middle of his chest, and little beads of moisture gathered on his upper lip.

Andrea didn't move. Robert wished her knuckles would start hurting and she would ease up and back off. He glowered back at her, narrowing his eyes.

What's with this staring at me forever shit? It's just like Alex.

Eventually, she pulled up and softened. "I hope that's true. Your life depends on it. Mine too, perhaps."

"I'd never let anyone harm you if I could stop it."

Andrea barked. Not a laugh. A bark with a bit of a snort thrown in for good measure.

Robert wiped his lip and rubbed his chest.

"Ah, Robert, you're a gas." She continued to bark/snort and then halted abruptly. "We missed our workout this morning. We'll resume tomorrow. I'll see you at 6 a.m. at your place. Afterward, we'll visit a rehab center with Lamai."

"Sure, sounds good," Robert said to her back as she walked out, leaving the door open.

Time to get to work, doing some research on the drug trade. Robert connected his terminal to the mainframe they used. He missed the faster speeds of his DC office, but at least everything functioned. Then, he had an idea he should have thought of sooner. He typed in a few commands, searching for a way to enter the police force's computer via a bulletin board. If he could gain access, he might find out about the police raids earlier than their notifications to Alex. Before leaving for the day, he had found something that helped him.

CHAPTER 9

After work, Robert hailed a *tuk-tuk* and returned to his apartment. He took a nap and woke in the early evening. An exploratory walk around his neighborhood brought him to a low-cost hotel, the Crazy Bird—one step up from a backpacker hostel—that catered to budget travelers from Europe and America. Its small restaurant served traditional Thai dishes and alcohol. He sat down at the bar next to a big pillar and ordered a beer and green curry.

The bartender, Chai, knew some English, so Robert chatted with him. They exchanged names and discussed their cocktail preferences. Robert, the foreigner or *farang*, preferred the Thai traditional welcoming drink, Sabai Sabai, made with Mekhong, the local liquor, plus lemon juice and basil leaves. The barkeep, however, favored Mekong in an Old Fashioned. Chai moved constantly, serving customers, clearing tables, making drinks, washing glasses, and—when there was nothing else—wiping his counter clean.

The place wasn't much. Four stools stood at the bar, and six tables filled the dining area, which opened onto the street. An awning protected the diners from the rain and sun. Chai took care of everyone—people seated at the tables and those at the bar. The kitschy décor—garish paintings of Asian women with low-cut dresses—enlivened and tainted the walls. The place was lit by an overwhelming number of low-hanging paper lanterns with incredibly dim bulbs, which would keep it shady even in the middle of a sunny day and rich in shadows in the evening. Robert had to weave and dip his way through the drooping lamps, which were at the height of his forehead, when he walked past the tables. A couple of young English blokes sat next to him for a time, but they were pretty absorbed in a conversation about the local temples, or *wats,* and the giant solid-gold Buddha they had visited during the day.

The food was simple, but surprisingly good—better than he could cook at home. He left a tip for Chai—enough that he would remember Robert's name. After reviewing the menu and seeing they served an American-style breakfast, he resolved to make a habit of coming in each Sunday morning to quench his longing for food from home. He now had a local.

That night, Robert dreamed he was sitting at the table in his old place in Surat Thani, a one-room studio. Someone was knocking on the door, but he couldn't get up; his legs wouldn't respond. The pounding persisted, and he could hear a woman whispering to him, calling him by someone else's name. He awoke and looked at the clock: 6 a.m. Then he remembered where he was and rose to open the door for Andrea. She charged into the room, bumping him aside as she entered.

"You're supposed to be ready now. You don't look ready," she barked.

Robert looked down at his pajamas and closed the door.

"Got any coffee?" Andrea asked.

"Yeah. Hello to you too. I'll make some."

"Good."

Robert entered his kitchen area and put a pot of water on the stove, spooned some grinds into it, and rubbed his face with both hands.

"Hobo coffee?" Andrea asked with her familiar disdain.

"It's all I've got."

"It'll do," she said with a grunt of disappointment.

"I've only been here a couple of days," Robert said in his defense.

"How's it been? Enjoying it?"

"Oh, yeah, a riot every minute."

"Good. Get used to it. It only gets worse." Andrea paced to the couch and flopped onto it.

"Thanks for the pep talk."

"Anytime," she said, waving her long arm expansively.

The water boiled, and Robert poured two cups through a sieve. They sat in silence at the kitchen table. Robert was still waking up, and Andrea didn't like small talk.

After their coffee, he flung on his clothes and grabbed his gym bag. Today's workout would set the pattern for most of their days. They would run around the racetrack twice and then, while Andrea worked out in the weight room, Robert had Muay Thai training and conditioning. For Robert, this included shadowboxing, rope jumping, weight training, medicine ball, and abdominal exercises. Rope jumping tripped him up at first as he tangled the cords, but it helped strengthen his ability to bounce on his feet, something essential for attacking and dodging hits.

Robert had taken a variety of fighting courses over the years—karate, jujitsu, and even boxing lessons—often with Jermaine. But once he got marginally competent at them, he became bored and dropped out. He knew that sticking with a formal martial arts training program and focusing on one type of fighting would be a good way to become a better combatant. The DEA course comprised generic self-defense and offense drills. With Muay Thai, there were specific punches and kicks using elbows, fists, feet, shins, and knees. The attacking moves had defensive countermoves. Chakan, who spoke only minimal English, guided Robert through everything with physical movements, emphasizing maintaining balance. From a poised stance, he could deliver punches and kicks with power and block or render ineffective his opponent's blows. At the end of each session, they sparred for twenty minutes.

After their workout, Andrea and Robert picked up Lamai at the office and went to the main Orson Group rehabilitation center. Lamai guided them through the building, explaining everything. The local manager tried to accompany them, but Lamai dismissed her after they visited one room, telling her she should return to her work. Robert listened intently while Lamai described the rehab process, struggling to absorb the flood of information. She provided statistics on the success rate of the clinic, the number of people currently occupying the unit, the number attending AA-type meetings regularly, staff turnover, etc. The employees treated Lamai with great deference, bowing deeply when they greeted her, thankful to be recognized. She was their manager's boss, and they wanted to impress her. Lamai stopped and questioned them discreetly from time to time, informing herself about how well things were running. Robert listened while pretending not to understand but learned how Lamai inspired her staff to improve their performance. He also saw the respect Lamai's staff had for her in the intense way they listened to her every word, nodding. In one instance, a worker explained with pride an art therapy project she had devised that had proved successful at calming the new clients after their withdrawals. Another boasted about being able to place recent "graduates" into jobs in their local communities.

After the tour, Lamai disappeared for a minute and returned with two teenagers, a boy and a girl. The young woman, Mai, bowed deeply to Andrea, then grinned at her. Andrea responded with a warm *wai* and an equally broad smile.

The boy, a slim, wiry youth of about fourteen years, looked confused as he shifted his gaze from Lamai to Robert.

"Robert, I'd like you to meet Samak. You'll be Samak's mentor."

Samak bowed to Robert and said, "Mr. Robert, call me 'Sam.'"

Robert returned the appropriate *wai* for an adult to a youth, with his clasped hands at his chest level, his head bent toward Sam. "And you can call me 'Robert.'" He threw a quizzical glance at Andrea, seeking her attention, but she continued chatting with Mai and ignored him.

"The Orson Group has a program of mentoring young adults," Lamai said. "We have chosen Sam for you because he speaks some English."

Robert's discomfort became apparent to Lamai, and she asked, "Alex didn't tell you about this process?"

"Uh…no."

"It's simple. You meet with Sam once a week and do healthy activities—visit a *wat* or museum, enjoy a bike ride, or perhaps buy an ice cream and talk, so Sam can practice his language skills. Your job is to keep him off drugs and out of trouble."

"It's easy," Andrea said. "Even I can do it. Though I'm lucky to have Mai."

Robert stared at Andrea, mouth slightly open. She and Mai were locked in a beaming lovefest. Where did this Andrea come from?

"So, we'll come here on Saturday mornings. I'll drive you. It'll be fun."

Lamai had more work to do at the clinic, so Andrea and Robert walked back to the car, Robert in near panic. Sam was young enough to be his son, but he hadn't dealt with teenagers since his Surat Thani days, and he wasn't sure he could provide guidance to him.

"So, how's it work with you and Mai?" Robert asked, his voice creaking.

"It's a walk in the park. She adores me. I train her in self-defense. We talk…you know…about girl stuff. And I told her if she ever does drugs again, I'll beat the shit out of her."

Robert nodded but felt anything but reassured. "That's easy enough for you, but I have to keep my language skills hidden, and it's been over a decade since I worked with young people."

"You'll do fine. It's not as stressful as fieldwork. Put it in perspective, Robert," she added scornfully.

Robert flushed. She had a point. Dealing with Sam would be a lot easier—and safer—than dealing with drug gangs.

The next day, they had another team meeting in Alex's office. Sakchai had confirmed the location of Wang's headquarters. Alex wanted the three of them to force an entry surreptitiously and gather any information they could about the large shipment coming from the Golden Triangle in February. Their international DEA sources had told them it was arriving at Wang's warehouse before being transported to the US.

"You'll have to plan the break-in down to the last second, making sure you know every guard's coming and going," Alex said. "If we're lucky, they may feel they're so powerful and protected, they have no vulnerabilities. Any questions?"

"I have a question, but only somewhat related," Robert said.

"Yes?"

"Um. We had this operation this week…you know…and…uh…I was wondering… if this has been a typical week?"

"It sure has, Robert. And you'd better get used to it," Alex ordered.

The room was quiet for a moment.

"Hah! He's just kidding," Andrea said, slamming her left fist into Robert's right shoulder. Robert reeled back a foot from the blow, then came upright again, like a boxing dummy.

"No, this *was* unusual," Alex said. "But things have been heating up lately, so you'll need to be ready for these kinds of operations. This burglary will be dangerous, but the more we know about the February delivery, the better we'll be able to thwart it. I don't, however, want the three of you to go in if it looks fatally dangerous. I can't spare anyone now. Or ever, for that matter. Understood?"

Sakchai, Robert, and Andrea nodded.

"Good. Start your surveillance of the warehouse next week after getting a good rest over the weekend…Class dismissed!"

In the hallway, Robert asked Sakchai, "Does he always joke about everything?" Sakchai looked at the floor but said nothing.

"He's never been in the field. Can't you tell?" Andrea asked. "He's always been a manager. That's why I lead our operations. We'll go to the warehouse area today and find a good place to observe everyone's work shift. Sakchai will take Monday night, I'll take Tuesday, and you get Wednesday. After a week, we should know enough to break into the place with minimal risk…I hope."

Robert rubbed his sore right shoulder and said, "Sounds good." Sakchai just dipped his head.

Wang's warehouse was in the Bangkok port area, along with dozens of other storage facilities. His depot was toward the end of the port, where the Phra Khanong canal flowed into the Chao Phraya River. The buildings were arrayed along a straight feeder road. The structures opposite them were few and far between, offering a clear view of the storehouses. On the river side, only a service road stood between them and the water. After driving close to the warehouse, Andrea spotted a likely place for observing it—an abandoned office block across the feeder road. They drove to the back of the structure, broke in, and took the stairs to the top floor, which had windows with a clear view of Wang's warehouse, perfect for their surveillance. Andrea tested the binoculars she had brought and determined they needed a stronger pair, since their lookout spot was three hundred yards away from their target. After dropping Sakchai off so he could get home on public transport, Andrea and Robert picked up some field glasses at a specialty shop. Andrea also bought a miniature Minolta camera and film. The shopkeeper showed them how to load the film into the tiny device.

"I feel like I'm an actual spy now," Robert said as they approached their car. "Camera, binoculars, gun. Now, I just need one of those fountain pens that shoots bullets. And by the way, where's our Austin Martin?"

"It's Aston Martin, you twit." Andrea punched him. "And you wish. Only in the movies. Here, in the real world, we make do with off-the-shelf merchandise and a beautiful, red Toyota Corolla." Andrea spread her arm wide as if she were a used car salesperson offering a reconditioned Mercedes up for Robert's inspection.

He examined the vehicle. The sun had faded the paint job, and no surprise given Bangkok's chaotic traffic, there were dents on every panel. The back bumper had crumpled and rusted from a long-ago collision, and the hood had a scratch across its entire length. They climbed in, and Andrea drove like a swallow, flying and swerving through the traffic to deliver him to his apartment.

"Tomorrow's Saturday. We'll have the morning with Mai and Sam. See you at eight!" Andrea commanded as Robert got out of the car.

"Yes, sir!" Robert said. Andrea glared at him. The Look. Robert, cowed, slunk to his apartment door.

The next day, as Robert climbed into Andrea's car to go to the center to pick up Mai and Sam, he asked, "What am I supposed to do with this kid?"

"You used to teach Thai teenagers, right?" Andrea asked, exasperated.

"Yes." Robert sighed.

"You've done this before. It's no different. Exercise, maybe teach him some Muay Thai, talk to him so his English improves. Don't complicate it!" Andrea sneered.

"You're right. I'll treat him like a student," Robert said, his voice faltering. Teaching was one thing, life guidance, another. On the other hand, Andrea—hardly a touchy-feely person—handled her mentee without a problem, so he should be able to help Sam.

After picking up the young adults, Andrea drove to Rot Fai Park and brought the car to rest on the road that ran along the grounds.

As they scrambled out of the car, Andrea pointed and said, "You can rent bikes over there." Then she strode off with Mai.

Robert watched the two disappear down a path, holding hands, a common custom with females in Thailand. *Where'd she learn that?* he wondered. *She can't even bow properly.* He shook his head and turned to his charge. Sam looked like a kid who was being forced to take medicine.

"Shall we ride bikes?" Robert asked, throwing enthusiasm into the question.

"OK," Sam said in a monotone, his face blank.

They walked toward the bike rental, trudging over the green strip known as Chatuchak Park before crossing the road into Rot Fai. "Do you like riding bikes?" Robert asked.

"Yes."

"When did you learn to ride a bike?"

Sam looked puzzled, and then his face brightened. "Five."

"You were five years old when you learned?"

"Yes."

Robert took a deep breath and let it out in quick puffs, relaxing his muscles to avoid showing his annoyance. Sam seemed to understand everything he asked, but he wasn't giving up much information. He tried a more open-ended question as they selected their bikes and Robert paid. "Tell me about your family."

Sam scrunched his brow, concentrating, before he replied, "I love my mother."

"What about your father? Do you have brothers and sisters?"

"No," Sam said, making a wan face, but then he turned his head and smiled.

"No siblings or a father?"

"No."

Robert noticed Sam had no difficulty with the word "sibling" and realized the young man found his awkwardness amusing.

As they mounted their bikes, Robert said, "I'll tell you a joke about a little old lady, a donkey, and a chicken." He pedaled down a path without looking back. Trees and benches flashed by. Sam raced to catch up. As they cruised down the trail, Robert would from time to time stand up and push ahead, but Sam always pumped his feet harder to catch up with Robert and hear the entire story. When Robert finished the tale, which concluded with the elderly woman using a chicken feather to tickle the nose of the stubborn donkey, Sam frowned.

"That wasn't funny," Sam said.

"It was as amusing as I could make it; I made it up on the fly," Robert said, grinning.

"On the fly?" Sam asked, his eyes narrowing.

"It means I created it just now to test your English. You have great comprehension."

"Yes. I get it now." Sam sighed. "I fooled you, so you tricked me."

"Yes, I think we'll get along fine now. Deal?" Robert gave a *wai* appropriate to a peer, clasping his hands together, thumbs on his chin, fingers to his nose.

Sam looked startled, then reciprocated, a wide grin crashing his face.

"I've been taking Muay Thai lessons. Would you like me to show you a few moves I've learned?" Robert asked, after they returned the bikes.

"Yes!" Sam said, grinning and nodding his head.

They walked to an open, lush green field so they'd have plenty of room.

After they bowed to each other and Robert showed Sam a couple of boxing moves, he asked, "So, why were you hiding how well you speak English?"

"It's what got me into trouble." Sam's face fell. "I learned to speak it to help my mother out in the shop she manages. A lot of American tourists buy there, and she encouraged me to study it. She speaks only a little. I picked it up quickly and had fun chatting with the *farang*. They found me cute, and Mom said they bought more stuff because of that."

"How'd that get you in trouble?"

"It's a long story, but not as lengthy as your chicken joke," Sam said. Robert was impressed with his sarcasm; this kid really spoke English well.

"Touché. Go on," Robert said, smiling and shaking his head. They strolled down a path shaded by large tropical trees with wide umbrella-like crowns.

"Some kids I hung out with got me addicted to opium. I couldn't get enough." Sam's head slumped to his chest, and Robert strained to catch his words. "That led to heroin," he croaked. They came to a small wooden bridge over a pond and crossed into Queen Sirikit Park. In stark contrast to Sam's tale of woe, birds were chirping in the rain tree branches that drooped over the rails of the bridge. A laughing thrush with its distinctive white crest squawked and jabbered at them.

"Then they told me I couldn't have it anymore unless I helped them steal. They'd heard about my language skills and wanted me to distract tourists. I'd talk to their marks on the street about…whatever. I'd touch their arm or stomach to slow them down, and that's when my gang pickpocketed them.

"Two of us got caught. My mom pleaded with the judge, and because I was never in trouble before and only fourteen, I got the Orson rehab center. The first week was hell." Sam grimaced and rocked his head in his hands at the memory. "But I've been clean ever since." He raised his head and straightened his back.

"Good, and we'll keep it that way. OK?"

"Yes!" Sam said emphatically. Robert smiled at his determination.

They did more Muay Thai training. Robert, though he felt he had been improving well with his boxing, discovered Sam had a talent for street fighting and caught him off guard twice, giving him a sharp kick in the thigh and later a punch to the chest. Robert wondered if he would learn more from Sam than Sam would from him. After a good hour of that, they found a food stall near the Chatuchak market and bought grilled pork skewers, sticky rice, and roasted vegetables for lunch.

They drifted through the park to the north end and, when they found an unoccupied bench overlooking a pond, sat down in a glade of trees. Grass, dirt, and fallen leaves covered the ground. Ducks bobbed in the tiny lake. Robert could smell decomposing flora, the freshness of the water, and the faint scent of bougainvillea. Birds' cries punctuated the muffled sound of distant traffic. Robert again asked about Sam's family.

"Not much to tell. I never knew my dad. Mom says he died when I was little. If he had a family, I don't know them. I have an aunt, Mom's sister. But she's not married, so I don't have cousins, and my grandparents also died when I was young. My mom's store sells Thai silk to tourists. That's about it." Sam turned his attention back to the tasty morsels on his pork skewers.

"I'm sorry to hear you have such a small family. Mine's small too. But what about school? What subjects do you like, and how are you doing?"

Sam laughed. "I'm good at English and Thai, but not math."

"If you like, I can help you with that," Robert said, eager to support Sam in his area of expertise. He scooped up a spoonful of rice and popped it into his mouth.

"I like biking and boxing, but yeah, we could do that. I need to learn how to do Mom's accounts." Sam shook his head. "This life of mine, and I nearly threw it away."

Robert considered Sam, who looked across the water at the buildings on the other side. Sam's tone had been wistful but genuine. The comment showed a depth of maturity that Robert knew he didn't have at Sam's age. His protégé had lived a rough life, and now Robert partially held Sam's fate in his hands. He hoped he could provide the help he needed. Sam was worthy of it; Robert could sense Sam's grit and resolve. A fast learner, he'd picked up boxing kicks and punches after one demonstration.

Later, they found Andrea and Mai waiting by the car on Kamphaeng Phet 3 Road. Robert said goodbye, saying he would make his own way home.

The following week, the three of them rotated through the stakeout starting on Monday. Each night, one of them observed the warehouse from midnight to 3 a.m. On the nights Robert had the watch, Andrea excused him from their morning workout, but otherwise she never failed to pick him up at 6 a.m.—even after her observation evenings. The guards had a routine. At midnight, a new guard relieved the exterior guard and then presumably lasted until morning. Sometimes they observed one person, always the same guy, emerge from the warehouse to talk to the outside man. This occurred between midnight and 1 a.m. At 3 a.m. a van pulled up, the driver stepped out, woke up the guard and checked inside to make sure all was well. Then it left. Andrea concluded 2 a.m. the following Wednesday would be an ideal time to enter. The exterior guard usually slept from 1:30 a.m. to 3 a.m., and they assumed the interior guard would be tired, if not asleep.

They were ready to break in.

CHAPTER 10

After picking up Robert and Sakchai, Andrea drove to the warehouse. She parked behind a shipping container, out of view of the guard, and well away from the target building. The dark, cloudless sky pushed the oppressive humidity down to street level. Andrea could smell rotting fish, engine oil, and rusty metal coming from the nearby docks. The distant, muted sound of Bangkok traffic came from the city behind them. On the other side of the row of buildings, the Chao Phraya River imparted an eerie stillness to the night.

Andrea reviewed her plan with Sakchai and Robert. She knew her plans sounded like she winged it, but she'd found that no strategy, however meticulously detailed, ever worked as originally envisioned. She preferred having a loose framework, remaining flexible, and dealing with the inevitable surprises as they came up.

They put on their balaclavas and got out of the car. Andrea peeked around the corner of the container that obscured their Toyota from the guard, who sat on a chair near the door. Even from two hundred yards away, he looked wide awake as he drank from a thermos.

They waited.

And waited.

Finally, after fifteen minutes, he leaned back and fell asleep as soon as his head hit the wall behind him. Andrea inched up on him, poured some chloroform from a bottle onto a cloth, and placed it over his face, holding her head away from the fumes. He awoke and grabbed her arm. Panic blazed in his eyes as he struggled to comprehend what was happening. Then he crumpled in a heap, nearly sliding to the ground. Andrea grabbed him by the shirt and righted him to make sure he didn't fall out of his chair.

She picked the lock and entered. Robert followed but stayed near the door. Sakchai, as the lookout, hid behind another container, equidistant between the guard and their vehicle.

Andrea crept like a cat into the cavernous space and sidled along the wall of the warehouse, searching for the other sentry. The interior had a series of tables where during the day Wang's minions cut, mixed, and packaged the drugs when a shipment was being prepared for distribution. Andrea walked counterclockwise, bending over to look under the tables as she passed them. She didn't need her flashlight; moonlight streamed in from the ventilation holes in the ceiling. Nothing on the first wall. She turned left at the corner, moving with longer strides. They would be short on time if she didn't find the guard soon. She finished the second wall, and still no watchman. But when she turned that corner, she stumbled upon a mattress on the floor. A dark blanket covered the sleeping caretaker, barely visible in the dim light.

She worked her way around the table near his bed, poured more of the knockout drug on the cloth, and leaned over. His head and torso shot up, and he shouted, "Aiee!" He looked straight ahead, eyes wide open. A nightmare. Andrea grabbed him by his hair and slammed the chloroform rag into his face. He struggled as he awakened, but he proved to be no match for the powerful anesthetic.

Andrea let out her breath and lowered the sentry back into his bed. He breathed raggedly, and his body twitched, but he wouldn't wake up soon. She darted to the front door and whispered the news to Robert, who followed her to the office. They climbed the stairs to the windowless room, and Andrea unlocked the door. Red, black, and gold dragons painted on the sides of the furniture greeted them when they turned on the light. Ignoring the décor, they found two gray filing cabinets with hundreds of folders. They pulled some out, looking for one with information on a large shipment. Only Robert could read the Thai, so Andrea helped by getting files out, opening them, and laying them on the desk and table. Robert flipped through file after file.

It was already 2:45 a.m. They needed to find the right document and photograph it.

Andrea jerked her head over to watch Robert, who stared at one folder. He'd found an invoice, entirely in Thai, describing a sixty-ton shipment of rice destined to arrive in Bangkok on February 12 from Chiang Rai, a city in the middle of the Golden Triangle. Heroin would be hidden in the shipment, and the trucks would pick up a special drug in northern Bangkok before arriving at Wang's main warehouse. Robert nodded at Andrea, confirming he had what they were looking for. He laid the sheets describing the cargo out on the office's conference table and arranged them to photograph a page at a time.

"I'll go keep watch on the guards downstairs," Andrea said, heading for the door. As she stole down the stairs, she heard Sakchai whistle a warning. She sprinted to the front door, and Sakchai pointed to the outside sentry, who was rolling his head around, shaking it. She splashed some chloroform onto her rag and clasped it to his nose. He slumped in his chair. She then ran into the warehouse to check on the other guy, who was also stirring. Had the chemist diluted the drug? She poured the remaining liquid onto the rag, grabbed the guard by his head, shoved the cloth into his face, and held it there. After counting to fifteen, she let his head drop. He was still breathing but knocked out.

She heard Sakchai's whistle again and dashed to the door. In the dimness, she tripped on some equipment and fell hard on her knee. Pain shot up her entire right side. She picked herself up, limped to the front door, and peered out.

She couldn't see Sakchai anywhere.

After Andrea left the office, Robert pulled out the Minolta and almost dropped it. The heat in the warehouse had seeped into his body, and his perspiring hands made his fingers slippery. He set the camera down, wiped his hands on his trousers, and prepared to photograph the pages. There were ten. He photographed the first one. Then the next one.

A man came out of a doorway at the back of the office.

Shaking his head, he rubbed his eyes in the light, then gawked at Robert and the files spread out on the desk. "What are you doing here?" he shouted in Thai and leaped at Robert, who stood gaping at him.

Robert fell backward, landing with a noisy thump. A sharp bolt of pain burst in his hip. The camera slammed onto the wooden floor and clattered across it, hitting each gap in the floorboards. As the man jumped on him, Robert reached for his gun even as he felt the man's hands on his throat, choking him. He lifted the gun out, but the man grabbed it from him by twisting his hand down and away.

At that moment, Andrea was searching out the front door for Sakchai and wondering about his whistle. Hearing the ruckus in the office area, she hesitated, then leaped up the stairs, fighting the ache in her leg. She opened the door and saw Robert on his back. A Thai man straddled him, one hand on Robert's neck, the other waving in the air, holding a pistol. Both of Robert's hands clutched the Thai's gun-wielding wrist.

Andrea rushed over to the struggling pair. The Thai looked up just in time to receive a powerful punch to the face. He sprawled backwards, dropping the Beretta. Robert scrambled up and seized his gun. He stood up.

The man looked at Andrea, then back at Robert, both clad in menacing balaclavas, and jumped to his feet. Robert whacked him on the head with the butt of his gun as he ran for the back door. He fell in a heap, eyes rolling back, out cold.

"Chloroform?" Robert asked.

"All out," Andrea said, slicing the words at him. Then, looking at the Thai on the floor, she added, "You're going to have to get better at fighting. That guy is way smaller than you."

Robert's shoulders slumped. Then he grabbed the camera from the floor and took the remaining photos, but the shutter clattered instead of clicked. He replaced the files and said, "Shall we go?"

"I don't know where Sakchai is," Andrea said, still angry. "He whistled, but I couldn't see him out front."

"Do we go out the front or the back?"

"Let's try the front."

But as they approached the door, they heard a truck pulling up, a vehicle louder than the Toyota.

Sakchai was monitoring the door, the guard, and their car when he saw the sentry awakening. He raced to the front door and whistled to Andrea, who came immediately and drugged the sentry a second time.

Later, still watching for trouble, he saw two men approach their vehicle from the shadows and jimmy the driver-side window. He ran to the door of the warehouse and gave a second whistle, then to the container, which obscured him as he looked around to see the thieves attempting to enter their car. They would soon be in the Toyota.

Sakchai took a deep breath. Gun or hand to hand? A gun would be too noisy.

He ran around the corner of the container at full speed. One man had just opened the door. They both looked at him, mouths slack. Sakchai slammed the car door and piled into them, landing a solid blow to the first one's head. That one reeled backward, bouncing off the car, but the other one jumped on Sakchai's back, trying to knock him over while hitting his head. Sakchai grabbed the man's head and flipped him off and onto the ground. The thug jumped up and attempted to kick his adversary, but Sakchai grabbed his leg and counter-kicked to the groin. The man crumpled, and the Thai-born DEA agent put him out with a kick to the gut and a punch to the head.

Which is when the other man got up, drew a knife, and came at Sakchai.

Sakchai pulled out his gun. "Drop the knife!" he growled.

The man threw the knife down and turned to run. Sakchai clipped his heel, sending him sprawling, then used his gun to knock him out.

Just as Wang's relief truck pulled up to the building.

At the front door, Andrea glanced out and saw Wang's vehicle arriving. She motioned to Robert to grab one end of a nearby table. They moved it in front of the door, flipping it on its side to provide some extra resistance. As Robert sprinted toward the back door, Andrea limped after him. Andrea saw the worry in his eyes when he glanced back. He came back to help her.

"Get the back gate open!" she hissed. She could hear the men at the front door rousing the guard, who was mumbling and slurring his words. They had just reached the garage door when they heard scraping from the table on the floor as the thugs forced the entry open. The giant gate at the back was bolted on the inside. Robert flipped the lock mechanism and leaned into the heavy metal door, creating a space for one person. Andrea hobbled out, followed by Robert, who shoved the huge steel slab shut. She looked up and down the road.

No Toyota.

"Now what?" Robert asked.

"He'll come from this way," Andrea said, pointing to the right. She began shuffling in that direction. Robert ran to her side and linked his arm in hers to help her move forward. She shoved him away so hard his knee hit the ground.

"I don't need help," she spat. Her leg fired darts of agony to her temples.

"OK. Sorry!"

"Never mind." Andrea kept limping toward where she willed the car to appear from a gap in the line of warehouses.

Sakchai's throat constricted at the sight of the van, and as three men emerged from it, his stomach clenched. At this distance, they'd hear him start the car. He jumped into the driver's seat, released the hand brake, and put the gearshift into neutral. Immediately he got out and leaned his shoulder against the door well, pushing while holding the steering wheel.

The car didn't budge.

He ran to the front of the car, dug in his heels, and shoved with all his strength.

The car rocked.

Sweat streamed from his forehead. He took a deep breath and rocked the car back and forth to get some momentum, and it rolled. He jumped to the driver's door, his hands shaking, and shoved hard to keep the car moving along the road. A hundred yards later, satisfied with his distance from the warehouse front, he started the car and raced to the back of the warehouse.

He sped around the corner so fast, two of the vehicle's wheels lifted into the air. Turning into the skid, he kept the car upright and screeched to a halt when he saw Andrea limping toward him, Robert at her side. Sakchai sped to the left of them, placing the Toyota between them and the exit gate of the building. Leaning back, he flung open the rear door.

Shouts resounded from inside the warehouse as the gate rolled open. More screaming. Andrea piled into the car and Robert clambered on top of her. Sakchai spun the Toyota around, rubber burning, and pointed it away from their pursuers. Andrea and Robert tumbled and rolled into the back seat as the vehicle sped away.

"Get off of me!" Andrea said, shoving Robert toward the floorboard of the cramped back seat.

Shots broke the silence of the night. Sakchai heard two thuds at the back of the car. He zipped around the corner and up the alley. Emerging from the narrow side road, he saw the thug's van still parked in front of the warehouse. He sped to the main road and merged into the late-night traffic. They'd escaped.

Andrea swiveled herself into place behind the passenger seat. Robert scrunched himself into a ball and squeezed himself onto the seat behind Sakchai. They both removed their masks and breathed in the air from the open windows.

"Where to?" Sakchai asked.

"My place," Andrea answered. "I want to develop the film and see what damage we have on the car."

Robert was still struggling to catch his breath and calm down when they reached Andrea's place. Sakchai drove into Andrea's garage and she closed its door behind them. After Sakchai and Robert wedged themselves out of the car, Robert spotted two bullet holes in the back of the Toyota.

"What do we do about them?" he asked.

Andrea went to the passenger side, opened the glove box, and took out some tourist stickers. She covered the holes with the decals, concealing the openings.

"Why didn't the bullets come through to the back seat?" Robert asked.

Andrea opened the trunk, lifting its lid. "Because of that metal plate. It doesn't make the car bulletproof, but at least it provides some protection."

Robert felt somewhat relieved but then added, "As long as some-one is shooting from straight behind us," he observed. *Sometimes you just need luck,* he thought.

Andrea took off the license plate, bent it in half, and threw it into the trunk. She retrieved another plate from the trunk and replaced the old one. She did the same at the front and then shoved Robert and Sakchai into her apartment. Andrea scowled at them. A hot cloud of rage emanated from her. Was she angry with them or about her leg?

Andrea stalked into the living room. "Camera."

Robert handed her the Minolta, and he and Sakchai followed her upstairs. She showed them her darkroom before ordering them to go to the kitchen and make tea. They slumped downstairs, made tea, sat down on the sofa, and waited. Robert's exhaustion made him shudder. He put some sugar in his tea to restore his energy. He noted Sakchai's pale face and damp hair.

Before long, Andrea came down to the living room with some photographic prints flapping in her hands. Her cheeks were deep red, and fury and disappointment contorted her features.

"The good news is…I could develop the film," Andrea said. She flung the prints onto the table, and Robert and Sakchai peered at them. They were all the same—black. "The bad news is…the camera broke and exposed the film, making the pictures garbage. We're going to have to rely on Robert's memory of the contents, since we can't rely on his fighting skills to protect the camera!" She slouched into the armchair opposite Robert and Sakchai and glared at the wall behind them.

CHAPTER 11

As Alex walked to his front door the evening after the break-in, he hung his head, despondent about recent events. The mission had been successful at getting into and out of the warehouse, but they didn't have documentation about the February shipment of drugs.

He'd been easy on Robert. Andrea hadn't; she ripped into the recruit in front of him and Sakchai as if he were a child. She was unhappy with his hand-to-hand combat skills, implying a better fighter would have been able to protect the camera. But Alex and the team needed Robert, and deflating him wouldn't do any good. Alex had cut off Andrea in mid-scold, stating Robert was getting training and would improve.

At least Robert had read part of the document he had photographed. The shipment was scheduled to arrive in Bangkok at Wang's main warehouse on February 12, less than four months away. Wang's drivers would transport it on two trucks with freight containers containing sixty tons of rice and two tons of heroin. The trucks would stop somewhere in Bangkok and pick up sixty kilos of a street drug known as Black Dragon. But no address was listed. After the two narcotics arrived in Bangkok, Wang's crew would mix the additive into the heroin for immediate shipment to the US. Combined, the drugs were worth about twenty million dollars at wholesale prices, $112 million at retail. He told his team he needed time to prepare a request for a special team from DC to aid them in capturing such a large shipment.

With his current three agents, Alex felt like he was juggling mixed props—a hammer, a beanbag, and a softball—and dropping one thing or another from time to time. They did their own thing if you didn't guide them with a subtle flip of the hand. Andrea pounded on about Robert and his incompetence; she even speculated she might do future assignments with Sakchai only. But Robert's Thai fluency counterbalanced his mushiness as an agent and had proved its worth when he discovered the destination of last month's drug shipment and the plans for the coming one. OK, he was trigger-shy and still improving his fighting skills. Hopefully, he'd get over that, but they had destroyed the consignment on the earlier mission—a minor victory, but a victory, nevertheless.

Robert needed encouragement, and he could learn. An atypical agent, he'd never served in the military or worked as a police officer. He was a research analyst who liked to expound on political and economic topics a bit too much, a minor flaw. But his marksmanship distinguished him…if he would only fire the gun! And Andrea needed a third person on her team.

Sakchai served as the bedrock of the unit, providing solid work performance in every area. His detective skills were excellent, and he had a great sense of strategy and a terrific memory, which he used to compete in bridge tournaments and often win at the city level. But he was enigmatic. He'd have something important to reveal about local customs, what's happening on the street, his views, whatever. Did he bring it up? No. Not until you asked him. And sometimes Alex forgot to do that. Why couldn't he just speak up?

At least he didn't have any difficulties managing Lamai. She was competent. Also, she spoke English well, and such people were hard to find in Thailand.

Yep. With the team, it was like juggling diverse objects. The analogy fit.

He opened the door of his small house, stepped inside, and set down his briefcase.

"Daddy, Daddy!" His two young kids, Al and Sally, ran to greet him. One grabbed his left leg, the other his right. He put down his briefcase and hugged their backs. To extricate himself from their clench, he tickled both of them in the ribs, and they fell to the floor, writhing and giggling.

"Where's your mom?"

"In the kitchen," Sally said, still gasping for breath from laughing. "She's making dinner."

"What were you doing before I got home?"

"We were playing Monopoly," Sally said.

"She always wins," Al said, crossing his arms, his face a harrumph. Al was five, while Sally was seven years old.

"You'll win someday, I'm sure," Alex said, ruffling Al's hair with his hand.

"Daddy, when are we going home?" Sally asked.

"Let me talk to your mom about that." Alex frowned at the often-heard complaint. He knew his kids suffered from living overseas, away from their grandparents and the children they had played with in their old neighborhood. But he expected this assignment would land him a promotion, returning them to DC. If they destroyed the February shipment, it would be the biggest drug bust in history. "Why don't you continue with your game while we prepare dinner?"

"OK," Sally said, grabbing Al's hand and dragging him away.

"Hi, honey," Alex said as he entered the kitchen and gave his wife a quick peck on the mouth.

"It's a good question," Shirley said. "When *are* we going home? Aren't we due at least for an extended home leave by Christmas?" Turning to focus on the stove, she stirred the beef stew and asked Alex to fix a salad.

"We have to take at least ten days, so the holidays would be a good time."

"Could we visit my family in Minneapolis this time?"

"Sure. That should work." *Agree, agree, agree. Minneapolis in December—ugh!* "It would be warmer in Florida, where my folks are. Maybe we could fly your parents down there for a family reunion."

"That didn't work out so well last time. Our parents argued constantly."

Alex opened the fridge and got out lettuce and a tomato. "Maybe you're right." *What did I just say to myself? Agree!*

"Besides, I miss the snow. I grew up with it, and it's traditional for me. You know the song." Shirley hummed the tune before lifting out a spoonful of stew to taste. "Mmm. Just right."

"Sure. 'White Christmas.' Bing." *You didn't marry her for her preferences in the weather or songs.* He patted her bottom and kissed her cheek.

"What's that for?" Shirley turned, examining her husband, who was not known for being affectionate.

"I was thinking of how much I love you," Alex said as he began slicing the tomato.

"Hmm. But it's Minneapolis, right?" Shirley swiveled again, and Alex sensed she was watching his back as he worked on the salad.

"Minneapolis. I'll get Lamai to book the flight," Alex said, without looking at her. *Minneapolis, frigging, frigid Minneapolis. And her oh-so-delightful parents. At least there'll be eggnog and maybe a whiskey or two. Make that three.*

"How's work?"

"It's fine," Alex said, then looked up at the wall in front of him. On it a large, round, elementary-school clock told him it was 7:32 p.m. "Actually, it's a disaster but nothing I can't handle."

"A disaster?" asked Shirley, alarmed.

"Yeah, we thought we had photos of some information we needed, but the camera broke, exposing the film."

"Oh, shame!"

"Yes. Not good. But we can recover. I'm hoping the major operation in February will be the thing to get me promoted. It will just be more difficult without the info we lost."

"A promotion would be nice. And well deserved." She took off her apron and crossed the kitchen floor to give him a hug and a proper kiss. "Then we could return to DC, right?"

He turned and squeezed her with his elbows, keeping the knife he held well away from her body. "Yep. Should work. But I may need to ask for a team from the US to come help us out. It's a big undertaking."

"But would you get credit for the success of such a venture if you used an external team? Or would they get most of the glory? It's sort of like you couldn't handle it and needed someone to help. Isn't it?"

"I hadn't thought of that. You may be right." *That's why I married her—she's smart.*

CHAPTER 12

The next morning, with his team arrayed in front of him, Alex sat at his desk drumming his fingers on it. He rearranged some papers in front of him for the third time, and at last spoke. "As I mentioned yesterday, that mission didn't go exactly as we had hoped. We don't know the route of the trucks into Bangkok or where they are supposed to stop first and pick up more drugs. We only know when they will arrive and where they will unload them—Wang's headquarters. This means we can't seize the shipment before it's delivered. Also, without documentation, I'm not sure how supportive headquarters would be of sending additional help. They'd want to run the operation, I'm sure, if they did." Andrea emitted a low, guttural growl. "However, I could still make the pitch. We'd likely be heavily outnumbered taking on a well-guarded warehouse full of drugs. Suggestions anyone?"

"I don't like the idea of headquarters running an operation here in Bangkok," Andrea said. "They don't know the territory or the opponents as well as we do."

"We wouldn't be able to make that decision, but I'm sure they'd want to have your guidance and expertise during any undertaking here."

"I don't get it," Robert said. "The three of us are supposed to go up against an entire gang?"

"It's what we have to work with," Alex said.

Robert let out a derisive burst of air and shook his head.

"Sakchai, you haven't commented. Any thoughts?"

"Perhaps, Mr. Butler, we could create a diversion that would lure many of Mr. Wang's operatives away from the warehouse."

"I'm listening."

"The gang that most concerns Wang's Dragons is the Scorpions. They often fight over territory in the poorer neighborhoods of Bangkok."

"Yes…?"

"If Wang thought the Scorpions were making a raid on his Phra Khanong warehouse on the day we planned to attack his primary warehouse at the port, he would likely send many of his fighters there."

"And how do we convince the Scorpions to help us out?"

"It is only necessary that Mr. Wang *believe* the Scorpions are going to attack his other facility."

"Go on."

"Perhaps Police Commissioner Amonsak Suwannarat might be of assistance."

"But he'd just…Oh, I get it. We lead Amonsak to believe that the Scorpions are planning to attack Wang's other key warehouse, and he informs Wang. When Amonsak asks the Scorpions if they are *actually* planning a raid, they'll say no, but he won't believe them. Amonsak and his crew are tight with the Dragons but not the Scorpions. There'll be distrust all around." Alex bounced his fingertips together. "You know, it might work. I'll have to think of a way to get Amonsak to drag the information out of me, so he believes it. He seems keen to protect Wang's interests."

"Yes, Mr. Butler. You are astute and clever. The plan is sure to be a success."

"Ha! Flattery will get you nowhere, Sakchai."

"He often has good ideas," Andrea boasted. Sakchai listened with a trace of a smile.

"So, we're back to square one, but now maybe with better odds?" Robert asked.

"I can still request a team from the US. If I succeed in getting them here, the odds will improve further," Alex said. *Of course, my chances of promotion might diminish,* he thought, and then wanted to kick himself for thinking such a thing.

Alex stood and paced in the area behind his desk, pausing sporadically to stare out the window. Walking and looking at street scenes always helped him think. On the one hand, he wanted to keep his family happy and get back to the US. For that, he needed more success here in Thailand. Blocking the February shipment would do that, but at what cost? Could he keep his agents alive and get promoted back to the Stateside? Finally, Andrea's tapping foot caught his attention, and he ceased his contemplation.

"Yes, it might work. Rather than making a special appointment with Amonsak, I'll just hint at something in our next scheduled meeting. Yes, yes." Alex looked at his team's expectant eyes.

"Yep. Back to work!"

Robert followed Sakchai and Andrea into her office.

After they were seated at her conference table, Andrea said, "Sakchai, that was a brilliant idea you had, but I think we'll need to help Alex flesh it out."

"I think Mr. Jordan should accompany Mr. Butler when he visits Amonsak," Sakchai said. "Since he doesn't know Mr. Jordan speaks Thai, we may learn something extra about their thoughts on our, how should I call it, intrigue?"

"But you usually accompany Alex to translate. Won't he be suspicious?"

"I can conveniently be sick that day, and Alex can use it as an excuse to introduce the commissioner to our new agent."

"Can you do that, Robert?"

"I've trained myself not to react when people speak to me in Thai. I just go blank and provide no facial expressions—no matter what people say."

"Sakchai had a good idea. What about you, Robert?"

"I've hacked into the police department's computers, so we should be able to get some additional information on their thoughts and actions from that source," Robert murmured, unsure of the response this news would get.

"What? You've hacked their computers? No one told me that was one of your skills."

"I don't normally talk about it, except with my computer buddy, Jermaine. It's something we do for fun—just to see if we can do it. We don't disrupt any of the programs or systems. We only see if we can find interesting information." Robert was sweating. *Maybe this is a skill I shouldn't talk about.*

"So, where have you broken into, aside from the local government?"

"I'd rather not say."

"Isn't it illegal?"

"It's a good question," Robert said, rushing the words out. "I don't think so. Not yet anyway. Not as long as we avoid disrupting anything."

"Show us," Andrea said, rising to her feet.

"Sure. Come to my office. It's easier on my terminal." Robert's heart skipped a beat. Could this be something that impressed Andrea?

As Andrea and Sakchai watched over his shoulders, Robert brought up the login page of the nonpublic police site. A second later: *Access Granted.*

"How do you get in?" Andrea asked, with shock and wonder.

"I got some police names from the newspaper and tried their first names and last names to gain access. People are amazingly lazy about creating passwords and changing them. I've been using this one for a couple of weeks. But let's try Pravat's account." Robert kept typing and brought up Pravat's login page. He tested a few passwords, but none of them worked.

"What else do we know about Pravat, Sakchai?"

"His wife's name is Kanchana."

Robert typed in the name. "Bingo! We're in his account now." Robert beamed.

"Wow," Andrea said. "But what does that get us?"

"The information he has about police activities, including drug raids," Robert replied.

"Have you told Alex that you have penetrated the police's computer?" Andrea asked, her brow furrowed.

"No. And I hadn't planned to do so, either."

"Why not?"

"I'm afraid he'll tell me to stop doing it." Robert recalled the time he had told his boss in the US about his talent. His boss had ordered him never to do it again. Of course, he ignored him.

"Good point. But I think Alex would be happy with any advantage we can get on the police and the local drug lords."

Andrea regarded Robert. "Sometimes you're all right, Robert," she said, smiling, and she punched him in the shoulder. Robert rocked from the tap, winced at the pain, but grinned from ear to ear.

CHAPTER 13

The following week, Robert accompanied Alex to his regularly scheduled meeting with Police Commissioner Amonsak Suwannarat. After they waited in the vestibule for about thirty minutes, Amonsak's secretary showed them into his office, a grand suite. Amonsak sat behind a six-foot-wide desk that held only a green paper blotter bordered in leather, a pen case, and a small Thai flag. A few expansive paintings of the countryside adorned the walls. His chief of staff, Prin Anurak, sat to his right, sitting upright, his expression empty and uninviting. Both Thais rose and gave Alex and Robert each a *wai*. The two DEA agents followed suit. Then Amonsak signaled for them to sit across from him. The sun poured in from two large windows behind the Thai officials, making Alex and Robert squint into the glare.

Alex introduced Robert and explained Sakchai couldn't make it today because he was ill.

"Oh? Does Robert speak Thai?" Amonsak asked.

"No, but he's our new guy, and I thought you'd like to meet him."

"It's a pleasure to meet you, Mr. Jordan," Amonsak said, nodding. He then spoke to Prin in the local language, his words pronounced slowly and distinctly. Robert looked at Alex, perplexed, but Alex shrugged his shoulder and waited patiently until Amonsak and Prin finished their discussion.

"Well, we've had a few developments since we last met, eh, Mr. Butler?" Amonsak asked.

"Yes, we were there on the successful capture of drugs by Colonel Pravat. Congratulations!" Alex said. "I couldn't take part, but Robert observed it."

"Yes, along with Agent Cannon and Sakchai. Colonel Pravat informed me. But I'm not sure it was that successful. Someone later stole the drugs from police protection and killed one of our night watchmen."

"Oh, really?" Alex asked, expressing shock. "I'm sorry to hear that. Please accept my condolences. We heard the Scorpions suddenly had an increase in supply. Do you think it could be related?"

Amonsak nodded again and turned to Prin for a discussion that lasted at least a minute. This time the words were a rapid staccato. Robert gazed at the landscape pictures, feigning boredom.

"We did not hear that, but it is possible. Can you tell me your source of information?" Amonsak asked, probing.

"I'm sorry, Mr. Suwannarat. I can't reveal that because I don't know. Sakchai has a good ear to the ground here, but he protects his sources."

"Yes, he is a most interesting person, your Sakchai." Amonsak straightened in his chair, becoming even more erect.

"We're lucky to have him."

"Indeed. We also have good contacts. We heard from our sources in the Dragons that there was a break-in at their large warehouse and two tall non-Thais were involved." Amonsak's narrowed eyes seemed to be trying to pierce Alex's mind to gauge his reaction.

"Interesting," Alex said. The hair on the back of Robert's neck bristled, and his heart raced. "What do you suppose it was about?"

"We thought you might help us. Both agent Cannon and agent Jordan are tall."

"Mr. Amonsak, I hope you are not suggesting that my team broke into a Dragon stronghold without informing you! I assure you if we knew anything about anyone breaking into one of Wang's buildings, you would be the first to know," Alex said, leaning forward and looking Amonsak straight in the eye.

While Amonsak consulted with Prin, Robert shaded his eyes and looked out the window, his face expressionless. When he glanced at Alex, he saw a picture of firm consternation. At last, Amonsak turned and looked at Alex.

"Very well, Mr. Butler," Amonsak said. "We'll assume it's an odd coincidence. But I trust you will keep us informed if you learn anything further about the theft of the confiscated drugs or the break-in of the Dragon headquarters."

"Of course, as always," Alex said, eager to please.

"What news have you heard from your contacts?"

"Not much. You know, the usual street noise," Alex said in a casual, breezy voice. Robert watched as Alex shifted uneasily in his chair.

Almost imperceptibly, Amonsak's brow knitted, and his eyes narrowed. "Nothing at all?"

Alex squirmed in his chair. "No. Nothing unusual."

"You wouldn't hide anything from us, would you?" Amonsak said, glaring at Alex.

"Me? No. Of course not. Never," Alex said, shaking his head and waving his hands to say no.

"Did you want to mention something about the tension between the Scorpions and the Dragons?" Robert asked, with innocence and confusion.

Alex swiveled and scowled at Robert for less than a second, then appeared to catch himself. He looked up, reflecting on the ceiling. "Oh. Yes. Robert reminds me that we've heard there's increased mistrust between the Dragons and the Scorpions. Perhaps aggravated by the Dragon's loss of that drug haul? Nothing definite. Nothing unusual. We're monitoring it." To end the conversation, Alex affected boredom with his last three sentences.

"Interesting," Amonsak said, leaning back and touching the tips of his fingers together. "We've heard nothing of this, but please keep us informed if you get more specific information. That can be through me or directly to Colonel Pravat."

"I will certainly do that."

"Is there anything else, Mr. Butler?"

"No, that's all we have. I wish we had more," Alex said, with the breezy tone again.

They bowed to each other. As Alex and Robert departed the room, Alex bent over and whispered something harsh into Robert's ear.

When Robert and Alex got to their building, Alex called Andrea into his office for the debrief. Sakchai was still at home, pretending to be sick.

"Do you think our ruse worked?" Alex asked.

"I think we got them interested," Robert replied with a slight grin.

"Me too," Alex said. "We'll have to dribble out the information." Alex leaned back in his chair, basking in the moment.

"Congratulations!" Andrea said, sweeping her arms in a gesture of approval.

"Thanks, Andrea. But what did they say?" Alex leaned forward, directing his eyes at Robert, who stood in front of his desk with Andrea.

"Their first conversation was about how ugly-looking Americans are. Prin said he had heard the men have tiny penises. Amonsak compared us to pink pigs. Both noted that we never learn the local language."

"Really? That's obnoxious," Alex said from his chair.

"I'm surprised you didn't react," Andrea said, nudging Robert with her elbow. He ignored her.

"I think they were trying to provoke me in case I knew Thai. They spoke leisurely and graphically—slow enough for someone who had just learned the language to grasp it. Later they talked rapidly, more naturally."

"Go on."

"They clearly don't trust us and suspect we stole the drugs and destroyed them after they disappeared from their warehouse. No one knows where those narcotics went. We're also suspected of being behind the break-in at Wang's main warehouse. They don't have any proof, but they don't know of anyone else who would do it. We are the only group with an interest in these things. Everyone else is benefitting from the drug trade."

"Hmmm. Anything else?"

"Yes, they'll cut us out of any drug raids in the future. We'll hear about them after the fact."

"Ouch," Alex said. "I could tell they didn't trust us, but I wouldn't have known about the decision to keep us away from the drug raids. Thank you, Robert. You continue to earn your keep."

"Thanks, Alex," Robert replied. He grinned, basking in the glow of the praise.

"But we'll still know what the police will be up to," Andrea said, pushing out her chest. "Tell him, Robert."

"Yes, I've hacked into the police computer." Robert gulped. "I even have access to Pravat's account."

"Excuse me? You what?" Alex asked, struggling to comprehend what Robert had just said.

"In DC, a friend and I hacked into government accounts for the fun of it," Robert said, hastening to add, "We never stole anything or disrupted anything. We only searched files."

"OK. I didn't hear that. Let's get back to Bangkok." Alex rubbed his forehead with both hands. "You can hack into the police accounts?" Alex looked at Robert. "Is that legal?"

"Officially, it's not illegal unless I disrupt something. Not even in the US. At least not yet."

"It sounds like it *should* be illegal," Alex said. "But this could be very useful." He mused aloud, "My new guy knows three languages—English, Thai, and computers." He shook his head in wonder.

"Any word about getting support from the US for the February shipment?" Andrea interjected, trying to bring Alex back to their current tasks.

"I thought you didn't want help from headquarters?" Alex asked.

"I want the mission to be successful and my team intact," Andrea hissed.

"OK. Fair enough. No, I just filed the report on Monday, and it went out in the diplomatic pouch yesterday. I don't know when they'll reply or how they'll respond."

"OK. Let us know when you hear."

"Sure." Alex held up his hands, dismissing them.

In the hallway, Robert didn't resist as Andrea shoved him into her office.

"Will you be able to spot a police raid from what you can get on your computer?"

"I should," Robert said. "The information for the raid where we took part was up the week before it occurred. I hardly think they are going to change their documentation procedures." Robert spoke with confidence, even though he knew he couldn't guarantee this would be the case. He didn't want to lose the warm glow he felt from being appreciated.

"But the police are full of leaks," Andrea said with scorn.

"Yes, that's why it's good that I have access to Pravat's account—I can find information there that's not widely shared."

"OK, keep me informed." Andrea nodded, satisfied—and pleased—with Robert's response.

"Absolutely."

Robert returned to his office and fired up his computer. He searched through everything but could find nothing new about police operations.

On the Sunday of his fourth full weekend in Bangkok, Robert went to the Crazy Bird, as usual, for breakfast. Chai greeted him by name and welcomed him to sit on his favorite barstool. He didn't need to order; Chai knew his regular Sunday morning meal—an American breakfast of eggs, bacon, toast, and hash browns. The other three chairs at the bar were taken. Two Australian women were reenacting a football (soccer) match, probably the first leg win of South Melbourne over Sydney Olympic. They would twist their torsos and fling out their feet in a frenzy of motion. Afterward, they'd shake their heads in amazement and gulp some beer, even though it was only 9 a.m.

A slim and stylishly dressed Thai woman of about thirty also sat at the bar. An untouched cup of tea rested on the counter in front of her. As Robert slipped into his usual seat, which was next to her, she turned to him and asked expectantly, "Gerard?"

"No, I'm Robert." They were sitting so close, he could only give an awkward *wai* and couldn't fully turn to see her.

"Fon," she said, introducing herself. She bent her head and clasped her hands in front of her face. "I didn't mean to bother you; I'm waiting for someone, and he is late."

"Sorry to hear that," Robert said as Chai set down a coffee for him. He could see the woman in the mirror, and she looked distressed as she turned to see if anyone had walked into the café.

Fon nodded and said, "I was supposed to meet a man named Gerard here, but he is over thirty minutes late. So, I think it is unlikely that he will come now."

"Oh, I see," Robert said, opening his eyes wide and scanning Fon for clues of her employment. She wore a white dress with short sleeves, simple and elegant, that draped down below her knees. It fit her body nicely, showing her curves without being too snug. But she didn't look like a prostitute.

"It's not what you think. I work for a tour guide company." Fon gave Robert her business card: Fon Chongrak, Tour Guide, with her company's name and phone number. "We take tourists around to the best sights—the *wats*, the Grand Palace, the markets, the food stalls, and restaurants. I thought something was wrong when I came here. Most of our clients stay at hotels like the Mandarin Oriental. This is…uh…"

"Yes, definitely déclassé," Robert said, looking at the dusty paper lanterns and the tawdry poster of a young Thai woman. "But I like it and the food's good. Evenings, Chai mixes a mean Sabai Sabai, and the beer is always fresh."

"This is what you call your 'local?'"

"Yes, I live nearby and come here often. Your English is fantastic."

"Yes, we have regular English lessons at my company, so we can improve."

"Can I buy you breakfast? Who knows, maybe Gerard will show up before we finish eating." Robert yearned to talk to someone other than his colleagues, where only work subjects prevailed.

"Thank you. That is kind, but I have eaten."

"A drink then?"

"Yes, thank you. It's a bit early for a Sabai Sabai," she said, with an impish smile. "I'll have an orange juice."

"An orange juice, Chai." Chai gave a thumbs-up and brought the drink.

"Why don't we find a table? It's noisy here." If the Australians heard him, they paid him no mind.

Robert found a spot, and Chai brought her juice and his mug of coffee while he carried his plate and cutlery. Seated across from Fon, Robert could view her better. She had a round face and dark-brown hair pulled into a bun. She had blackened her eyelashes, rouged her lips, and darkened her eyebrows into a long curve. He breathed in her perfume—jasmine.

While Robert ate and Fon sipped, they talked about their lives. When Fon told him she had grown up in Surat Thani, he had to bite his tongue to keep from saying anything about his time with the Peace Corps near that city. He knew it well. Her dad owned a popular restaurant there, the Khrua Ohm, a place Robert had eaten at once. It made enough money to educate her and her two brothers. Her younger brother worked with her dad at the restaurant. But her older brother had a severe case of hepatitis and liver problems. His expensive medication was one reason she worked in Bangkok—to make extra money to send home for his drugs and treatment. She had studied English at a technical school and gotten the job as a tour guide after graduating. Robert told her about his family, how his father had died when he was ten and his mother had raised her three children while working as an accountant. She had died when he was thirty. He said his brother, Matt, had tragically died recently of a heart attack. His only remaining family, his sister Robin, worked in health care. He enjoyed giving a partially accurate account of his background, with changed names and details. Lying about his entire history would've been awkward.

Her brother's illness sounded like it might have come from sharing needles, a common transmission mechanism for hepatitis C, but Robert said nothing. Such a comment might make him sound knowledgeable about drug usage beyond his supposed background. He told her his cover story about his work in Thailand and some of his research work.

She asked him what he had learned about Thailand while working here. He discussed the prime minister, Prem Tinsulanonda, and his economic and political policies and how the economy prospered despite—as one could find in any country—some corruption.

Robert blushed from Fon's keen interest in his work. She expressed admiration of his knowledge of Thai politics and the economy. She said she didn't follow these things carefully in the newspapers. But she knew that her father's business thrived—people had more to spend on eating out—so much so that he planned to open a second restaurant.

After they finished eating and drinking, Robert asked, "Do you see your Gerard?"

Fon scanned the restaurant area, but there were no single foreign males to be seen. The young people at the café were in groups of two or more.

"No, I do not see him." Fon stood to leave, so Robert also got to his feet.

"Well, how about you give me a tour instead?"

"Oh! I'd be delighted to do that, but I must first check in with my office," Fon said, looking grateful to have a client for the day.

She used the phone at the bar and returned to Robert, her face cheerful. "Shall we go? I have already planned the day," she said and winked.

CHAPTER 14

After Robert stopped at a cash machine and paid Fon, they went to the Grand Palace. When she walked away from him to buy their tickets, Robert promised himself that he would look more at the sights than at Fon but knew it would be difficult. He smiled and raised his hand to his forehead to block the sun's glare as he looked at the palace entrance.

"Let's first go to the Wat Phra Kaew, the Temple of the Emerald Buddha," Fon said.

After they entered the complex containing the *wat*, they approached the temple, took off their shoes, and walked into the shrine. Robert inhaled the woody scent of frankincense wafting from burning joss sticks set alight as an offering to the spirits. A breeze rustled their clothes. The green jasper Buddha statue was small—a little over two feet tall. But Robert's eyes widened in wonder when he looked up at such a large piece of semiprecious stone clothed in gold vestments and framed by a structure that stretched to the ceiling. The statue was the country's palladium, protecting the nation. When he turned to Fon to gauge her reaction, he caught her looking at him, assessing his response.

Leaving the Buddha, they examined the scale model of Angkor Wat, the famous Cambodian Hindu-Buddhist temple. The details of the miniature made Robert want to visit Cambodia to see the shrine, which covered over four hundred acres, a sanctuary so vast it would take days to view.

Fon then led Robert to the nearby Phra Mondop, with its sumptuous entrance. Its sixteen columns, each covered with multicolored tiles, stretched forty feet to support the roof. By now, many tourists were jostling for space, taking photos, and gawking at the tall gold entry with its red ceiling.

In the Queen Sirikit Museum of Textiles, they found a large area filled with a wide variety of Thai textiles. Particularly stunning were the shiny silk dresses, draped over headless mannequins. The costumes intrigued Robert with their meticulous designs in so many hues and styles.

Fon directed Robert to the Pavilion of Regalia last, to view the coins and royal artifacts. Its exhibits included many national treasures of Thai history and art, showcasing its cultural heritage. Robert, of course, examined the coins with great interest; their descriptions strengthened his understanding of Thailand's economic history.

Fon described the sights well but surprised Robert with her frequent references to her notes, detailing the palace's history. She sometimes fumbled with her cheat sheet and became nervous.

The sun blazed down on them as Fon led them to a pleasant, quiet nearby restaurant.

"Have you been a tour guide long?" Robert asked after they seated themselves.

"No!" Fon responded, her cheeks flashing pink beneath her soft brown skin. "This is only my second week. I'm still on probation. And I sometimes get nervous. Was I OK?"

"You were fine. Somehow, I got the impression you had been doing this work for a long time."

"No, I'm still learning. I've been on tours with my colleagues, but I have not yet memorized the—how do you say it? Patter?"

Robert laughed. "Yes, that is the exact word. Or spiel."

"Spiel?" Fon asked with a tinge of puzzlement.

"And what do you do for fun in your spare time, Fon?"

"Oh, not much. I am careful with my spending habits, so I can help support my family. I save as much as possible also because I would like to visit the US someday. My teachers, who have traveled there, tell me it is a fascinating country. Wealthy and unimaginably large."

"Yes, there is a lot to see in the US. One of my favorite memories is riding mules down into the Grand Canyon with my brother. Mom and my sister stayed up on the ridge. The cliff's beauty is spectacular—so humongous and colorful. Plus, the crazy surefootedness of the mules, keeping you on a narrow path where a slip would mean sure death as you tumbled into the depths below. Wild! We also went to Bryce Canyon and later visited some Native American ruins." Robert, thinking he'd been enthusing too long, shifted to asking about Fon. "But surely you must have friends."

"Yes, we meet for meals, and sometimes we go see a film together. When I get a chance, I visit my family in Surat Thani."

Robert studied Fon as she spoke, and he could see that Fon's family was very important to her. When she spoke of them, her voice changed, softening with respect and affection. She yearned to have more time with them, to travel to see them. Beneath her formal sentences and calm appearance, he sensed nervousness, like a bird trapped in a cage, flying from one side to the other, seeking to escape. But he couldn't determine the source of her unease—was it her inexperience as a guide, him, or something else?

"You changed your hair," Robert said, noting that she must have let it down when they entered the restaurant.

"Yes," Fon said, flicking her hair to the right to get it out of her face. Then she put her elbow on the table and rested her chin on the back of her hand. "Do you like it?"

"Very much. It's lovely." *Is she flirting with me?* His stomach tightened, and a fluttering thrill raced through his heart.

Fon straightened her back, folded her hands in her lap, and gazed into Robert's eyes. She smiled. "Thank you."

The Thai menu had no pictures, so Robert asked Fon to order for both of them, which she did. When Fon asked what he liked, Robert told her he ate everything.

"Everything?" Fon asked.

"Yes. Everything."

Robert let his eyes roam around the room while Fon spoke to the server. He knew what she ordered, but faked surprise when the food arrived. For starters, Fon chose ant eggs in curry sauce and steamed wasps wrapped in banana leaves. Her eyes widened as she watched Robert eat the food. He pretended never to have tasted either, holding the wasps up to his eyes for inspection before nibbling on them. After the unconventional beginning of the meal, Fon switched to standard Thai food—pad thai and a red chicken curry, the specialties of the house.

"Delicious!" Robert announced at the end of the meal.

"Yes, I was impressed with the way you handled the insect dishes. You said 'everything,' but I didn't believe you. I enjoy teasing people. It's naughty, I know. I shouldn't have."

The word *naughty* caught Robert's attention, but he didn't think it polite to ask about her playful habits. "Oh, no problem. But what was the first dish—the curry one? The wasps I recognized."

"Ant eggs."

"OK," Robert said, bobbing his head as if this information shocked him. "What would you have done if I had refused to eat them?"

"I would have eaten them myself and ordered something bland for you. You're paying," Fon said with a coquettish smile.

"Yes, that makes sense." Fon's pink-rouged lips made Robert forgive the trick she had played on him. He admired the arch of her neck and the blush on her cheek highlighted by the overhead lights.

Robert had to stop himself from saying he'd eaten these dishes before; that he was being "naughty" himself. Why was he so tempted to tell Fon about his past?

Later that afternoon, they strolled to the nearby Wat Phra Chetuphon with its giant reclining Buddha covered in gold leaf. When they had seen the solid gold Buddha at the Wat Traimit, Robert said he was done with *wats*—their beauty and colorfulness had become overwhelming.

To finish their tour, they attended the last Kohn performance of the day at the Sala Chalermkrung Royal Theatre. The dancing mesmerized Robert and Fon. Garbed in ornate, sparkling costumes, the actors paced through the elaborate sword fights with acrobatic dignity. Robert recognized many of the moves from his Thai boxing lessons, but what he saw was much more stylized. The Thai music accompanying the show tinkled and clinked, tickling the audience's ears. Musky incense wafted through the air, enhancing the otherworldliness of the act. Robert found the performance to be more refined and intricate than anything he had seen in his Peace Corps days.

After the half-hour show, Robert asked to visit a food market with Fon so she could help him buy the ingredients for Thai curries.

"You cook?"

"Yes, I enjoy cooking," Robert said. "It's fun and relaxing. I might have a Singha beer or two with it to enjoy a quiet evening at home."

They went to an open market near his apartment block that had plenty of fruits, vegetables, poultry, meat, seafood, and curry ingredients for sale. The market exploded with smells, colors, and the cacophony of street markets worldwide. They entered at the end of the market that had flower stalls. Robert picked out an enormous bunch of yellow daisies and asked Fon to carry them. Next, he spotted a merchant selling baskets, so he bought a woven grass one with leather shoulder straps to carry his food.

At a fruit trader, Robert asked Fon to order about half a kilo each of oranges and limes and a kilo of bananas.

"What about this papaya?" Fon asked, pointing to a ripe-looking specimen.

"Sure!" Robert responded as a merchant pushing a cart full of onions passed behind them.

When they arrived at a vegetable dealer, Robert wanted green beans, a small cabbage, and carrots. As Fon ordered, another customer stepped up and made a rapid-fire series of requests. Fon objected, and the merchant served them first.

Robert purchased onions, garlic, scallions, and shallots from one merchant, and they moved toward a vendor selling the ingredients for chili paste. Walking to it, they avoided a motorbike and rider winding along the aisle, dodging shoppers.

The seller had a wide variety of green, red, and orange peppers, both large and small. Robert wanted to make a Thai green chili, so he asked Fon to get him kaffir lime leaves, galangal, lemongrass, and Thai sweet basil.

"You know how to make a curry paste?"

"Yes, I took a class when I arrived. It lasted a few hours. But I was pleased my dish came out so well." He knew how to cook Thai food from his Surat Thani days but had taken the class soon after his arrival to bolster his local cover.

"Impressive," Fon said, a little awed, since most Thai men didn't cook at home.

Robert shook his head, grinning. "Not really. I'm a huge fan of my cooking, though. Just biased, I guess."

Fon expertly ordered the various required fixings for the chili in precise quantities, and the seller placed them in plastic bags, then handed them to Robert, who paid for them. Fon watched as the money exchanged hands, making sure it was the correct amount, then nodded with satisfaction and thanked the merchant with a quick *wai*.

"You should come back to my place and help me prepare the meal."

Fon's head arched back, and her eyes widened at Robert's forwardness. "That would not be proper."

"Oh, sorry!" Robert's face flushed red. "I wasn't thinking. Of course, you're right." Rushing to recover, he added, "I could take you to dinner if you like."

"No, I must be getting home," Fon said firmly. "My roommate is expecting me. We're eating out tonight."

"That's good. Enjoy your evening. But…when will I see you again?" Robert asked, his voice a little scratchy.

Fon had turned to leave but now examined Robert. After pausing, she said, "I'm available for a tour next Saturday, if you like."

"OK, I'll arrange that on Monday with your agency."

"I'd like that. Good night, Robert."

"Oh, wait! Take some flowers." He grabbed half the daisies and handed them to Fon. She smiled as she took them in her hand, holding them up to her nose to smell, her face lighting up like a yellow lantern. Then she bowed, turned, and walked away.

Robert watched Fon disappear into the crowd at the market, observing the sway of her hips. *Wow, does she always walk that way?*

CHAPTER 15

On Monday, Robert was still smiling from his day spent with Fon; the image of her face filled his mind as he anticipated the coming weekend. Back in the office after his workout and training, he checked Pravat's account for any upcoming police activity and discovered some startling information.

"Whoa!" Andrea said after Robert pushed open her door and entered her office, excited to tell her about his discovery. "Turn around, go out, and knock before you enter."

Robert started to blurt out his news but thought better of it and did as she instructed.

"Enter."

"I found new information about that chemistry lab in Bangkok. The one where they manufacture the drug additive, the Black Dragon," Robert exclaimed while rushing to her desk.

"What information?" Andrea said, her voice hoarse with irritation.

"They mention it a few times," Robert said. "They add this dragon stuff to heroin. But if they put in too much, it's deadly."

"Where did you find this out?" Andrea seemed to warm to the idea.

"Pravat's computer account," Robert said, his palms sweaty.

"Where's the lab?"

"It doesn't give an address, but it's somewhere in the metropolitan area. They mention a chemist, but not the guy's name."

Andrea's eyes lit up as she said, "OK, get Sakchai and let's develop a plan."

Sitting at his desk, Alex reviewed the report he had filed that requested support for the upcoming February raid—the big one. He checked, for the umpteenth time, to see if it struck the exact balance that he wanted, even though he'd already sent it out. When he heard a knock on his door, he put it in his top right-hand drawer and shouted, "Come in!"

"Robert has found some evidence about Wang's Bangkok lab. They have a chemist there who manufactures the drug added to heroin, giving it an extra, but sometimes lethal, kick," Andrea said after they had filed in and lined up in front of Alex.

"Whoa. What's this about?" Alex said, holding up his hands as if to slow the flood of information. "And where did you find this, Robert?"

"I was searching the police files on my computer, and I learned of a factory that synthesizes an opioid," Robert said. "Wang adds it sometimes to the heroin he ships to the US. But this drug is powerful, and if too much is in the mix, overdoses increase."

"Go on," Alex said.

"This must be the place where the February shipment will stop and pick up extra drugs," Robert said, leaning forward.

Alex studied Robert. Then he stared at Andrea and finally glanced at Sakchai. These revelations made him uneasy. He knew they were building a case for taking action, and he didn't want to risk his team on anything small. He needed them fully intact for the raid in February.

"What do your Scorpion sources tell you?" Alex asked Sakchai.

"They are unaware of any lab, but they know Wang has something more potent than plain heroin."

"Andrea, what do you think?"

"I think we should find the lab and destroy it." To Andrea, this was clear.

"Robert?"

"This is the stuff that killed my brother," Robert said, placing his hands on Alex's desk. "So, I agree with Andrea."

"I'm uncomfortable," Alex said, knitting his eyebrows. "My biggest concern is being ready for the big delivery early next year." Alex put his hands flat on his desk, reclaiming it. Robert leaned back and straightened to his full height.

"We shouldn't stop everything and wait until February rolls around," Andrea said, punching the words out. "We work well as a team, and we can accomplish some tasks before that one."

"Yes," Alex said. "A talented team and often squabbling about your partner's performances," Alex snapped. He'd been listening to Andrea's complaints about Robert for the last month. Although he had hoped she would get past it and he should now be pleased, this sudden newfound camaraderie irritated him.

"It's a good crew," Andrea said, her jaw set. "Not perfect, but good."

"I'm glad to hear that. OK. What do you propose?" Alex took a deep breath.

"Sakchai will use his detective skills to locate the lab," Andrea said. "Once we find it, we could do a stakeout in February. When the trucks carrying the shipment stop there, we could capture them and the drugs."

Alex nodded. "I like the idea of capturing the shipment before it arrives at Wang's warehouse. There'd be a lot fewer thugs guarding the drugs. But I need to talk to headquarters. It's not the same thing as a drug shipment; it's a manufacturing facility. Also, I know my boss is keen to stop this additive and the overdoses it causes. I'll see what he says."

Late that night, Alex phoned his manager, who startled him with an immediate and emphatic decision: locate the lab, destroy it, and capture the chemist. His supervisor said he would arrange for the CIA to assist Alex and his team in kidnapping the scientist and transporting him back to the US for trial. And he emphasized that he wanted it all done *yesterday*.

Alex grabbed his head. Two thoughts made it ache. First, this killed their opportunity to waylay the shipment before the drivers delivered it to Wang. Now, not only would they have to burn down this lab, they'd have to attack Wang's warehouse directly since it was the only other known stop for the shipment. Second, sometimes it's just stupid to call headquarters.

After their Saturday session with Mai and Sam at Rot Fai Park, Andrea took the kids back to the Orson rehab center, leaving Robert on the roadside. He took a *tuk-tuk* to meet Fon at the Royal Barges National Museum. She wore something similar to a Ruean Ton, a businesslike traditional silk outfit. Its shiny light-blue top had long sleeves and buttons down the front. Instead of a skirt, she wore trousers that plunged to her ankles in straight, tight lines. She'd had her dark hair cut and styled since they'd last met. Cut shorter, her hair framed her face with slightly longer hair in the front that swept forward to a point below her cheekbones.

Fon guided Robert through the eight barges displayed in the museum, explaining the meaning of the bow ornaments. Small waves from the Chao Phraya River lapped at the boats' hulls. The smell of salt and fish floated off the water. The figureheads were so stunning, Robert could barely listen to Fon's talk. One had seven golden heads of naga—serpent creatures—with bared pearly white teeth, and red tongues.

Large pointed scales ran down the back of their necks, and green and gold scales decked their chests. Another had the Monkey King with his hands on his hips, head thrown back showing the red roof of his mouth. The barge adornments competed, demanding attention.

Afterward, Robert hailed a taxi that took them to the Wat Arun, the typical destination for the royal barges when they were carrying the king for the Kathina Ceremony. As they got out of the vehicle, a man approached Robert, gave him a deep *wai*, and began speaking rapidly in Thai. Robert recognized him; it was Ko, one of his former students from his Peace Corps days. Robert could understand everything he said, but stood silent, his mouth open, stomach clenched. When Ko said, "You fixed your nose!" Robert involuntarily moved his right arm toward his face, thinking he would touch his nose, but stopped midway in the gesture. He closed his mouth and composed himself. Robert sensed Fon staring at him.

Taking his eyes off Ko, Robert turned to Fon. "What's this man saying?"

"He thinks he knows you. He says you are Thomas, his Peace Corps teacher from ten years ago."

"Tell him I'm Robert. I've never been in the Peace Corps, and I don't know him."

Fon explained this to the man. Ko's face clouded, his brow furrowed, he shook his head a few times, made a deep *wai* three times at Robert and one to Fon. Then he turned and walked away from them.

Robert's stomach turned. He would have liked to have taken Ko to lunch and reminisced about his Surat Thani days. He would have quizzed Ko on his math skills and asked if he ever used what he had learned. Robert must have impressed him; Ko's excitement revealed admiration.

"That was weird," Robert said to Fon, his voice trembling, as they turned to go into the *wat*. "I've been mistaken sometimes for someone else, but he seemed convinced I was this Thomas guy."

"Yes, I'm not sure he believed us when I told him you were Robert."

Robert's head swiveled toward Fon. "No?"

"He seemed saddened that you were pretending not to know him."

"Odd. Did he say something about my nose? He pointed at it."

"He said you must have had surgery to straighten it."

"Double odd. Anyway, never mind. Let's see the Wat Arun." Robert straightened his head and gazed at the *wat*, a sight less colorful than the golden temples—or the barges, for that matter. Robert and Fon climbed up the steps of the white and black main *prang*, a conical tower, to the circumnavigation level and walked around it. Robert's thoughts kept racing back to Ko, and he grimaced; finally, he pushed it from his mind and calmed his face. Later, they spent some time listening to the monks chanting mantras in an active part of the temple. A breeze from the nearby river cooled them as they sat.

They visited two more of the lesser *wats* that afternoon. The tour completed, Robert asked Fon if he could take her to dinner. His head jerked back, and he smiled when she accepted. And of course, she knew an excellent restaurant nearby.

Once they sat down, Fon said, "I am not so fond of insects. I was only seeing if you would eat them last week after saying you ate 'everything.'"

"I was trying to impress you."

"You succeeded," Fon said and briefly struck a pose, with her elbow on the table, batting her eyelids, her chin on her hand, teasing him with a flirtatious attitude. Sitting back, she continued, "Tonight, we'll have more traditional dishes. We'll share a green papaya salad for a starter. And we can share our main dishes, a massaman shrimp curry and *tod mun pla*, fishcakes. For dessert, we'll share a mango sticky rice."

"Sounds great. You're spoiling me. Please order a couple of Singha beers too."

"Two beers for you?" she asked, cocking her head and *tsk*ing.

"One for each of us. I was hoping you'd join me."

"I will. Thank you," she said, her eyes smiling through her eyelashes. She turned to the server, ordered, and then asked Robert about his work.

"It's pretty boring. I research the Thai economy and politics and write reports."

"That must be difficult without knowing how to read Thai."

"We have a couple of people who can help me with that in the office. It's awkward, but it works. I have the analytical skills, and they have the language skills. What about you? Is this the job you love? Or would you rather be doing something different?" Robert had learned to deflect conversation away from himself and redirect it to whomever he was speaking with.

"I once thought I would like to be a doctor, but that is unattainable. Perhaps a nurse. That is a respectable profession."

"Why is becoming a doctor unattainable?"

"I am not that good at the sciences—biology and chemistry." Fon ducked her head and frowned.

"Ah. I guess that could be a problem. And nursing?"

"For now, I enjoy taking tourists, such as you, around Bangkok," Fon said, with a note of triumph and a sly smile.

"And I'm glad you do!" Robert laughed, marveling at Fon's beauty and coy playfulness.

Outside after their goodbyes, Fon walked off in the opposite direction from Robert's apartment. He couldn't help gazing at her disappearing figure. She was certainly attractive, and Robert enjoyed her intelligence, quick wit, and liveliness. As he turned to head home, he wondered where their meetings would lead them.

On Monday morning, Robert followed Andrea into Alex's office after their boss called them in for a meeting. Sakchai was out in the field searching for the specialized drug lab. They stood in front of a jubilant Alex.

"Why are you so happy?" Andrea asked, looking puzzled.

"All the polls say Ronald Reagan will be reelected tomorrow!" Alex exclaimed, startling Robert and Andrea. "Our funding will continue, and his threat to cut aid to uncooperative governments should help us get more collaboration from the Thai police."

Robert blew out an unimpressed breath, while Andrea showed no emotion. Their unease and indifference registered with Alex, dampening his enthusiasm.

"How's the investigation going?" Alex asked as he sat down and sighed.

"Sakchai has just begun his search for the lab," Andrea said. "He's working his detective magic as we speak."

"OK, keep me informed," Alex said.

"Yes, definitely," Andrea said, irritated. "Is that all?"

"Yes, you can get back to work now."

Robert's assessment of their "meeting" was that Alex wanted to share his happiness about Reagan's pending reelection. But he sensed also something personal in his joy. Maybe he thought this increased his chances of a promotion? When Alex spoke of his family in private moments, he revealed a deep love that endeared him to Robert. The team knew Alex didn't want to get away from them; he wanted to make his family happy by getting back to the States. Robert hoped he succeeded. He hoped they all succeeded.

Robert returned to his office, shaking his head. He was glum about Reagan; he didn't think his war on drugs was working. But he consoled himself with the security of their jobs, while doubting Thai police support would improve. His thoughts turned to Fon. Remembering their first meeting, something troubled him. Was it really a coincidence? He was at the Crazy Bird every Sunday morning. Was he flattering himself in thinking she was interested in him? He searched the police computer for information about Fon Chongrak. No police record. No arrests. No record on her at all. Robert let out his breath in a long blast; he hadn't realized he'd been holding it in.

Feeling better about the day, Robert turned his attention to finding more details on the lab north of Bangkok. He couldn't find anything new; he'd given everything he could to Sakchai already.

CHAPTER 16

To pinpoint the place that manufactured the deadly heroin additive, Sakchai reviewed Robert's information about the lab's location. None of the five mentions from various reports had a specific address. But by combining the minimal evidence, Sakchai concluded it was in the Pathum Thani Province of the Bangkok metropolitan area.

After that, it was basic gumshoe work for Sakchai. He visited the government department with company registrations. Fortunately, the files were organized by district and industry. He plowed through the set of massive binders for Pathum Thani. Each company had one sheet describing its activities, its address, telephone number, and industrial code. He found seven chemical companies: four were petrochemical firms, one was a fertilizer plant, another made aspirin, and a final one made pesticides.

Sakchai went to the garment district of Bangkok and bought a brown coverall. With that, he visited his costume designer, Chariya, from his police days.

"Chariya, I need some labels for this boilersuit."

"Ooh, you make mischief, Detective Sangthong?" Chariya asked with her head lowered and her eyes teasing him.

"I'm no longer with the police force, but I will, as always, rely on your discretion to keep this between us," Sakchai said, opening the bidding.

"Mmm. What do you need?"

"I need a uniform of a safety inspector from the Ministry of Labour. Here is their official seal." Sakchai handed a photo of the seal to

Chariya. "That would go on the back and be about this big." Sakchai held his hands ten inches apart. "On the front, I'd like two labels. For the right side, it should say 'Inspector, Worker Safety, Ministry of Labour.' On the left side, a name tag saying, 'Sakchai Suwannathat.'" He placed the tag descriptions on the counter between them.

"Hee-hee, new name, new job. You pose as a government official, Detective Sangthong?" Chariya asked, estimating the cost of the disguise and raising her bid.

Sakchai almost corrected her again on his old police title but decided it was useless. "Let's just say I'll be acting as one in a neighborhood play that I'm in."

"Interesting. You always good actor," Chariya said, grinning.

"And I need the outfit by tomorrow, if possible."

Chariya's eyes widened, and her face lit up. "That cost extra."

"Yes, but it's a simple task for such a gifted fashion designer as yourself."

"You try, but no discount for flowery words," Chariya said as she bent over a receipt pad and made a great show of her elaborate calculations. She named a price, Sakchai countered, and she came back at him. Bid. Set. Contract.

The next day, Sakchai had use of the Toyota, so he picked up his new uniform and changed clothes in Chariya's back room. He'd already produced multiple inspection sheets, making them as official looking as possible, and carried a clipboard and pen with him.

When he arrived at the first petrochemical plant, the guard at the gate asked if he had an appointment. Sakchai barked, "I need to see the manager. I'm here on behalf of the Ministry of Labour to make a snap inspection of the worker safety at this plant. It's a surprise. I'm not meant to have an appointment!" The guard opened the gate and directed him to the office.

After introducing himself, Sakchai used his stern police-investigation persona to grill the supervisor. "Have you installed any safety features for workers recently?" Of course, they hadn't, so Sakchai demanded to inspect the plant and directed the boss to accompany him.

The plant was in a large rectangular building, and they needed to wind their way through the various operations. The workers created the plastic in one area, heated it, and then sent it through the stamping machinery. As Sakchai and the manager moved about the plant, plastic bottles poured off the assembly line, and the laborers made sure they landed in the boxes neatly. The regular staff ignored him, but the administrator jumped after him, attempting to glimpse what notes Sakchai scribbled on his clipboard. But Sakchai hid his writing, holding the forms' text facing his leg.

"Do you have any other rooms for making anything?"

"This is it," the manager said, spreading his arms and looking worried and baffled.

Indeed, the few doors they had were emergency exits—Sakchai noted each one approvingly—and there weren't even closets. The cleaning materials and equipment were stored in a corner. Sakchai scrutinized the inspection dates tagged onto the many fire extinguishers and again showed his satisfaction.

At the end of the tour, Sakchai said, "Everything seems in order, but I can't guarantee what the chief inspector will conclude. You'll hear from us next week only if there is something amiss. If you don't hear from us, you've passed the inspection. Good day!"

He toured the other three chemical companies next, followed by the fertilizer plant and the aspirin factory. They looked legitimate, leaving only the pesticide facility. He'd left it to last because he loathed the smell of bug killer.

He drove up to the property through a wide-open gate. The minuscule building faced him. He double-checked the address against his notes, but this was the place—a small, bland building which couldn't be more than a thousand square feet. The other plants he had visited had tens of thousands of square footage.

He knocked on the metal door and listened, his knuckles smarting from the effort. No response. He pounded and shouted that he was a government inspector. The entryway opened a crack, and a pair of eyes squinted at him. A heavy chain prevented anyone from easily kicking the door open. It closed, and Sakchai could hear metal clank against the wall. The steel entrance swung open.

"May I help you?" asked a squat *farang* man.

"I'm Inspector Suwannathat from the Ministry of Labour here to inspect the safety of your plant," Sakchai snarled, speaking English like a commanding general.

"I'm Dr. Golovanov," the man said, stretching himself to his full height—four and a half feet. "There's no need for that. I'm the only person working here, and I'm fine," Golovanov said, closing the door.

Sakchai set his foot into the gap and his shoulder against the metal. "I'll be the judge of that. I must conduct my investigation."

"No one gave me any notice of any inspection." Golovanov again attempted to shut the entrance.

"It's a snap inspection allowed under Rule 34.2 of the labor code!" Sakchai claimed, shoving past the diminutive man as he made up a number.

"*Hmmph!* Very well. Inspect!" Golovanov said, thrusting his arm to the side in exasperation.

"What type of doctor are you?" Sakchai asked in a soothing tone, hoping to put Golovanov at ease.

"I have a PhD in chemistry."

Sakchai waited for him to add the name of his university and, when he didn't, concluded Golovanov's degree was self-bestowed.

"What's this?" Sakchai asked as he approached an elaborate three-tier jewelry case displaying dozens of small bottles.

"I couldn't invent an insecticide that made any money, so now I produce perfume in small batches for select clients." Golovanov pulled a set of keys from his pocket, opened the case and, with a wave of his hand, invited Sakchai to smell the contents.

Sakchai chose a random tiny flask, unscrewed the lid, and sniffed. Patchouli. He smelled another. Sandalwood. And so it went—they were common scents, some of flowers, such as jasmine. But one vial contained a scent that reminded him of his sister Kalaya. He hastened it back into the cabinet but couldn't stop the flow of memories of her demise.

Kalaya's boss had recognized the value of her beauty and befriended her. He invited her to lavish parties, where he eventually introduced her to a magical powder that you inhaled through a straw. The drug had transported Kalaya to another world both beautiful and deadly. She'd told Sakchai that she'd never known such bliss and happiness. Her worries about money and taking care of their parents disappeared, leaving only a warm feeling of contentment. Of course, it was heroin, and unfortunately for Kalaya, it overwhelmed her—she never wanted to be without it. Once her boss had her hooked, he withheld the drug from her unless she performed special services for some of her male clients. She became a prostitute full of shame. Only the white dust made her forget her disgrace.

Kalaya reached out to her brother Sakchai—they had always been close. He arranged for her to go to a clinic, but she didn't stay long; they couldn't hold her against her will, and her addiction to the drug overpowered her. She returned to her new line of work. Her parents heard about her misfortune from a cousin who lived in Bangkok and had learned about her plight through his friends at work. Kalaya had become well known as one of the top courtesans for foreigners in Bangkok.

When her parents visited to help her, Kalaya became furious and screeched at them, asking if the money she sent them—a great deal more than she had sent previously—wasn't enough. She told them that if they didn't like what she was doing, she would be happy to cut them off.

Sakchai had visited her shortly after their parents returned to Chiang Mai and found Kalaya in a deep depression. Her work and addiction humiliated her, but she couldn't miss her daily fix. She threw herself on Sakchai's shoulder, wailing in desolation. He tried to console her, but to no avail. She said she needed to use the bathroom, but when she came out, narcotics had transformed her. Speaking in a calm, confident tone, she told him how much she loved him and her parents. She was sorry they didn't approve of her life, but she was going to continue it. As long as she had her fairy dust, she would be happy.

Two weeks later, when he went to her apartment, he found her in bed. A syringe lay on the floor, her arm draping toward the needle, just inches away from her hand. A fragment of a smile creased her calm face.

She was dead.

Sakchai, still a homicide detective, suffered a cruel twist of fate— she died in his jurisdiction. His boss, remembering his insubordination over a previous case, spitefully sent him to investigate her death. Sakchai searched methodically for any indications of foul play, interviewing her colleagues, her manager, and her neighbors. Her boss was upset, distraught—he'd lost his most prized asset. Her neighbors and colleagues mentioned her bouts of despair related to her occupation. Sakchai concluded it was suicide. Kalaya had saved up the small doses her boss doled out and made sure she had more than enough to kill herself. Her last several days must have been a gruesome withdrawal from the usual dosage of the drug, followed by one short, incredible—and fatal—high.

Their folks had taken the news particularly hard. Kalaya was their favorite because she had been cheerful, optimistic, and funny. A lively person, she wore her beauty with modesty and had always been highly respectful of her parents and elders in their neighborhood before her addiction.

A month later, Sakchai heard that the Orson Group was looking for a trained police officer to help with their security. He'd had enough of investigating murders, suicides, and drug overdoses. When he learned what they were really doing, he felt it was serendipitous. He believed it would finally be a base from which he could better fight the poisonous trade in narcotics. And honor his sister.

"Yes, very nice," Sakchai said to Golovanov, being careful not to sound suspicious as he shook off the nightmarish memories while replacing the vial.

"If you like, I could mix up something for your wife?" Golovanov asked, his voice lilting with hope.

"I couldn't accept it," Sakchai said, with a sharp edge.

"No. Of course not. But I didn't mean it that way," Golovanov hurriedly assured him.

Sakchai glared at Golovanov and said, "Now I'll inspect the working area." He strode toward the only exit from the front office, the chemist scurrying behind him.

"No need for that. Nothing exciting there."

Sakchai ignored him, opened the door, and stepped through into the lab. Rows of tables greeted him, all covered with test tubes, flasks, beakers, and other chemistry paraphernalia. A centrifuge rested on one table, an incubator stood in the corner, and a couple of Bunsen burners were off to the side under a ventilation hood. It looked a lot like the police lab in his old precinct. Golovanov had laid out the equipment neatly, and everything looked to be in perfect order. Sakchai saw clear-plastic bags of white powder stacked in two corners but pretended not to notice them. He walked around the room, making a show of his fascination with the gadgets. At the end of the first row, he found a door. Looking inside, he found Dr. Golovanov's living quarters, with a bed, a small kitchen, and a bathroom. He walked down the other row back toward Golovanov and realized something was missing.

There was no smell.

Sakchai beamed at Mr. Golovanov and said, "Well, everything is well organized, and you have no workers, so I'll relay that to my superiors in my official report, and I'm sure you'll pass inspection. Good day, Dr. Golovanov." Sakchai gave him a *wai* and strode out the entry toward his car. There, he pretended to make notes on his clipboard while Dr. Golovanov watched him from the front door. Then he drove away.

It was late. The fake inspections had taken the entire day. His visit to the government customs office would have to wait until the next morning.

Sakchai arrived at the import data building when it opened at 9 a.m., dressed in his best business suit. A young man greeted him with an ingratiating smile and bowed deeply.

"I'm looking for the import data of these seven firms," Sakchai said, laying a slip of paper on the counter between them.

"Oh, that might take a long time," the man said, bending to peer at the list. Then he picked it up, and the two-hundred baht note underneath the document disappeared into his pocket. "But I'll collect them for you quickly. Please have a seat."

Sakchai sat on one of the three chairs in the waiting room. Before long, the clerk returned with seven files and plopped them on the counter. Sakchai took them to the photocopy machine and, using coins, he copied several pages—one or two from each folder. Many of the papers had elaborate names of chemicals, while others had details of the compounds. The forms for the perfume company had long names and the molecular formulas of the substances. Everything looked proper. He returned the records to the archive worker, who again smiled and gave him a *wai*.

"Why is there a red check mark on this file?" Sakchai asked, pointing to the pesticide company.

"Oh, that means I stopped entering its data into the computer one night. It helps me pick up where I left off the next day."

Next, Sakchai visited a fruit market and purchased four ripe dragon fruits. Then he traveled to his former precinct to visit Ratanaporn, the head chemist of the police lab.

He met Ratanaporn in his office, which had a large window looking over a workroom similar to Golovanov's. Papers splashed across a desk on one side of the room. The walls were lined with bookshelves filled with technical journals and textbooks. In one corner, a large white refrigerator with rounded shoulders gleamed at them. A sink was next to it.

After handing the box of fruit to him, Sakchai bowed to Ratanaporn, addressing him with the respectful *Khun*. His former colleague returned the *wai* with a perfunctory dip of his head before ripping open the box and grinning like a cat that had just caught a bird.

"Thank you, Detective Sangthong," Ratanaporn said. He turned and picked up a huge scalpel, placed a fruit on his desk, and sliced it evenly. Clutching one half in his palm, he again turned and selected an instrument with a spoon at one end and a spatula at the other. He began eating the magenta flesh of the fruit. "Mmm. So delicious!" A dribble of red juice trailed from his mouth to his chin.

Sakchai waited patiently while his friend enjoyed the treat. Ratanaporn knew Sakchai was no longer with the police force, but if he wanted to think of him as a detective, he would not object.

Having finished the half, Ratanaporn wrapped its pair in plastic and gently placed the remaining fruit in the fridge. After wiping his face with the sleeve of his lab coat, he asked, "What can I do for you today?"

"Khun Ratanaporn, I want to determine what these chemical companies are manufacturing. I have their customs invoices, which detail their imported ingredients, but I am no chemist. Could you enlighten me?" Sakchai laid the stack of forms in front of the scientist.

"Hmmm." The chemist examined the first six documents with a cursory glance, turning them and snapping them down on the counter. "The first four make plastic goods, the fifth is a fertilizer plant, the sixth makes aspirin pills, but to tell you about the last one I'll need to check something first." He walked to the bookshelf and pulled one off.

"These are pharmaceuticals. This benzyl compound would react with the anilide one to produce a drug." Ratanaporn flipped through the tome, almost tearing the pages. "Ah, yes, here it is! Combined, these two would produce a painkiller." He looked up at Sakchai. "It would kill so much pain, it might kill you!" he said, cackling.

"Anything else, Detective Sangthong? I should get back to work."

"No, that's everything I need to know. Thank you for your time, Khun Ratanaporn." They bowed to each other, then Sakchai grabbed the papers, returned to the car, and drove as fast as he could to the office.

CHAPTER 17

Back at headquarters, Sakchai walked directly into Alex's office without knocking.

Alex's head jerked up when he saw Sakchai striding to his desk. Sakchai knew he was acting like Andrea, surprising himself as much as Alex.

"Yes, what is it, Sakchai?" Alex asked, sounding concerned.

"I have conclusive proof of which factory in Pathum Thani is making drugs," Sakchai announced. "It's a small company, registered as a pesticide manufacturer, and falsely claiming to be making perfumes but importing powerful pharmaceutical chemicals. There's only one worker there, Dr. Golovanov."

"What evidence do you have?"

"I have the customs documents on their imports, and the head chemist at the police lab, Ratanaporn, says the combined imported substances would create a potent painkiller. A deadly one."

"Good. I'll call the CIA now. My boss got their agreement to help us. I want them to take the lead on this raid, so if anything goes wrong, they can deal with the ramifications. We don't have the authority to kidnap people. We need to stay clean to pull off that February raid." Alex called Lamai, who connected him to the CIA. After briefing them, he cupped his hand over the receiver and asked Sakchai, "Is there any urgency to nabbing Golovanov?"

Sakchai racked his brain for clues about Golovanov's intentions. "I don't think he was suspicious of me," he said uncertainly.

Sensing Sakchai's unease, Alex spoke into the phone, stressing the urgency of the matter, but the response disappointed him.

"Sorry, Sakchai. The best I could do was this evening. The CIA agents assigned to us aren't available until tonight."

"I hope that's soon enough," Sakchai said, swallowing his frustration. "He lives there, in an apartment at the back of the shop." He had envisioned his team racing up to arrest the chemist. His performance as an inspector at the narcotic factory hadn't been as convincing as he would have liked; the chemist might become apprehensive as the day dragged on. The memory of Kalaya's lifeless body in bed flashed through his mind. He'd hate to miss a chance to strike another blow against the drug trade.

Alex conferred on the phone and, hanging up, said, "The two operatives will come here at 6 p.m. to accompany you to the factory. Inform Andrea and Robert to be ready."

Sakchai grimaced, his hands trembling. He left to apprise his teammates of the latest developments, choking back his resentment at the CIA delay.

Sakchai and his colleagues were waiting in Alex's office when the two spooks arrived at 6:00 p.m. and not a second earlier. They wore dark suits and black ties. Their jackets bulged under their left armpits. Both were wearing flesh-colored earbuds in their right ears, and Sakchai spotted tiny microphones pinned to their lapels.

One was tall, with broad shoulders and blond hair. A leading man from a romantic thriller. He stepped forward, exuding calm and authority. The other was short, skinny, and unable to keep still, touching his pockets, pinching his nose, and tapping his hands on his thighs. His left eyebrow had a tic, like a little jitterbug. They didn't introduce themselves, offer to shake hands, or *wai*.

"Who are we working with?" Blondy asked Alex.

Alex rose from his desk. "Let me introduce you to Sakchai Sang-thong, Andrea Cannon, and Robert Jordan," Alex said, gesturing to each from left to right. "They'll be assisting you in the abduction."

"OK," Blondy grunted in disdain. "We'll need to stay in touch with your team, but we only have one extra communication device." He held out his left hand. Twitchy scrambled to get the gadget out of his pocket. Then he placed the electronic gear in Blondy's palm.

Blondy stepped forward to give the equipment to Robert, but Andrea strode in front of him and held out her hand, staring him in the eye. Robert remained still, looking impassive.

Blondy glanced at Alex, then swiveled his gaze to Andrea. "Here. This goes in your inner pocket and this earbud—"

Andrea swiped up the apparatus, flipped the control box into her jacket pocket, put the bud into her ear, and clipped the mike to her lapel in one smooth motion. She stepped back, but now she stood a little in front of Sakchai and Robert.

"Good," Blondy said. "That's settled. The transmitter is in our car. We'll test it before we leave. To get to the target, we'll follow you."

"Here's the address in case you lose us," Sakchai said, stepping forward and handing a paper to Blondy.

"We won't lose you." Blondy crumpled the note in his beefy fist and jammed it into his coat pocket.

Outside, Sakchai, Andrea, and Robert climbed into the Toyota and waited until an enormous black BMW pulled alongside.

"DEA-one, can you hear me?" Blondy asked, eyeing Andrea from the passenger seat, his window closed.

"Loud and clear, CIA-one," Andrea said flatly, without looking at the agent.

"Lead the way then."

Andrea put the Toyota in gear and flew out of the parking space. She wove in and out of the Bangkok traffic, zipping north to Pathum Thani. Though the Beamer was a much more powerful vehicle, its size hampered its forward progress. Still, when Sakchai looked back, he could always see the enormous orbs of light emanating from the black behemoth. They parked a block from the small building housing the drug factory, and a few seconds later, the BMW parked behind them.

The three DEA agents got out of their car, and Andrea led the way to the gate. Blondy pulled a hydraulic bolt cutter from the BMW's trunk, and the two CIA men followed them. By the time Blondy and Twitchy had reached the fenced entrance, Andrea had picked the lock, and Sakchai and Robert silently swung open the entry. Blondy tossed the tool aside and signaled to Twitchy, who ran around to the back of the building, moving like an ostrich—wings flexing, head bobbing but on stealthy feet. Andrea and Blondy arrived at the front door together, with Sakchai and Robert behind them.

Blondy turned to Sakchai and said, "Tell them to come out with their hands up." Then he pounded on the door, drew his pistol, and pointed it at the lock while Sakchai shouted the instructions.

Andrea tapped Blondy on the shoulder and held up her lock pick to stop the spy from shooting the metal latch, which could have resulted in a ricocheting bullet. He shifted back, bowed, and swung out his arm in a mock display of graciousness.

With a couple of twists, Andrea turned the knob and, in one motion, threw open the door, pulled her gun, and stepped to the side.

There had been no response to Sakchai's command, and the shop remained dark.

Blondy crouched to the left of the entry, Glock extended in front of him. He nodded to Andrea, who stood to the right of the entrance, and then ran inside with his gun swinging to catch any targets.

Andrea strode in behind him and turned on the light.

Blondy leaped behind the desk for cover and screeched in a whisper, "Why'd you do that?"

"No one's here."

"How do you know?" Blondy spat the question at Andrea.

"I can sense it." Andrea took two steps past the fragrance display to get to the inner room and flipped another switch, illuminating the factory floor.

"Are your senses ever wrong?" Blondy growled. Rising, he shouldered his weapon.

"Not when they're this strong," she said, striding into the chemist's lab.

Blondy, Sakchai, and Robert followed Andrea into the space, which had been trashed. Papers, a couple of broken beakers, and dust covered the floor. With no equipment, the place looked like an empty cafeteria without seating.

Sakchai walked on tiptoes to avoid damaging any of the potential evidence strewn across the surface. He entered the studio apartment and opened the back door. Twitchy leaped in, gun drawn, swirling it at everyone before holstering it, his brow scrunched in puzzlement.

"What did this look like earlier today, Sakchai?" Andrea asked.

"There was a full chemistry laboratory on these tables and bags of white powder, here and there," he said, pointing.

"This is a total fuck-up!" Blondy hissed. "You idiots must have a mole in your organization. Come on; we're outta here." He waved at Twitchy, and they left.

Sakchai could see Andrea's face redden in anger. Was it directed at him, the CIA operatives, or both? He said, "Please don't touch anything. Let me listen to the messages on Dr. Golovanov's recorder."

Andrea and Robert trailed Sakchai into the bedroom. Sakchai approached the answering machine, whose blinking red light he had noticed when letting Twitchy into the building.

Sakchai pulled on rubber gloves from his backpack and pressed the play button.

They listened as a Thai person, in halting English said, "Dr. Golovanov? Sorry to bother you. I phoned you, exactly like you said I should, to tell you that someone pulled your import records. So when can I expect my payment? I'm short on cash and was hoping you could get it to me this week. Thanks."

"Who is it?" Andrea asked when the voice stopped.

"This is a message from the customs clerk I saw this morning," Sakchai said.

"Shit. That explains this," Andrea said, sweeping her arm toward the chaos of the middle room.

"Yes, that red check—I should have guessed," Sakchai said, slapping his thigh in dismay.

"Red check?" Robert asked.

"Golovanov's customs folder had a red check on it. It must be the clerk's indicator to himself to phone the importer about any investigation of their goods."

"Don't be hard on yourself," Robert said. "You couldn't have known."

"Now what do we do?" Andrea asked.

"We conduct a forensic investigation. We need evidence in case we can track down Golovanov." Sakchai placed his knapsack on one table and handed gloves to Andrea and Robert. "First, I'll gather some of the powder from the floor. Then we'll dust for fingerprints."

Sakchai stooped in one corner and brushed a small amount of residue onto a mini dustpan. After placing the white particles into a plastic bag, he sealed it, labeled it, and put it in a case. Then he handed out the dust, brushes, and tape for gathering prints. They found plenty. Finally, they picked up the papers from each room and secured them in a plastic folder.

The next morning, Sakchai visited the fingerprint expert at his former police precinct. As a special favor, the forensic professional agreed to check them that evening after he had finished his regular workday.

Sakchai then visited Ratanaporn, his chemist buddy. This time Sakchai was armed with a bag of mixed fruit.

The scientist grabbed the sack from Sakchai, poked his head in, and seized an orange from its interior. Setting the packet aside, he peeled the fruit. "What brings you to see me this time, Detective Sangthong?"

"I'd like you to analyze this powder for me to determine what the substance is." Sakchai handed over the evidence bag.

"Let me guess. You suspect this is what results from mixing the two compounds you asked me about yesterday?" The chemist pulled off an orange slice and popped it into his mouth. Then another and another in rapid succession until his mouth brimmed with fruit and his chewing emitted tiny sprays of juice.

"Yes, that's correct. I'd also like to know how powerful you might think it is."

"Finding its molecular structure will take time, but we can test it on Francis."

"Francis?"

"Francis is one of my lab rats." Ratanaporn bounded over to his sink, washed his hands and face, then leapt into the lab behind his office. Moments later, he emerged with a single white rat in a clear plastic tank, open at the top. He set the case on his desk.

"I'll mix a bit of this powder with peanut sauce and give it to him." Ratanaporn used a tiny measuring spoon to put a precise quantity of the drug on a small tray. He added the peanut paste from a jar using a separate instrument, stirred the mixture, and set it in the transparent box. "Francis loves peanuts. Don't you, Francis?" he asked, peering into the top of the cage.

The rat lunged at the sauce, and it disappeared after a few licks. Then it jumped to the side of its prison, sat on its haunches, and wiped its face with its tiny paws.

Ratanaporn dug a banana out of the fruit bag and relieved it of its skin. "Now, we wait. What can you tell me about this mystery drug, detective?"

"You know I can't tell you anything about our investigation."

"Yes. Always secretive." Half the banana bulged in the chemist's mouth, but he continued. "We just analyze here in the lab. Only when there is a trial and I testify do I learn about the usefulness of my work. Often, I hear nothing after giving you police officers my results."

"Usually, we have nothing to tell you because we can't bring a case," Sakchai said. "In our inquiries, we have a policy of telling only those who need to know. Besides, we don't want to bias any forensic work."

Ratanaporn guffawed, spraying bits of banana from mouth. "You could never bias my results. My work is always about the science, nothing more, nothing less." He looked over at Francis. Grabbing the container by its sides, he shook it. Then he took a long spoon and poked the rat. The animal lay motionless on its side, its stiff legs poking straight out.

Francis was dead.

"Poor mouse," Sakchai said, his brow furrowed with concern.

"It's a rat, and Francis was old. This is not a great loss. I gave him five milligrams—like twenty grains of salt. We can conclude that this is a potent drug."

"What have we learned from the evidence you gathered?" Alex demanded that evening. He sat at his desk, his hands flat on its surface and his back straight, glaring at his team standing before him. He'd heard from the CIA station chief that afternoon, and the conversation hadn't been pleasant.

"The drug is very powerful," Sakchai said. "A tiny dose killed a rat almost instantly. We'll know in a couple of days what the compound is. On the fingerprints, I expect to get a report any moment now."

While shifting from one foot to the other, Robert said, "I looked through the papers we gathered from the drug factory, but there was nothing of interest—utility bills, some government forms, some literature on how to make perfumes, but nothing related to narcotic manufacturing."

The phone rang, and Alex picked it up. "It's for you," he said, handing the receiver to Sakchai.

Hanging up, Sakchai said. "It was the fingerprint expert. He said he couldn't find a match with any of the prints they have on file."

"Shit!" Alex pounded the desk with both fists, rose, and went to the window, turning his back on his staff. He put his hand on the latch of the double-hung window and peered out. An old lady carrying a water jug crossed the alley below him. "So, we know we had the right guy, but we have no leads on where or who he is," he said, defeated. "That will be all." He continued to stare out the window as Andrea, Robert, and Sakchai filed out of his office.

"Oh, wait!" Alex said, turning to face his team. "Robert, we need to go to Amonsak's office tomorrow. He has some important information about a drug delivery happening soon. He says he wants our help on it."

CHAPTER 18

Alex steeled himself inwardly for this meeting with the police commissioner. He plastered on a professional face before they approached the chairs in front of Amonsak's desk. He gave a *wai* to him and to Prin, who had risen from his seat for the greeting.

"Welcome," Amonsak said. "Come in and have a seat. I'm so glad you could come to visit us on short notice. I see we have agent Jordan, not Sakchai?" Everyone sat down. A large, benevolent smile slashed across Amonsak's face. Prin remained prim.

"No, Sakchai had a family emergency today," Alex said, by way of an apology.

"I'm sorry to hear that."

"Me too. But it couldn't be helped, and Robert is good at listening and writes up the meeting memo for me."

"Oh, we warrant memos, do we?"

"Bureaucracy—the rules of our mission. We must document our government meetings. I'm sure it's the same for you." Alex spoke in the bored voice of an official.

"Yes, precisely why I always have Prin at my side," Amonsak said. "Before I get to the main matter, I was wondering if you have heard anything new on the theft of drugs from our airport warehouse in early October?"

"No. Our sources still tell us the Scorpions stole it," Alex said with conviction.

"We have uncovered nothing new either. Shame." Amonsak turned to Prin and whispered in his ear. Prin responded in the same manner.

Amonsak's smile disappeared, and his face clouded. "Gentlemen, I will get straight to the point. We are overcommitted now and would like your help on a matter of great importance."

"We are always happy to help if we can," Alex said, his gaze direct, his back straight.

Amonsak placed both hands on the table and retrieved his broad grin, which soon faded as he became serious. "We have some information about a drug deal with the Dragon gang. In about three weeks, we expect a large shipment. We don't know where it is coming from or when. Nor do we know which warehouse Wang will use to process it. That's where we'd like your help. If you could look into this and find out the details, we'd greatly appreciate it. Of course, when the police decide to confiscate the drugs, we'll ask your team to join us. That way, we can share in the glory. What do you say?"

"We're a small group, but we'll do our best. We'd like to hear of any further information your officers might gather," Alex said, with a lilt, expressing hope.

"Of course. We'll share everything we know. But that's what we have right now. We value your support on this major case." Amonsak stood, reproduced his munificent grin, and gave a *wai*, dismissing them.

In the taxi on the way back to the office, Alex attempted some small talk. "What are you up to this weekend?"

"A friend and I are going to visit some sights of Bangkok together."

"A friend? That's good. How did you meet him?"

"I met her…she's a tour guide. I took a couple of tours with her and…uh…now we're friends."

Alex could see Robert's hands quivering in the air when he spoke of his new friend.

"Friends? I see." Robert's flapping hands and weak explanation didn't reassure Alex. Then he gave an order. "You should have her checked out. Make sure she's an upright citizen, that sort of thing."

"I did. I checked…I looked her up on the police computer. She's clean. No connection with the drug trade. No arrests. You? What are you up to this weekend?"

"What did you find out precisely?" Alex asked, watching Robert's hands bouncing on his thighs.

"She didn't have any record for anything, not even a traffic ticket."

Alex said nothing until Robert repeated his query.

"Me? Oh, the usual," Alex said, his voice softening. "My family and I will go to the club, play some tennis, go for a swim, and dine at the restaurant. The kids enjoy it—it's something special we weren't often able to do when I worked in DC."

"Sounds great," Robert said, releasing a gust of anxious air.

"It is. Yes, it is."

Once they were back at their building, Alex ushered Robert into his office and asked, "What did you think about our meeting with Amonsak?"

"Well, there are not many opportunities for me to translate anything. They now whisper, and I couldn't hear what they said. That shows a lot of distrust. Either they suspect I speak Thai, or they think we're recording them."

"Yes, it's clear they're suspicious of us." Alex sighed. "Let's get Andrea and Sakchai in here." Alex buzzed Lamai, and both agents soon arrived.

"OK. OK. Let's review the facts. They don't trust us; both Robert and I agree on that. But then they say they need our help on a surveillance operation. What are we to make of that?" Alex searched the faces of his staff.

"They want us to work with them on something?" Andrea looked incredulous.

"It could be a trap," Robert said.

"That's what I thought also," Alex said. "Sakchai, any thoughts?"

"I agree with Robert," Sakchai said.

"OK. Well, I'll leave you three to sort out the details of how we proceed. But please err on the side of caution. Sakchai and Andrea, could you please stay behind? Thank you, Robert."

Alex waited for Robert to leave and then asked, "What do you know about Robert's female friend?" Andrea's head jerked back and swiveled to look at Sakchai.

"Sakchai?" Alex asked.

"He has a female friend?" Sakchai shifted his feet and examined Andrea, his eyes widening into a question mark.

"That's how he refers to her—friend. He says she's a tour guide. He says she's clean. Andrea, do you know anything?"

"It's the first I've heard of it, sir."

Sir? Alex thought, his brow knitting. Andrea rarely called him sir.

"You can leave us now, Sakchai. Let me know if you hear anything about Robert's new friend." Alex paused while Sakchai left the room.

"I don't like it, Andrea," Alex said. "Find out what's going on. Is this woman clean or not? We can't have Robert sleeping with the enemy. It won't be the first time we've been infiltrated this way. You remember what happened to Colson?"

"Yes, that wasn't pretty," Andrea said, the memory still bitter.

"You? Any boyfriends I should know about?"

"No, sir."

"Girlfriends?"

"No." Andrea's eyes narrowed into slits as she spat the word.

"Good. It would be prudent to keep it that way until we get through the big operation in February. Agreed?" Alex sharpened his look at her.

"Agreed," Andrea said with resignation and a tinge of resentment.

"Don't leave this hanging."

"I won't."

"OK. And keep me posted on your plans for finding out about this Dragon deal."

Robert had barely turned on his computer when Lamai popped her head in to tell him Andrea wanted to see him in her office. When he arrived, he found her seated behind her desk. Her lips were pursed, and she glowered at Robert. She kept that up for a full minute.

"What's this about a girlfriend, Robert?"

"She's not a girlfriend—just a friend." Robert hurried his words out. His hands went up as he spoke, shadowboxing. "We go sightseeing together. She's a tour guide. I paid for a couple of tours. Now, when she has time, we hang out together."

"You told Alex she had no record?"

"Yes, she's never been arrested and has no connection to the drug trade."

Andrea kept staring at him. Hard. "Agent Jordan, please make sure your…what's her name?" Andrea flung the question at Robert.

"Fon," Robert said. Her short name popped out of his mouth, and his spirits lifted.

"Please make sure Fon knows nothing of your language skills, nor what you are really doing here in Bangkok."

"I will. I've been very careful," Robert said, eager to end the conversation.

"How'd you meet her?"

"In a bar."

"In a bar? Classy. What type of bar?" Andrea's sarcasm crackled as she leaned forward, placing both hands flat on her desk.

"My local. It's connected to a hotel near where I live. It's a legitimate place. One of her tour clients stood her up."

"A likely story."

"She gave me a card. I checked out the agency. It's legit. And she actually works there," he said in a rush, still keen for closure.

"Oh. Goody for her," Andrea said, the derision palpable. "Look, Jordan, here's the story." Andrea's voice softened. She sighed, and she leaned back in her chair, folding her hands in her lap. "You remember I told you about Colson's death? What I didn't tell you is how he and I got into that situation. We'd scouted the warehouse, finding it unguarded. Our sources said there were only a few kilos of heroin stored in it, so Colson intended to grab it by himself. At the last minute, I decided to accompany him since I wasn't busy that evening. But here's what went wrong: Colson liked the nightlife here in Bangkok. Long story short, he had a girlfriend, and we found out later that she betrayed him, tipping off the Dragons about where Colson would be that night. Tianhao stabbed him before I could intervene. We don't know if his lover was a plant from the beginning or if they began paying her after she befriended him. Afterward, she disappeared—left town, we assume. Bottom line: I don't want to lose another agent! So, be careful, Robert," Andrea said. Andrea turned away from him to look out the window, shaking her head.

Robert walked home that evening, an hour-long stroll, but he needed to think. He had been looking forward to seeing Fon at the Crazy Bird that evening, but now he felt uneasy. No one in the office liked the idea of his seeing her. How could something that felt so good be bad? But it was a weird coincidence that she was sitting at that stool on the day he always had breakfast at the Crazy Bird. If not a fluke, then she had targeted him. But why him? OK. Sakchai and Alex are married, and Andrea's a woman. He was the logical person to connect with if you wanted to monitor the Orson Group. The single guy. The newcomer.

The story about Colson disturbed him, as well. His girlfriend had betrayed him to the Dragons, but now they had a bigger problem—the police. The drug squad knows what the Orson Group does and suspects the mission has changed to destroying drugs. Any compromised officer getting kickbacks from the drug trade would want them out of the way. Permanently.

Robert slumped into the Crazy Bird. Fon sat at the bar, waiting, and spotted him in the mirror. She turned to greet him, a huge smile beaming from her face, then rushed toward him and flung her arms around him. He hugged her back, breathing in her warmth and happiness. Clouds parted in his mind, and he kissed her head, then her lips when she looked up at him. She kissed him back with a joy he had never felt before from anyone.

"I'm no longer on probation at the tour agency! I have the job permanently! And your tours helped me! Thank you so much!" Fon wriggled closer to him.

They had a cocktail to celebrate, followed by a spicy curry dinner washed down with beer. At the end of the meal, Fon surprised Robert by saying she'd like to return to his apartment with him.

CHAPTER 19

From the shadows, Andrea followed Robert and Fon as they left the café. She watched and waited for three hours to see if Fon would emerge from Robert's building. She didn't.

Andrea walked back to the Toyota and climbed into the driver's seat. Even though the traffic was light, she dawdled while driving home, thinking about what had happened. She could see the attraction—Fon was beautiful. Andrea also understood the need for companionship; she felt the urge frequently. But it was so risky here. Even legitimate friends could pose a problem. They might innocently talk about you to the wrong people, and you couldn't control what they said to whom. You never knew. Not that she had any. Friends, that is. She had the gym, trips to the countryside or sightseeing, but no one to do anything with, except Mai. With Mai, she felt she could remake her own childhood and create a better person. The guys she had met at the club, presumably less risky than a local, seemed afraid of her. Why? She didn't bite. Such wusses. If she saw the Butlers at the club, she'd wave to them but wouldn't approach. She didn't want to get involved with his family. What if they asked her to babysit? Yuck!

The only friend she'd had while in Bangkok was Colson. They used to go for a beer after work, play tennis, work out, go to parks, and bike ride together. That dropped off when he met Kamlai, his girlfriend. For a time, Colson invited Andrea along on some of their dates. But she didn't enjoy being in the way of their lovey-dovey relationship. So sappy. She should have suspected Kamlai would betray him. She seemed shallow. Colson adored her, however. Shit! Why didn't she warn him off her? Hell, he wouldn't have listened…

Who needed friends anyway?

When she got home, she parked in her garage and slammed the door of the battered Toyota. She stomped into her home. What's Robert thinking? The same stupid thoughts as Colson? They weren't thinking. They were acting just like any man in the face of an attractive and willing companion.

Overall, as an agent, Robert had progressed well, improving at Thai boxing and gaining strength. He always did well at target practice but needed to be tested again at using his gun in the field. She hoped she would be there to protect him because she'd hate to lose him. But she would never say that to him.

She poured herself a mango juice and sat on her sofa, struggling to calm herself. With a big gulp, the drink disappeared. She banged the glass on the coffee table.

The entire team could be in danger because of this Fon. She might lose Sakchai, an outstanding agent, dependable, and quick to follow orders precisely. Always calm and respectful. With a wife and son. At the thought of Sakchai's small boy without a father, she swiped at her eyes, took a deep breath, and let it out slowly.

When she was eleven, she'd lost her parents in a car accident and moved to Abilene to live with her spinster aunt. Auntie, much older than her mother, walked cautiously and slept late. She taught Andrea never to rely on anyone else. If you wanted something in this world, you'd better figure out how to get it yourself. No one ever handed you anything on a silver platter. Or a tin plate, for that matter.

In Abilene, tall for her age, Andrea looked like a rival to the toughs in the school. On the first day of high school, one bully, Sharon, shoved Andrea aside as Andrea stepped through the door at school. Confused and upset, Andrea clipped Sharon's heel. Sharon turned around and slammed her meaty fist into Andrea's face. A burst of pain blasted into Andrea's brain as her nose swelled and bled. A crowd gathered, but Andrea, though taller, faced a girl who was heavier and more mature. Her face flushed with shame, she broke through the crowd and ran away from the shouts of "Chicken!" behind her.

When Andrea heard about a karate class in town, she went to sign up. The instructor, Jake, laughed at her and said he didn't have any girls in his class. She begged him for a chance to show him how much she wanted to learn. He eventually agreed to spar with her on the large mat in the studio. Andrea attacked and kept attacking, and Jake kept sending her to the floor. Again. And again. Finally, Jake flipped her forcefully onto her back, but Andrea—panting and sweating—still persevered, stumbling to her feet for yet another assault on him.

In the end, Jake let her into his beginner's class.

Andrea learned quickly, and she moved into Jake's intermediate class within a year. Soon she moved up to his top-tier class and earned a black belt. By far the best in her weight class, she even held her own against some of the heavier boys. Her speed, agility, and growing strength got her to the state finals, where she placed second. Against the boys.

So, when Sharon bullied her again just before graduation, Andrea challenged Sharon to meet for a fight at a secluded practice field. A crowd of Sharon's friends gathered around them. Andrea didn't have a supporter among them.

Sharon charged at Andrea, arms swinging. But Andrea stepped aside and flipped Sharon onto her back. Sharon shook her head in disbelief, got up, and approached one small step at a time, fists up. Andrea waited, and when Sharon punched, Andrea swiped away her blows and karate boxed her sternum, then moved closer, pulling up Sharon's right arm, and tripped her to the ground with her right leg. Sharon rolled off her back, jumped up, and rushed at Andrea, who tossed her down and stomped on her gut as she lay sprawled on the ground. Sharon doubled over, groaning, rocking, and wheezing for air.

"Want more?" Andrea challenged in a calm, confident, and menacing voice. She imagined herself breaking Sharon's neck. Her breath quickened and her nostrils flared as she remembered the time Sharon had embarrassed her on the first day of school.

"No! You win. I'll never bother you again," Sharon panted.

"Good. And if I see you bullying other kids, I'll step in. Understand?" Andrea's breathing slowed, and she pushed her dark thoughts away.

"Yes." Sharon nodded as if her life depended on it, still clutching her stomach.

Andrea turned to the group surrounding them and walked straight at them. The girls parted, pushing each other to make room for her to walk by.

College was better. She had friends, both men and women. Sometimes she'd be in a relationship, but it never lasted long. She never became close to anyone. Nothing endured. People moved on.

Family? The closest thing she ever had to a family was her teams. The latest, Sakchai and Robert, were her family now. She felt most comfortable when the three of them were in the field together. Most happy. Most alive.

Andrea shook her head, clutched her stomach, and rocked on the couch. What if something happened to one of them?

CHAPTER 20

Robert opened his eyes. He blinked and looked to his left. Fon snuggled against his shoulder, sleeping, her face placid and calm, as her shallow breathing swished the hairs on his arm. Everything felt so *right* about her. He couldn't imagine her causing him harm and chided himself for even thinking about it. Sneaking his leg out of the covers and placing his foot on the floor, he slid out of bed.

In the kitchen, he made coffee with his new French press. Moving on his stockinged feet to his bedroom, he peeked in at Fon and smiled. Still asleep. He closed the door and returned to the living room, sat on his couch, and picked up a paperback copy of John le Carré's *Tinker Tailor Soldier Spy*. But he couldn't concentrate. Thoughts of the upcoming drug delivery, the Dragons, and their raid kept banging into his mind. He'd double-check what the police knew about it on Monday. Maybe they were holding something back. Eventually, he pushed that aside and dove into his book.

He was engrossed in his reading and didn't hear Fon sneaking up on him to tickle his ear.

"Hey!" Robert said as Fon hugged him from behind and kissed him on the cheek.

"Hey, yourself."

"Did you sleep well?"

"I had a beautiful sleep, thank you. I smell coffee, but do you have some tea?"

"Sure. I'll make some for you."

"That's nice, but I can make it myself."

"No, that's OK." Robert put the kettle on to boil, got the jar of loose Thai black tea from the cupboard, took the condensed milk—already opened—from the fridge and placed it, the sugar bowl, and an extra spoon next to the tea.

"You know how to make Thai tea?" Fon asked. Robert's head jerked around to look at Fon. *Shit! Of course, I know how to make it; I used to live here.*

"Sure," Robert said, pausing to think. "I learned how to make it as soon as I arrived. Thais like their tea with milk and sugar. Often cold also, but usually warm in the morning, I understand. You?"

"Yes. Hot in the morning and cold for the rest of the day. And for me, always with milk and sugar."

"No wonder you're so sweet." Robert wrapped his arms around Fon, looking down at her, then he kissed her. A long, slow, seductive caress.

"Mmmm. That was lovely." Fon rested her head on Robert's chest and sighed.

"Do you have to work today?"

"No, I have the day off. What should we do?"

"Do you want me to hire you so you can guide me somewhere?"

"No. You are no longer my client. You are my lover. That would not be appropriate," Fon said. "But you can buy me lunch and din-ner," she said, laughing with her eyes and crinkling the corner of her mouth as she looked up at him.

"Sounds good to me," Robert said, grinning in anticipation of another evening with Fon. "But before lunch, I need to meet with Sam. He's at one of our rehab centers, and I'm his mentor."

"Oh? How does that work?"

"Each of us at the Orson Group is assigned one of our promis-ing charges to make sure they stay off drugs, study diligently, and become—I don't know—productive members of society? So, we hang out and do healthy things—bike ride, Thai box—you know, guy stuff."

"You box?"

"I'm taking lessons, so I teach him the moves I'm learning. Truth be told, he's probably a better fighter than I am, but he enjoys learning the techniques."

"Good for you." Fon seemed pleased and surprised to hear about Robert's charity work.

During breakfast at the Crazy Bird, Robert smiled at Fon and said, "I'd like to make curry for you sometime. To see what you think of my efforts. But we'll need to go to the market."

"I can do that this morning while you're with Sam. After lunch, we can stroll in Lumphini Park. It's very romantic."

"Romantic. I like that." Robert leaned over and kissed Fon across the table.

After breakfast, Robert left Fon in his local market and went to meet Sam at the clinic. Since it was near Rot Fai Park and a pleasant day, Robert wanted to walk there, though Sam seemed reluctant.

"What's up?" Robert asked, sensing Sam's unease as they wound through the streets.

"This is my old neighborhood," Sam replied, swiveling his head, searching the faces of the surrounding pedestrians. "I thought I saw someone from my old gang."

"Who? Where?" Robert jerked his head to look behind them. He couldn't see anyone who looked sinister. Everything was peaceful. The few people on the sidewalks seemed to be shoppers going about their business, and the park was close by. But to get to their destination quicker, Robert directed Sam to a shortcut through an alley.

Big mistake.

Three thugs had spotted Sam and had been shadowing them for a couple of blocks. Two had run ahead and were now walking toward them, blocking their way. The third came up behind them.

"These are the gang members who got me into trouble," Sam said, his voice quavering.

"OK. We'll get out of this," Robert said, with more confidence than he felt.

The leader loomed in front of them, a knife scar stretched across his left cheek. A guy with a white T-shirt and cauliflower ears stood to his right. Scarface shouted he wanted Sam to come with them and leave this dirty *farang* behind. Sam rushed out a translation—needlessly—for Robert. The thug behind them, a tall, scrawny man dressed in black, raced forward, picked up Sam, and ran around behind the other two, before Robert could react. Sam screamed and kicked, twisting away from his captor, who struggled to keep hold of him. Scarface and Ears approached Robert, their fists clenched, jaws set.

Robert dropped into his boxing stance, but he'd never trained at fighting two opponents. He backed up a step but stopped as he watched Sam wriggling and lurching with the skinny guy. His gut clenched and his muscles stiffened; he couldn't let them take Sam away! Skinny was straining to hold on to Sam, a whirlwind of motion, kicking and punching, preventing the goon from escaping with him.

Scarface laughed when he saw Robert in the classic Muay Thai pose, with his right leg behind him, knees bent, and fists up. He and Ears moved forward, crouching. Robert scooted back a bit, feigning a retreat, and they both came forward. Adrenaline coursed through his body. Instinctively, before the two of them could attack him, he hit the leader first. He landed a sharp jab with his left fist, but when he tried to follow through with his right, Scarface had bounced backward, and Ears struck Robert on the right side of his face. Twisting and shielding himself, Robert deflected his next blow and countered with two quick punches, left and right. Scarface came at him, but Robert surprised him with a kick to the stomach, pushing him backward. He tripped over a bump in the pavement and landed on his butt. Sam squirmed away from the third punk and jumped into Ears's back, sending him sprawling at Robert. Robert grabbed his arm as he came toward him and used Ears's momentum to swing him around and smash his head against the wall, knocking him out.

Skinny pounced on Sam, who lay on the ground after pushing Ears. The leader approached with more determination and less arrogance. He and Robert traded blows, and Scarface attempted kicks. Robert defended well against kicks, but couldn't counter-kick effectively, so he retreated. Scarface intimidated him with rapid punches, but Robert's longer reach kept him at bay, and Robert backed him up while Skinny and Sam struggled on the ground. When Sam kneed Skinny in the groin, he broke free and flung himself into Scarface's ankles, tripping him from behind.

Robert leapt over Sam and attempted to strike Scarface in the stomach with his foot, but he rolled away, so Robert kicked him in the head before he could get up. Scarface lunged at him, trying to tackle Robert. But Robert stepped back, grabbed Scarface's head and brought his knee up hard into his face. He crumpled. Skinny got up, holding his crotch, and staggered backward. Ears rose and wobbled away, clutching his bleeding head. Scarface got up, and Robert hit him hard with a left and then a right, and he stumbled into Skinny. They clung to each other to stay upright and backed away, watching Robert for any sign of another attack. Then they turned and fled.

"Are you all right?" Robert asked, looking at Sam for any signs of bleeding or injury. Sam had scraped his face on the pavement; tiny beads of blood dotted the cuts. Robert took some deep breaths to ease some of the adrenaline from his veins, relieved to see Sam standing and checking for injuries.

"I'm fine. Just this scratch and some bruises," Sam said, touching his cheek wound.

"Let's go back to the center and clean up. That's enough boxing practice for the day." Robert searched Sam's face for clues about what he was feeling. "Do you often encounter these guys?"

"I avoid this neighborhood."

"I'm so sorry. Please forgive me. I wasn't thinking. We'll take a *tuk-tuk* next time." Robert said, his face flushed with guilt.

"It's OK. You kicked their butts," Sam said, grinning.

"*We* kicked their butts. And we'll continue our boxing training so we can get better," Robert said, almost putting his arm around Sam. But he recalled that Thais don't touch each other and gave a respectful *wai* instead.

"Yes, I'm enjoying our Muay Thai training," Sam said, throwing two punches in the air, followed by a kick.

"We'll keep it up," Robert said, thinking of the peril Sam faced in the streets.

At the Orson rehab center, after they had washed themselves, Sam dug out the novel Robert had given him, Hemingway's *For Whom the Bell Tolls*. Robert had told Sam that his parents had named him after the main character. They read it for a while, and Robert explained some passages and words. Then as Sam asked for help in his math studies, he pulled out a tattered book from his cubbyhole and presented it to Robert—it was the same textbook Robert used to teach his students in Surat Thani.

Robert, still reeling from the fight, nearly forgot himself and launched into teacher mode. But he remembered it would reveal his language skills, so he asked Sam to translate some segments.

Sam watched Robert navigate easily through the book. Brow furrowed, he asked, "How come you know what this is about?"

"First, it's math, and that's a universal language. I can look at the numbers and symbols to understand the lessons. But also, it seems to be a translation of the math book I had in high school." Robert watched Sam's reaction, tensing. Was he too casual? He calmed down when he saw Sam had accepted the lie.

At lunchtime, Robert bought them curry from a street stall. He watched Sam finish eating before excusing himself.

From there, he took a *tuk-tuk* to Lumphini, an extensive park with paths and a lake, and met Fon at a restaurant.

"What happened to your face?" Fon exclaimed as Robert approached the table where she sat.

Robert explained the fight and Sam's role in it. "I couldn't have fought them off without his help. He's an impressive young man."

"He has an *impressive* mentor and protector," Fon said emphatically.

"Thanks," Robert said. "I'm not sure I'm that great, but I am glad I've been taking boxing lessons."

Feeling the heat of the bright sun on his back, Robert had to remind himself it was November, one of the coolest months of the year. Instead of walking along the paths, they went to the lake and rented a rowboat, Robert's preference over the paddle boats. He rowed them around the lake, pausing to watch birds in the trees along the shore and to observe the many flowers spread throughout the park. They passed a cannonball tree, its flowers bursting with a scent that hinted of magnolia and jasmine with a touch of lemon. Round fruit drooped from its trunk. A five-foot monitor lizard swam by their boat as they headed back to the rental agency. By the time Robert climbed out of the skiff, he was dripping with sweat. They hadn't escaped the heat on the lake; the cool water couldn't compete with the relentless sun.

As Robert and Fon strolled along the paths, they encountered more people enjoying the cooler breeze of the late afternoon. They walked by the giant palm trees, their trunks clothed in the stubbles of the long-gone fronds, like up-reaching hands. In the shady areas, orchids draped from the branches of trees. The smell of trees, grass, and sun-warmed flowers pierced the air.

Fon showed Robert the library on the grounds. Like the park, the library was the first public one in Thailand. Then Fon took Robert to see the monument to King Rama VI. The statue of the king, two-and-a-half times life size, stood atop a pyramid-like concrete base. Four bronze lotus buds marked the corners of a square that support-ed the statue's pedestal. In front of the monument was an area for worship, and one could get closer to the statue by climbing stairs on either side of the imposing structure.

Fon's voice grew proud and strong as she showed these Thai achievements to Robert. Assuming her tourist guide persona, she explained the history. In the late 1930s and early 1940s, the govern-ment planned to construct eight statues of former kings. Eventually, they erected them all, though World War II delayed their completion.

Another *tuk-tuk* took them home. When they were in the apart-ment, Robert turned on the air conditioner he had purchased. It took up a large part of one of his two windows but cooled the place to a reasonable temperature. He got out the fixings for the curry and began cooking the rice. After coarsely cutting the ingredients for the red curry paste, he placed them into a mortar and ground them with the pestle. He added oil, and crushed them some more, being careful not to splash any chili juice into his eyes.

Fon watched him, following his every movement. "You are quite an expert at cooking Thai food."

"Yes, it's been one of my favorite dishes since I…uh…since college. I had a Thai roommate in my first year at university, and he taught me a lot about his native cooking and culture. So, the course I took here was a refresher. There are some decent Thai restaurants in Washington, DC, where I lived before coming here. At first, Thai food was only available in Los Angeles and San Francisco, where the first Thai immigrants lived."

"You know a lot about Thailand."

"Well, as you know, I write reports about your country. So, yes, I do. But it's also true that I enjoy learning about the place where I live. I did the same in DC. Like here, there is a lot of history to learn in that city."

Robert finished cooking and put the dishes of food on the table.

"Bon appétit!" Robert said, sitting down. Fon, already seated, observed the placement of everything on the table.

"Why a French phrase for eating a Thai dinner cooked by an American?"

Robert laughed. "I have no idea. It's simply a fun way to invite people to begin eating."

"You have placed everything properly on the table. This is good. But you have only been here a short time?" Fon looked at Robert, her head cocked to one side.

"I observe what happens when I go to restaurants, and there seems to be a pattern of how they present the food, so I copied it."

"You observed well. Now, I must taste this curry. It smells delicious!" She scooped some rice onto her plate, followed by a generous portion of curry. Robert watched as she tasted it.

"It's yummy! You are a wonderful cook, Mr. Jordan."

"Please. Call me Robert," he said in a Sam Elliot tone, causing Fon to smile at the deep, faked voice of a movie actor she didn't know. They finished eating and retired to the bedroom.

In the middle of the night, Robert screamed from a nightmare, waking himself and Fon.

"What is it, Robert?" Fon asked, grabbing his hand.

Robert opened his eyes and looked around, surprised to find himself in his bedroom. He looked at Fon and hugged her. His breathing was rapid and irregular. "I'm sorry. Did I make a noise in my sleep?"

"You shouted in terror."

"It's a recurring nightmare," Robert said, rubbing his face with both hands. Fon looked unnerved by his shout.

"You scared me," she said. "Are you OK?"

Robert hugged her again, kissed her on the forehead, and said, "I'm fine. Sorry I woke you. I'm going to make some chamomile tea. Would you like some?" He started to climb out of bed.

"I'll make it. You rest," Fon said, pushing him back into a prone position.

After drinking the tea Fon brought him, Robert felt more relaxed and settled under the covers. Fon hugged him and snuggled into his side, clutching his arm.

Just as he was falling asleep, Robert's eyes popped open, and he burst out in sweat as he remembered what he had yelled: "Don't shoot me!"

But he'd shouted it in Thai.

CHAPTER 21

On the Monday ten days before Thanksgiving, Robert saw Andrea watching him and Chakan as he finished his workout. He smiled, glad she had caught him sparring well with his instructor. As he walked to the locker room, Andrea called to him.

"Meet me at the café in ten minutes."

Robert nodded and headed for the showers. Something was up; Andrea had spoken more brusquely than usual.

When they were seated at a four-chair table in a quiet corner of the sprawling eatery, she spoke without a greeting.

"First, what happened to your face?" Andrea asked.

Robert explained the fight and how he got lucky and, with the help of Sam, bested the three thugs.

"Couldn't have all been luck. I saw you in the gym."

Before Robert could say "Thanks!" Andrea interrupted him.

"Next, how serious is it with you and Fon?" Andrea demanded.

"I don't know. She stays over at my place sometimes. I don't pay her for tours anymore. We enjoy the city together. We visited Lumphini Park over the weekend." Sitting opposite Andrea, Robert didn't know what to do with his hands, so he stuck them in his pockets.

"Romantic," Andrea said, deadpan.

"It's a pleasant park," Robert said, pulling his hands out and setting them on the table between them. He put his hands back into his pockets. "We rented a boat, and we rowed on the lake."

"Charming. You enjoyed yourselves." It wasn't a question, just a flat, mocking statement. "Look. It can be dangerous here. We've learned that the hard way in this office. Be careful with Fon. You don't speak to her in Thai, do you?" Andrea asked in her usual harsh tone.

"No, of course not." *Technically, that's not a lie.* Robert's ears turned red.

Sakchai walked up and said, "Am I interrupting something?"

"No," Andrea said. "We're finished." Then to Robert she said, "I invited Sakchai to meet us here so we could start the week quickly."

"What did you learn over the weekend, Sakchai?" Andrea asked, still glaring at Robert, as Sakchai seated himself to the left of Andrea.

"I have two informants speaking about a large shipment to be delivered to the Dragons. It's coming in the week after your Thanksgiving holiday to be processed in their King Kaeo warehouse from Tuesday to Thursday."

"OK. What's our plan for raiding this place? Any ideas, Sakchai?" Andrea turned to look at him, ignoring Robert.

Sakchai looked from Andrea to Robert and back, then back again at both of them. "We should go in late at night. People need sleep, and they will be less alert at one in the morning."

"Go on." Andrea continued looking only at Sakchai.

"Balaclavas too. We need to keep them guessing about who is doing these raids."

"Yes?"

"We will need a safe house near the warehouse. If something goes wrong, we'll need somewhere to hide. It might be difficult for us to escape." Sakchai kept shifting his gaze between his two colleagues.

Andrea leaned toward Sakchai. "That's a good idea. We barely got away from them last time. And they'll have a more powerful car. We were lucky their vehicle was on the other side of the warehouse. I think we'll need to find two places. One we pass through if they're on our tails—to slow them down—and a second where we can vanish.

"Any thoughts, Robert?" Andrea turned her fierce eyes to him.

"Uh…I'll monitor the police reporting to see what they know about the shipment."

"Good. You do that." Andrea turned to face them. "I need the restroom, and then we can drive to the office."

After she left, Sakchai asked, "Do you and agent Cannon have a problem?"

"She's unhappy that I have a girlfriend."

"Yes. This complication led to the loss of Agent Colson. His girl-friend betrayed him. My informants told me about it a month after he was gone. People brag about their successes."

"I checked her out. She's not connected with any drug dealers and doesn't have a police record." His ears burned again.

"I hope that is the case, Agent Jordan."

"Yeah. Me too. How does one really get to know someone, anyway?"

"Yes. This is a mystery of life."

"You're lucky to have a wife and child. It must be a blessing."

"Yes, I am most fortunate." They gave a more formal *wai* than usual to each other and walked to the car where Andrea joined them.

Robert's thoughts turned to Fon. He moped about being unable to see her that weekend—she had two full days of tours lined up. He'd miss her.

Robert sat at his desk, both hands on it, drumming his fingers as if playing a tune on a piano. Still thinking of Fon, but reflecting on his colleagues' comments, he decided to double-check on her.

A scary idea occurred to him. What if her name wasn't really Fon Chongrak?

Remembering her father's restaurant, Khrua Ohm, he searched business directories for ownership. Robert's stomach lurched, and beads of sweat formed on his forehead. Sap Shinawatra owned the restaurant, and he had three children—two sons and a daughter named Fon. Like him, Fon had used her real background, but she'd slipped up and used the actual name of her dad's restaurant, probably thinking he'd forget it instantly.

He searched the police computer for information on Fon Shinawatra. What he found made his heart sink.

Fon worked for the police.

Robert slapped his hands to his head, then pulled at his hair. What was he going to do with this information? She served as a consultant to the Police Internal Affairs, the anti-corruption unit. What did that mean? Why would she be pursuing him? He wasn't a Thai police officer. Worse, he couldn't confront her until after Thanksgiving; he'd invited her to dinner on the Sunday after the holiday.

His hands shaking, he put the revelation aside; he'd think about it later. He needed to get back to work, so he reviewed the police reports in the drug section. What he found made the hair on the back of his neck bristle.

Another stomach-dropping find.

"We'll need a meeting with Amonsak as soon as possible," Robert said after he and his team arrived in Alex's office.

"What's up?" Alex asked.

"Let me show you on my computer," Robert said.

"So, here's the document that surprised me," Robert said moments later, showing his colleagues on his terminal after they gathered in his office. "We agreed when we last met with Amonsak that they would share information with us, and we would share it with them. But they've had the information about the drug shipment and the warehouse for over a week."

Alex thumped his finger on Robert's desk, absorbing the information. "We'll meet with them next Monday and ask them if they have any new information about shipments. I'll take Sakchai, and he can give them a minimal account of the news we have on the shipment. That'll be our excuse for a meeting. If they don't tell us anything, we'll know they are actively plotting against us."

In the morning before the Monday meeting with Amonsak, Andrea told Robert and Sakchai she had surveyed an alleyway over the weekend and found two adjacent abandoned buildings. They could enter the first one and then leap across the roof to the other one. It would have to work, should anything go wrong next week.

As the two DEA agents were getting seated, Amonsak and Prin greeted Sakchai enthusiastically and smiled at Alex. Alex guessed they were happy to speak their own language and let Sakchai translate.

After a few pleasantries in English, Amonsak said, "Thank you for coming to see us to share your information. We've heard about a shipment coming into one of the Dragon's storage buildings, but know little else. What can you tell us?"

Sakchai gave only the information about the shipment arriving next Tuesday and said that Wang's crew would process it by Thursday but said nothing about which warehouse. He translated for Alex, who blinked at Sakchai, a small sign of approval for withholding some intelligence.

Alex then stated, "We expect to learn the whereabouts of the drugs before the end of this week. But we won't be able to support any police action until next Thursday. We'll need to fully prepare for any raid, but we should be ready by then. Will your police be able to storm the building by then?"

"We cannot do any major police operation next week, but if you verify the warehouse for us, we should be able to break into it the following week." Amonsak was sympathetic, but firm.

"Our sources tell us it will be out of the warehouse by Friday," Alex said, testing for a reaction.

"If you can find out where it is going, we may be able to stop it before it leaves the country or they distribute it on the streets."

"Sure. We'll do our best. Please let us know if you learn anything new."

"We will. Thank you for sharing your informant's knowledge."

"Absolutely. We appreciate your cooperation and support," Alex said, without a trace of irony.

"You can count on us at all times," Amonsak said, appearing sincere. "If there is nothing else, I have another meeting. Thank you again for providing your intelligence to us."

Back at the office with his team standing in front of him, Alex said from his chair, "They withheld information about this drug consignment from us. They don't trust us, and they may be laying a trap for us." He kept shaking his head in disbelief and horror.

"What do you want us to do now?" Andrea asked.

"I told them we weren't able to support any raid before next Thursday, so we have to go in on Tuesday night, the first night the drugs arrive. It's our only chance to stop this shipment. We should be able to take them by surprise, which will give us the advantage," Alex said, with more hope than conviction.

"OK. We'll formulate a plan and see if we can't destroy the drugs. We may have to torch the warehouse," Andrea said, looking confident.

"I can't see why we shouldn't do that. We're on our own now. But we'll need to do everything we can to leave no trace of us." Alex's gaze drifted to the window, his forehead a mass of wrinkles.

"Understood," Andrea said.

Before Robert could get back into his office, Andrea summoned him and Sakchai into hers. He listened as Andrea went over her proposal to enter the warehouse. With a map, she showed them the planned escape route, should they need one, through the two empty buildings she had found. To Robert, the plan sounded haphazard and ad hoc. Also, the "getaway" office blocks were a significant distance from the target. But he liked the idea of the safe house as a backup. She ordered them to take turns monitoring the warehouse security. Sakchai took that evening, Robert got Tuesday, leaving Andrea with Wednesday, the day before Thanksgiving.

On Thursday morning, though a day off for their American company, Andrea had them meet again in her office. After they each detailed what they had seen during their separate surveillances, they concluded the guarding routine was the same every night. Andrea told Robert and Sakchai that they should take the rest of the four-day office vacation. Besides, Alex's wife had invited everyone to dinner that evening, an annual tradition.

Robert arrived a little late at the Butler's home, carrying flowers and wine. Alex greeted him at the door, shook his hand, grabbed the bottle and bouquet, took his drink order, and disappeared into the kitchen. The blue-clothed dinner table now dominated the living/dining room—Alex had added extensions and moved furniture to accommodate it. It held a sumptuous spread; Shirley had set the table with holiday plates and silverware. Gourds and eucalyptus created a colorful and fragrant centerpiece. In the remaining living area, Sakchai's family, Sirikit and Niran, occupied most of the couch on one side of the room, while Andrea, Sakchai, and Lamai took up the space near the bookshelves on the other. In the middle, Alex's children, Al and Sally, were playing a board game on the coffee table.

Alex returned with the drinks—a whiskey for himself and a Pinot Noir for Robert. "Happy Thanksgiving!" Alex said, raising his glass and clinking it with everyone, including Sirikit. Andrea sipped a Chardonnay while Sakchai, Sirikit, and Lamai were hitting the hard stuff—water with a slice of lemon. Andrea almost looked chic with her combed hair and a string of pearls adorning her neck. However, she still wore her uniform, a simple white blouse and dark slacks. In contrast, Sirikit and Lamai wore elegant formal Thai attire, with one shoulder bare and the other covered by a long shawl-like length of fabric. Sakchai wore one of his suits, so Robert was relieved that Alex, like him, sported casual clothes—khakis and a dress shirt, open at the collar.

"What's everyone doing over the long weekend?" Alex asked.

"My family and I will go to Lumphini Park tomorrow," Sakchai said. "It will be less crowded than on the weekend. And on Saturday, Sirikit and I will compete in a bridge tournament."

"Sounds fun, and good luck in the competition. Andrea?"

"I'm playing tennis at the club," Andrea said. "And will swim in the pool, jog in a park, the usual."

"Oh, is that a tennis 'date'?" Alex asked.

"Hardly. I played with a woman, Sandra, and it was embarrassing even though I went easy on her. Afterward, she suggested I play with her husband, Ken. She'll be there to watch us."

"You 'crushed' her?" Lamai asked.

"Yes, it wasn't pretty. Where do you learn your English phrases, Lamai?"

"I read American novels in my spare time."

"And is that what you'll do this weekend?" Alex asked.

"No, I'll spend this weekend with my friends. We eat and we chat. We'll likely go for a picnic."

"Robert? Any plans?"

"I'll spend some time with a friend of mine," Robert said. Alex hadn't invited Fon; he'd made it clear he expected him to show up alone, so he didn't mention her name.

"Of course," Alex said, patting Robert on the shoulder.

The conversation didn't improve after that—the weather, a bit on the Thai government, some tut-tutting over the recent assassination of Indira Ghandi and political affairs in India—so Robert joined in a game of Chutes and Ladders with Alex's kids. He enjoyed watching them react to the thrill of a long ladder and the setback of a slide. And they laughed at his antics when he lost. It reminded him of rainy days playing Monopoly with his sister, Maddie; they were evenly matched in their strategies. They played by the original rules, so it took a long time, and luck, to crush their opponent with rent. But the game always ended cordially; there would be a next time, with another chance to win.

Finally, they sat at the table, with Alex at the head and Al squeezed in next to him. Shirley sat at the other end with Sally next to her. Sakchai and Sirikit sat on Alex's left, with Niran in a highchair between them, while Andrea, Robert, and Lamai, were on his right.

Alex began with a thankful prayer, and everyone bowed their heads and said Amen when he finished. Then he asked everyone to say what they were thankful for, starting with Al.

"Cranberry sauce!" Al said, eyeing the bowl filled with red jelly.

Sakchai replied for his family that he was thankful for their health.

"My birthday!" Sally shouted, thinking ahead to the early December event.

Shirley was thankful for her lovely children and doting husband.

"My parents haven't disowned me, even though I am not married," Lamai said, laughing.

Picking up the family theme, Robert said, "I'm thankful for my sister, who has always been there for me."

"I'm thankful that I can share this holiday dinner with my colleagues and their families," Andrea said, lifting her glass in a toast. Everyone raised their drinks and took a sip.

Alex spoke last. "I'm thankful, of course, for my loving wife who prepared this fabulous feast, for my joyous children, Al and Sally, and also for my colleagues. With each passing day, they continue to improve individually and as a team. Happy Thanksgiving!" He raised his goblet of wine and said, "To us!"

Robert, seated in the middle, attempted to communicate on all sides. With Lamai acting as translator, he joined Shirley's discussion with Sirikit about raising children. He'd never thought much about having kids or getting married. He wondered if Fon would want to join him when he returned to the United States. Of course, he had to survive this mission first, and they had to become more honest with each other. One thing he was sure of: any children she had would be beautiful.

"Robert is improving rapidly at Thai boxing," Andrea said to Alex and Sakchai. "I watched him sparring, and he landed some heavy blows on his trainer."

"Gee, that almost sounds like a compliment," Robert said, and Andrea laughed as she slammed him with her elbow. He found it odd that she could brag to their boss about his skills but never say anything positive directly to him.

"Are you ready for next week?" Alex asked Andrea in a low voice, so the women at the far end of the table couldn't hear him.

"Yes, we have a plan and a great team." She grinned at Sakchai and slapped Robert on the back, nearly plunging his face into his plate.

"Good. I'm pleased to hear that," Alex said as he stuffed another bite of turkey into his mouth.

Robert looked up and saw Niran staring at him, so he winked at him—one eye, the other, then both. Niran giggled and buried his head behind his mom's arm and then peeked out. Robert repeated the gestures, sometimes covering his eyes, until Niran tired of the game. Robert realized he liked kids; he'd surprised himself earlier with how much fun he had playing with Al and Sally. He hoped he could help Sam stay off drugs and mature. *A lot of potential there,* he thought.

Toward the end of his play with Niran, Andrea spied his antics and looked at him like he was nuts.

"What on earth are you doing?" Andrea asked, shaking her head, bewildered.

"Playing peekaboo with Niran."

"You never cease to amaze me, Agent Jordan."

"I'm a man of many talents. Playing games with kids is just a minor one."

Andrea turned away to ask Alex a question.

Sakchai tickled his son's back to get his attention and made eye contact with him. Niran squealed in delight.

That Saturday night, Robert rolled restlessly in bed. He dreamed he ran down a dark alley, but his legs turned into two tuna, and he slipped and fell, sliding down the narrow passageway, ricocheting from one side to the other and bouncing off walls and garbage bins like a pinball. After he bumped into a crate, breaking it open, white powder spilled onto the asphalt. He skidded straight toward a fiery building. Above him, fireworks burst like giant, shimmering flowers in the black sky.

He shook his head when he awoke, relieved to be rid of his nightmares. He got up, made coffee, and ate a breakfast of *jok,* the Thai rice porridge dish topped with a soft-boiled egg. Then he went to the market to get the ingredients he needed for an improvised Thanksgiving dinner—chicken instead of turkey, but most of the rest of the trappings, except cranberry sauce. As usual, he eavesdropped on the Thai merchants. Today, they laughed at his mop of hair, so curly, like those silly American poodles. But they always served him with a smile and never overcharged him.

He'd invited Fon to dinner that evening—before learning of her police work—intending to impress her with his American-style cooking. She had clients on Friday, Saturday, and Sunday morning, so this was the earliest they could connect. Though he was unsettled by her duplicity, he looked forward to spending the night with her.

While preparing dinner, he mulled over his line of attack. It made his head throb. They both worked undercover. He pretended to be a charity worker doing research. She pretended to be a tour guide. But he had felt her genuine happiness at no longer being on probation. Why would she care? She kept her police work secret—a job focused on other cops. That meant that she was investigating him, a known DEA agent to the police. How was he going to wring that out of her—and not disclose his DEA status and actions?

When she arrived, he embraced her, taking in her scent. She must have been a tour guide that day; he detected the musky scent of a day outdoors in her hair, mixed with her jasmine perfume. He rubbed her back, kissed her, and then pulled away. He'd prepared the dishes earlier, so he served up everything and opened a bottle of Sauvignon Blanc while she set the table.

After they sat down, Robert asked, "So, have you ever worked in another job besides tour guide?" Robert knew he had neither talent as an interrogator nor subtlety.

Fon froze, fork halfway to her mouth, and stared at Robert. She set her utensil down. "Why do you ask?"

He'd overplayed his hand; she was already suspicious. But he needed to know where Fon's loyalty lay.

"I thought I saw you going into a police station the other day. The one where they have the Police Internal Affairs." This was a lie, but it got straight to the point without saying what he already knew.

Fon's hands flew to her mouth, and she sucked in her breath. Then she laid her hands flat on the table, took a deep breath, and asked, "How long have you known?"

"I learned last week, Fon Shinawatra," Robert said. Fon gasped, hanging her head.

"Yes. I have two jobs, one as a tour guide, the other with the police. My boss assigned me to learn everything I can about you. I don't know why. You're not a policeman. But I wasn't ordered to sleep with you. I *fell* for you. You must believe me!" Abruptly, Fon rose, rushed to Robert, and flung her arms around him, kissing his cheek feverishly. "I joined the police to help stop the drug trade, but I've done nothing but fall in love with you."

Robert set down his spoon, wrapped his arm around her waist, turned his head, and kissed her. "It's OK. I believe you."

After the meal, in the bedroom, Fon made love to him, giving everything of herself in a gesture of great anguish, striving to convince him of her love.

In the morning, Robert prepared breakfast, while Fon readied herself for a morning as a tour guide.

"When will I see you next?" Fon asked. She moved toward Robert, placed her hand on his waist, and looked up, desperate for reassurance.

"I'm very busy this week, but how about Friday?" Robert asked, showing his uneasiness but endeavoring to comfort her.

"That would be great!" Fon said, sighing in relief.

After Fon left, Robert washed the dishes, his stomach churning, and his shoulders slumping with remorse. Was he now using Fon for his own desires? Was he sleeping with the enemy? He really cared for Fon and wanted to believe her. Was love blinding him? He took solace in knowing that he'd fallen for her before knowing she worked for the police.

But their conversations niggled at him. Was Fon telling the truth, or was she just a damn good actress?

CHAPTER 22

On Monday morning, Hao Wang sat in his office reviewing accounting papers that evaluated his profits. He stroked the head of one Siamese cat on his lap while another paced across his documents. Though he sat upright, the picture of a businessman with his dark hair sparsely covering his skull and the thin mustache dirtying his upper lip, he had the aura of a panther, crouched and ready to leap onto its prey. Tapestries, paintings, and sculptures depicting dragons filled his office. Some dragons turned and twisted, others sat on their hindquarters, and a couple simply stood, magnificent, majestic, and menacing. In the right-hand corner, a black safe lurked, with—what else?—a gold-leaf dragon on the front. Two cat carrier cages were stacked next to it. To his right, Tianhao sat at a wooden table with four chairs.

Hearing a knock, Wang waved to Tianhao to open the door.

Wang stood, and the cats dove for the floor. He bowed deeply as Amonsak Suwannarat entered the room. Amonsak performed a similar *wai*, and they addressed each other with the respectful *Khun*.

"Please, sit," said Wang, waving his hand at a chair facing his desk. They spoke their customary English, the international language of business.

Amonsak sat, "Thank you. I have some urgent information on a likely raid on your King Kaeo warehouse."

"Please continue."

"Mr. Butler has suggested that his Orson Group team will only be ready to conduct an operation by this Thursday."

"Excellent! We'll prepare a trap for his people as we agreed."

"However, I suspect they may strike sooner."

"Oh?" Wang leaned forward, his scrunched brow emphasizing his query.

"Butler and his team are not fools. They suspect we do not trust them. So, when he *implied* it would be on Thursday, I immediately thought it would be sooner. Perhaps even tomorrow night when the shipment arrives."

Wang sat back in his chair, placing his hands in front of him with the fingers touching. Then he spread out his arms and shrugged. "This is not a problem. We'll be ready for them as soon as the drugs arrive."

"Yes. I agree. That would be prudent. I have some more information."

"Yes?"

"You remember the raid on our warehouse near the airport? The one we suspect was Butler's team?"

"Of course. How could I forget the loss of two hundred kilos of heroin? And your failure to secure it?" Wang couldn't resist the criticism. He'd never suffered such a loss before; even the Scorpions encroaching on his territory had not caused such a blow to his business.

"We never suspected they would steal from a police warehouse," Amonsak said, with thinly disguised anger. "They hadn't ever before confiscated drugs on their own."

"Yes, well. And what about it?"

"We had two security people in the building at the time. Not police officers, of course, but contractors."

"And?" Wang asked, tapping his finger on his desk.

"As you know, one of them died. But the other one didn't have a weapon, so remained hidden behind a crate. He observed the action that night and witnessed something unusual." Amonsak paused.

"Go on," Wang said, leaning forward, his hands flat on his desk.

"While the armed guard shot wildly at one intruder, the Butler agent held his fire, even though his gun was pointing right at our man."

Wang lurched backward. "So, how did your guy die?"

"It was another Butler agent who killed our night watchman. The person under fire, whom we suspect to be the new agent, Robert Jordan, never discharged his gun."

"He's getting shot at, and he doesn't defend himself?" Wang asked, puzzling over this development.

Amonsak nodded.

"That's odd, but it shouldn't matter after this week. We'll have a surprise for them whatever time they come for the drugs." Wang suddenly remembered something and held up his hand, asking Amonsak to wait. He rose, strode to his safe, unlocked it, and drew out a packet. "You've done an excellent job of luring our foes into a trap. Here is your usual payment. If they show up to raid us, I'll know that your deceit with them has worked, and you'll get another equally weighty envelope."

"That's fair. I'll see you on Friday to collect that."

Wang smiled at Amonsak's confidence. After they bowed to each other, Amonsak left.

Wang waved again at Tianhao, who walked over to the inner-office door and opened it, stepping aside for the people standing there.

"Did you hear all that, Mr. Volkovich?" Wang asked as a tall hulk of a man entered the room. Two even larger men with enormous heads but no necks, followed him.

"Please. Call me Vlad. Yes, I understood everything. I'll assume you'll resolve that by the end of the week." Vlad slipped into one chair in front of Wang, while his bodyguards stood sentry at the front door. "I congratulate you on your access to such a high-level government official. No wonder your operation is normally very efficient."

"Thank you. You've seen our facilities and now know how we work with the local authorities. Shall we discuss the other reason for your visit?"

"I haven't seen the lab where you create your mysterious added ingredient. It's this that worries me, because your Bangkok Dragon mix has led to an increase in overdoses. To be blunt, we can't sell drugs to dead people." Vlad sat up, straightened his back, and leaned forward. "It's not the quality of the additive I'm worried about; it's how much you put into the heroin, and you do that *here in this warehouse*," Vlad said, thumping his index finger on Wang's desk.

"I understand your concern perfectly," Wang said, unruffled by Vlad's menacing bulk tilted toward him. "Dr. Golovanov has suggested a safer dosage, and I personally will oversee the implementation of the additive."

"When can I see the lab and meet Golovanov?"

"Our lab needed to move in a hurry. Our chemist will inform us of its and his whereabouts once it is up and running again. I trust you are happy we have a Russian scientist working for us?"

"Yes, I'm sure he produces high-quality drugs. But why did you have to move in a rush?"

"The landlord booted us out, giving us only a day's notice. Such things happen in Bangkok when a wealthy client wants something. Until we hear from Golovanov, we won't know where he is located. He's operating that way for security reasons. After this week, we'll be able to produce the narcotic more securely. As an added precaution, we're importing the ingredients under false names."

"Why do we need this additive at all?" Vlad asked, not bothering to disguise his disdain.

"Ah, that is an interesting question," Wang said, picking a piece of paper from his desk and presenting it to Vlad. "Please review these numbers. In short, we can double our profits with this additive; it's that strong. Golovanov estimates it is up to fifty times stronger per milligram than heroin. And it's cheap to manufacture."

"I understand the finances, but I don't like it. Here's what we'll do. We'll buy your February shipment with the Bangkok Dragon additive, but if overdoses are too high, we'll only buy pure heroin in the future."

"That will work. I'm sure you will be happy with the product and the profits," Wang said.

The Russian stood up and held out his hand. Wang came around his desk and shook it.

"We'll see about that," Vlad said, gripping Wang's hand and squeezing hard. He turned and departed, his bodyguards trailing behind him.

"Tianhao, bring me some of our pure heroin and a packet of Golovanov's special mixture. We need to test the dosage of the additive on some of our local addicts—the ones who struggle to make regular payments. I don't want to disappoint Mr. Volkovich."

CHAPTER 23

Fon closed the door of Robert's apartment building and strode into the glaring Bangkok morning, already steamy. Dodging motorbikes and other pedestrians, she shut out the blare of the local traffic and the rank smell of the garbage in the gutter as she walked toward the Crazy Bird. She intended to use the phone there to make an appointment to see her boss, Head of Police Internal Affairs Kla Ritthirong.

While she strolled, Fon recalled an outing with her then-healthy brother, Jirayu. One weekday, they'd driven into Surat Thani from their village with a picnic lunch. After arriving at Koh Lamphu Park, they roamed around the entire island. As they wandered, they looked for birds and were happy to see a green-billed Malkoha, with its spotted tail, red eye "patch," and blue wings. The trees with gigantic yellow flowers were in bloom, their large petals giving off a light vanilla fragrance.

They settled down on a grassy area near the Tapi River on the north side. Jirayu had taken his special "medicine" that morning, so he radiated a relaxed glow. The January sun blazed, but a breeze off the water kept them cool. Fon couldn't remember what they talked about, but she could still see the trees on the opposite bank of the silver-blue river and the orange chest and blue wings of the kingfisher that briefly joined their picnic.

The recollection reminded her she should send more money to him. Her mother had written to her recently, informing her that his health deteriorated a bit each day, but the medications they bought with her extra money eased his pain.

At the Crazy Bird, she asked to use the telephone and paid a small fee to Chai. With a lift of her chin, she implied to him she needed privacy, and he moved away. She connected with Kla's assistant, who left her hanging on the phone while she conferred with their chief. When she returned, she said the earliest he could meet her was the next afternoon, Tuesday, at their usual rendezvous point. *Typical,* thought Fon, though she had stressed the urgency to meet, he'd made her wait. She knew he found her trifling, but still it irked. Having completed the call, she bowed to Chai and left the Crazy Bird.

To fill the hours before her appointment the following day, Fon threw herself into her tour job. She enjoyed the work, finding pleasure in the gratitude of her mostly American and British tourists. She'd worked hard to memorize the key points of each landmark, so she no longer needed notes to describe them. In her spare time, she read about the history and features of Bangkok's points of interest so she could answer any question her clients might surprise her with. Their rave reviews of her tours to Kla's sister, her manager at the agency, had ensured she ended her probation period, becoming a permanent employee. When she reflected on her customers' compliments, their kind words made her heart dance with joy. She'd collected letters of recommendation from some of them, in case she needed to change to a different tour agency.

And then there was the work with the police. At first, she relished it, because she thought she would be fighting against the police corruption that allowed the spread of narcotics in Thailand. She wanted to stop the scourge that had made her brother ill. She'd applied for work at many police agencies, but they always turned her away because she was a woman. Finally, Kla had hired her on contract as his assistant. She received no formal training—the police academies didn't allow women to enroll. But Kla made sure she had access to the manuals and had one trusted officer train her privately in their procedures and systems. He gave her a computer terminal, a telephone line, and a modem so she could work from home. He even gave her a revolver and paid for her training in how to use it. Usually, police officers had to buy their own weapons. She couldn't imagine a situation where she would need to use it, however.

Kla had also arranged with his sister, her tour agency's manager, to hire her as a cover for her police activities. But now she found working with tourists more appealing; she didn't understand her police work—what could Robert have to do with police corruption?

On Tuesday afternoon after leaving her last client for the day, she caught a bus and headed across town to Lumphini Park. As she entered it, Police Commissioner Amonsak Suwannarat passed her, striding with a military step toward an exit. She performed a *wai* as he passed, but he didn't deign to acknowledge her, keeping his eyes focused on the exit gate. A moment later, she saw her boss, Kla, sitting in the shade on a bench where they usually met.

Fon bowed deeply to Kla and took a seat next to him after he gestured for her to sit.

"What was it you wanted to see me about?" Kla asked, tapping the fingers of his right hand on his knee.

"Something may happen this week with the Orson Group…"

"Yes, and do we know what?" Kla asked, showing his impatience.

"First, I need to understand why I'm engaging with someone who is not a police officer and what you think he has to do with police corruption. I'm struggling to understand what I should look for exactly."

"It's enough that you report about Agent Jordan's activities," Kla said, biting the words. "I hope you haven't become emotionally involved with him."

"Of course not. I monitor him professionally," Fon said, straightening her shoulders with indignation.

Kla regarded Fon for a moment. Satisfied, he continued. "We suspect the Orson Group is collaborating with the police to extract part of the profits from the local drug trade. He's the weak link on the team, and your job is to find out what they are up to so we can catch them and some of our fellow officers taking bribes."

"Well, it is difficult to get information from him; he remains secretive about his activities. However, he appeared agitated yesterday morning when I met him for coffee. I have a strong feeling that something is up this week, but I don't know what or when. I'm sorry I don't have more."

"Hmmm. That's useful. Thank you. That confirms what my other sources also suspect."

"Yes. Something else. After a nightmare, he spoke Thai. 'Don't shoot me,' he said distinctly."

"That's odd. He may be more important than we thought. But I can't see how that can matter now. Did you have something else?"

"I was wondering about my pay."

"Ah, yes. Thank you for reminding me." Kla took two envelopes from his sport coat and gave the lighter one to Fon. He deftly returned the other to his inner pocket.

"You did well. Thank you," Kla said, standing.

Fon rose and they each gave the other a *wai*.

Kla took a step away and then turned and said, "By the way, there will be no need to monitor Jordan after today. I'll give you a new task next week. Unfortunately, I'm so busy I won't have time to assign you to a new project until then. Please make a thorough report on him this week."

Fon gazed at Kla. "Yes, sir." He strode away, and Fon sat down, as agreed, while he left the park.

That was odd. He'd only recently assigned her to Robert. Why would the job end abruptly? Did it mean she'd succeeded on her first mission? Assignment over, she looked forward to Friday evening with Robert. She could do the Jordan Report in the evenings and the tourism job during the day; the extra pay helped.

While waiting her required fifteen minutes on the bench—"standard protocol," Kla had instructed her—she reflected on her evening with Robert. She couldn't tell if he believed her when she expressed her passion for him. It sickened her to know that he had learned she had lied to him before she could tell him. On the other hand, he hadn't been open and truthful either. But his job required that. Her job targeted him for deception, making it personal. She needed to quit her police work; it wasn't what she had hoped for, and she wasn't good at it, anyway. She'd fallen in love with her first assignment. Pathetic. But so lucky that it was Robert!

As she left the park, Fon recalled the police commissioner striding to the exit.

She stopped in her tracks.

A moment later she ran to the curb, hailed a *tuk-tuk*, and directed it to the Crazy Bird. Hoping to spot Robert as he walked home from work, she took a table near the sidewalk. She ordered an orange juice and a snack. Then she waited. And waited. But Robert didn't pass by at his usual time. When she still had not seen him an hour later, she phoned his apartment, but he didn't answer.

Panic thrust up from her stomach to her throat. She dashed to the main street and hailed a *tuk-tuk* for home. Once inside, she turned on her computer and made a cup of tea. Her tea grew cold as she labored over her computer for the next two hours. At last, she found what she was looking for. She jumped up, turned off her computer, and raced to the kitchen. She wrote two letters and put each into a box; one she addressed to her brother in Surat Thani and stuffed the money from Kla in it. The other had only the note and the address. Then she wrote instructions for her roommate about what to do with the parcels.

She grabbed her gun and rushed out the door.

CHAPTER 24

Robert looked at Sakchai sleeping on the mattress beside him in one of their spare offices. Andrea had ordered them to stay at their office until they departed for the raid. She didn't want any slipups when they traveled to Wang's King Kaeo warehouse. For the same reason, she left the Toyota at home. While they rested, Andrea reiterated their simple plan: penetrate the building, verify the drugs were inside, torch it, and get the hell out of there.

At 1 a.m., a taxi dropped them about a mile and a half from the warehouse. Robert and Sakchai walked behind Andrea as she showed them the two office blocks that would serve as an escape route should they need it. The moon cast the buildings' shadows onto the pavement, and in the darkness, the scent of spilled garbage hung in the windless air. Bangkok usually bustled with noise, but tonight Robert heard no traffic. The scratching of rodents' claws on the pavement as they scurried unseen across the alley underscored the unusual stillness. The silence troubled him.

They each carried fireworks, a liter of gasoline, a BIC lighter, their Berettas, and two extra magazines. However, to avoid attracting attention, Andrea instructed him and Sakchai to use their guns only if necessary.

They approached the warehouse along a wide, straight alley with industrial-sized trash bins on both sides. The modest-sized target building loomed in the distance, directly at the end of the road. It had a large garage door opening with a wicket—a regular-sized door—for individuals to enter the warehouse. No guards were visible, but they knew there were at least two inside.

After putting on their balaclavas, they began their approach. They stole from one doorway or dumpster to the next, searching for lookouts. Andrea and Robert led the way, with Sakchai trailing behind. Andrea dashed down the right-hand side of the alley, and Robert and Sakchai slipped to the left. They moved on padded feet from one hiding place to another. Stepping into doorways or crouching behind dumpsters or shipping containers, they progressed slowly, taking no chances of a surprise attack. After fifteen minutes, they were within a quarter of a mile of their target. They inched forward.

Robert crept to within two hundred yards of the building. He ducked into a doorway. There was Fon!

"It's a trap!" she whispered. "They're going to kill all of you!"

"Why are you here?" Robert sputtered, his heart pounding ferociously as sweat poured from his brow.

"This area is off limits to police patrols this week. And my boss said you wouldn't be around next week. Then you didn't come home tonight. Get away while you can!"

"Fuck!" he swore. Turning, he yelled, "Pull back! It's a trap!"

At the sound of his voice, gunfire erupted. Shots blasted from the windows of two buildings near the warehouse, one on each side of the road. Andrea, Robert, and Sakchai pulled their guns from their shoulder holsters and fired at the windows. Robert watched as Andrea pulled back first, ducking behind a dumpster. Sakchai, still behind them, also fell back. Robert's turn. He pulled Fon's wrist. She twisted away and dodged back into the protection of the doorway.

"I'll cover you!" Fon said.

"Are you crazy?" And then he saw her revolver.

"Retreat!" Andrea shouted.

"It's Fon!" Robert shouted back.

"She betrayed us! I'll cover you."

Andrea began shooting at the windows. Frustrated with the eye openings of her balaclava, she flung it off to see better. Robert didn't want to leave Fon. He turned to retreat but hesitated. Just then, he saw a thug emerge from a doorway behind Andrea, a gun in his hand. But Andrea's large frame blocked his shot at the Thai.

"Duck!" Robert shouted. She flattened on the ground. He fired at the man's chest. The gangster collapsed, landing a few feet from Andrea. His gun slid from his hand.

Robert panicked and raced to Andrea, splayed on the asphalt. Was she injured? Had he just killed someone? He could hear Fon behind him shooting at the windows as he dashed across the alley. Bullets hit the pavement near his feet. Behind him. Ahead of him. But none hit their mark. He hunkered near Andrea behind the dumpster.

"Are you all right?" he asked Andrea.

"Yes, I'm fine," Andrea growled, lifting herself up. "What the fuck are you doing? You're supposed to wait for me to cover you before retreating."

Robert looked at the man near Andrea. "He's dead," Robert said, shocked.

"Yes, thank you," Andrea hissed. She shook her head.

Robert collected himself and recited a mantra for the dead Thai. "Fucking nutcase," Andrea muttered.

Another barrage of shots exploded in the lane. None hit near their dumpster. Robert turned away from the slain Thai and looked down the alley. Fon was running across it toward them. He began shooting at the windows to stop the hail of gunshots. Andrea pulled him back.

"What the hell are you doing?" Robert asked, infuriated. "She didn't betray us. Let go of me!" Robert shoved Andrea so forcefully she landed on her haunches. He resumed firing at the windows.

Some bullets struck the area around the dumpster and in the alley. Fon had made it to the middle of the passageway. A shell hit her in the back. She slumped to one knee, got up, and struggled forward. Robert continued firing at her assailants. Another shot slammed into her, and it was over. She fell onto her face ten feet from Robert. Two more slugs rocked Fon's body. She lay motionless, her white dress a mass of red Rorschach blots.

"Fuck!" Robert said, dropping behind the cover of the dumpster. He closed his eyes.

"What?" Andrea asked, glancing into the alley. She pushed him aside with a sweep of her arm. More ricocheting shots. "Remember, she's why we're pinned behind a garbage can right now."

"No! She covered me when I crossed the alley. She warned us this was a trap. She works for the police."

"Not anymore, she doesn't." Andrea peered out at Fon's lifeless form.

"Shit!" Robert said, brushing back the tears. His body shook. He pounded the dumpster, picturing Wang, the police, and the shooters receiving the force of his fist.

"Don't go nutso on me now!" Andrea said, punching him. He had tears on his cheeks, rage in his eyes. "Where's Sakchai?" Andrea turned to look for him and saw him struggling with a large Thai who wielded a knife. The two were locked in an embrace, twisting and turning, hands locked above their heads. But Andrea didn't have a clean shot. "Cover me!" she shouted at Robert.

Robert fired rapidly at the two windows. One side. Then the other. He repeated the shots while Andrea raced across the alley. His gun clicked empty. He ejected his clip and slapped in another magazine. He couldn't help seeing Fon's body. His aim wavered with his guilt and grief. He breathed in and out slowly and wiped his eyes. He focused and discharged two more bullets, which hit close to their targets.

As Andrea approached Sakchai, his opponent overwhelmed him and stabbed him in the stomach. Andrea came up behind the Thai and whacked him on the head with the butt of her gun, still afraid of shooting Sakchai. The Thai stumbled forward, flipping Sakchai between them to avoid being shot. He stepped around Sakchai's slumping body and knocked her Beretta to the ground. Andrea punched him square in the face with her left hand, drawing blood. He staggered back, glared at Andrea, then charged at her, pulling up and kicking. Andrea shifted to the side and with her left arm grabbed enough of his leg to pull it upward and away from her, tripping him. He landed on his left shoulder, giving Andrea enough time to kick him in the crotch. As he doubled over, she gave a fierce kick to his neck. It cracked gruesomely. She grabbed Sakchai and pulled him into a doorway for protection, hugging him and covering his bleeding wound with her hand. She kept him upright. They looked at the fallen Thai, his neck bent at an ugly angle. He wasn't moving.

It was Tianhao.

"Hold on, Sakchai. We'll get you out of here."

"Ungh. Thanks." His head rolled back and onto her chest. He wheezed.

"Robert, I need to get Sakchai to safety!" she screamed across the alley. "Cover me until I'm down the road. OK?"

"What about Fon?"

"She's dead. Can't you see that? Take Sakchai's gun. You may need it. It's a long way." She threw the pistol across the alley. "I won't be quick with Sakchai." Andrea flipped Sakchai onto her back, knocking his head against the doorway.

"Sorry!" she said to Sakchai.

"'S OK," he slurred, his head wobbling, his legs flopping.

"Ready, Robert?"

Robert nodded. He looked at the two windows. He fired at them, alternating his shots unpredictably. A couple of shots here, one there, pause, then shoot again.

Andrea staggered down the long, straight alleyway, Sakchai clenched between her muscular arms. Initially, she zigzagged. But then she rushed to put distance between herself and the Dragon thugs. Gang members emerged from the buildings at the other end of the alley, but Robert kept them pinned down. Andrea heard one gangster scream, then another. She smiled. Robert was finally using his shooting skills to their advantage.

After several minutes, Andrea—Sakchai flopping on her back—reached their two getaway buildings. Andrea opened the door, dragged Sakchai in and laid him down. She looked down the street. Robert was a distant speck.

"Damn!" she said. A mile away. "Run, Robert!" Could he even hear her? She strained her eyes, glad to see Robert dashing from one side of the road to the other, occasionally turning to shoot behind him. Then he broke into a sprint, getting a half mile closer.

He slowed.

Andrea could see his legs had gone heavy. What was wrong with his running?

"I have to go back to help Robert!" Andrea said to Sakchai, who nodded once.

Andrea sprinted back toward Robert, who lurched forward at a sluggish pace as the thugs gained on him. She pinned them down with some rapid shots while he struggled to run by her. Then she covered herself while he kept moving.

He made it.

She raced back and leaped inside the building, locking the door behind them.

"Bundle him up. He can't lose any more blood!" Andrea ordered.

She wiped her hand across Sakchai's shirt, getting blood on it. With blood dripping to the floor from her fingers, she went to the back door, opened it with her red-drenched hand, and shook her wrist on the outside, splattering a trail of blood.

Robert removed his backpack and set it aside, fighting to catch his breath. Using his undershirt, shirt, and jacket to wrap up Sakchai's wound, he contained the bleeding.

"Hurry!" Andrea urged as Robert flipped his backpack on.

Andrea grabbed Sakchai by his ankles. "You lead," she said. Robert clutched Sakchai's shoulders under his armpits and walked up the stairs backward. First one flight. Then a second. Finally, a third. Robert swayed, and Andrea let him rest a moment before they walked to the door at the end of the hallway. So far, no blood dripped from Sakchai's bandages. They stepped onto the roof, walked across it, and placed Sakchai near the edge. There was a two-foot gap to the next building's rooftop.

"I'll go first," Andrea said, leaping across the space like a leopard. "Stand him up and shove him at me."

Robert got on top of the shallow ledge, still winded from his run. He hauled Sakchai up behind him. He turned, and holding the Thai upright, he shoved his colleague toward Andrea. She grabbed his arms, swung him onto the other roof, and laid him down. Robert swayed and slipped. Andrea gasped. But Robert caught himself and jumped onto the other rooftop.

"We're almost there," she said, attempting eye contact with Sakchai. "Don't go dark on me!"

They descended the stairway into the building's interior. Then they walked down the hallway, carrying Sakchai between them.

Andrea opened a door, they entered, and she closed it. A cord hung from the middle of the room's ceiling, and a drop-down ladder gave access to a small attic area. After laying Sakchai down, Andrea pulled the cord and ascended the stairs.

"Lift him up to me," she said from the attic. Andrea watched as Robert heaved Sakchai upright, then raised him toward her.

Andrea heard a splintering noise when the thugs broke open the door in the adjacent building. Then there were noises of men racing out the back, while others clumped up the stairs, shouting. Andrea seized Sakchai's shirt and pulled him into the attic like he was a sack of potatoes.

"What are they saying?" Andrea asked.

"They're going to search the building, and some are searching behind it. They're looking for blood everywhere."

"Check the hallway and floor for blood."

Robert dashed into the hallway, and Andrea saw his torch flashing around. Then she listened as the door on the roof of the other building slammed open. More yelling. She turned to Sakchai and murmured, "Hang in there. You're going to be all right."

Andrea watched as Robert rushed back into the room and, using his flashlight, scanned the floor.

"Shit!" Robert swore under his breath.

He took out his handkerchief and wiped up the drips of blood on the floor. Andrea heard two men coming down the stairs from the roof.

"They're coming!" Andrea whispered.

Robert flashed his light across the floor one last time, then leapt up the stairs, handing Andrea the end of the rope.

Andrea jerked the rope, flipping up the lower half of the stairs. She caught the steps, folded them onto the upper half and pulled the whole thing up along with the cord, which she brought into the attic with her, leaving a small portion flat against the ceiling.

The door to the room burst open.

Through the cracks in the ceiling, Andrea and Robert could see lights from flashlights shining below them. They held their breath. Two men were talking. They swore in Thai. They jostled each other.

The door shut.

Andrea listened to the men searching the rest of the building. The last noises were on the ground floor. Then silence.

"We'll have to wait until they get tired," Andrea said in a hoarse undertone.

She turned to Sakchai, but she couldn't hear any breathing.

"Sakchai!" Robert said in a low, urgent voice. He checked his fallen partner's pulse. Then he put an ear to Sakchai's mouth. Robert lifted Sakchai's head to gaze into his eyes.

"Go in peace, my brother," he said, his voice cracking.

CHAPTER 25

"We'll have to take his body with us. We can't leave it here," Andrea murmured, thinking out loud.

The attic was shaped like a tent with nine-pane farmhouse-style windows at each end, which allowed a dim glow of moonlight. The space must have acted as a skylight before the owners converted it into a small storage area. Robert crouched near Andrea's feet, bent over Sakchai, mumbling a Buddhist prayer for the dead. Andrea stretched out her hand and stroked Robert's hair as he rocked over Sakchai. Robert didn't acknowledge her fingers. "We'll wait until we're sure Wang's thugs and the police are gone," she said.

As if on cue, Andrea heard the sirens of several squad cars approaching. She withdrew her hand and bent her head toward the noise. Most of the commotion sounded distant, probably in the middle of the alley where Fon lay. Andrea assumed the gang had picked up their fallen comrades. She thought she heard the police enter the building next to them, but it didn't sound like they searched every floor—only the ground one. In any case, it would have taken a clever cop to spot their hiding place.

His prayers finished, Robert maneuvered around the jutting stairs in the middle of their space. He flipped his backpack off and leaned his bare back against the opposite window. He stared at Andrea.

"I got Fon killed. She was there to warn us."

"Not your fault. If she worked for the police, she was a professional, and she made her decision. Don't worry about it. By the way, now we're even. You saved me from that punk who came up behind me."

"We lost Sakchai."

"It's done. We'll take him to a hospital where Sakchai's wife can claim his body. Alex will make sure Orson takes care of his family."

"Andrea?"

"Yes?"

"I killed a man."

"Yes. Thank you. You saved my life. A perfect shot. He died instantly." Andrea flung the words at him. *What's his problem?*

"I've never done that before. I also injured or slayed two others."

"You may be in the wrong line of work," she sighed, slumping further into the window.

"Stan never…" Robert's voice faltered. "Sakchai…Fon…"

Andrea saw the tears flowing. A trickle at first. But then he began blubbering. His sobs grew louder until Andrea crossed over to him and crushed him with a powerful embrace.

"Hush! We're not in the clear yet. We need to keep quiet."

Andrea pulled back to look at Robert, who struggled to make eye contact. He wiped his eyes with his bare arm, took a tissue out of his backpack, and blew his nose quietly.

"Some special agent," Robert said, his lip quivering.

"You're doing great. You've experienced too much, too soon."

Robert nodded.

"You'll be fine," she ordered. "Get some sleep." Another command. He needed rest.

An hour later, Andrea shook Robert awake. "We have to go."

"I fell asleep?" Robert asked, still groggy.

"Overload. It happens."

Andrea pushed the ladder and extended it to the floor. A few moments later, they had their comrade's limp body down from the attic.

Andrea hefted Sakchai's body onto her back in a fireman's carry.

"You sure you don't want me to do that?" Robert asked.

"You are stronger now from the workouts in the gym. But, no, I've got him." Sakchai was her team member, her responsibility. And she'd failed him. The least she could do was get his body to the morgue.

Robert opened the door, and they crept down the stairs together, Robert in the lead to catch Andrea and Sakchai if she slipped.

They exited at the rear of the building after scouring the back alley for any remaining police or gang members. Seeing no one, they made their way to a major street and, holding Sakchai upright between them, they hailed a cab and went to the nearest hospital.

CHAPTER 26

Alex got the call from Andrea in the middle of the night. He didn't have the heart or the energy to wake Sakchai's wife to tell her the bad news. It could wait.

In the morning, he rose early and put on his best suit. He contacted Lamai at home via a *tuk-tuk* driver he hailed on the street, asking her to inform Sakchai's wife, Sirikit, that they would visit her at home at 10 a.m. with news about Sakchai. He was thankful Lamai and Sakchai lived in the same neighborhood but frustrated that he couldn't get phones installed in everyone's home.

While he drank his coffee and ate a bowl of cereal, trying to grasp the loss of another agent, Al and Sally raced into the kitchen and gave him a hug. What a contrast to what he faced doing today—telling Sakchai's wife of her husband's death. He rose and poured them a glass of orange juice each, and they sat at the table with him. They were both quiet and respectful, not demanding attention or food. Did they sense he needed consoling? Soon his wife came in and looked at him with alarm; she knew what that suit meant.

"Who?"

"Sakchai."

"Oh, no!" she gasped, her hand flying to her mouth.

"What's wrong, Mommy?" Sally asked.

"Nothing, dear. Would you like cereal also? How about some Cheerios?" Shirley turned away from her children, fighting back tears as she moved to get breakfast for them. Cheerios were a special treat from her parents, sent to them via a friendly embassy employee.

"Yes!" Al and Sally said in unison.

Alex rose, put his bowl and mug in the sink, ruffled Al's hair, and gave Sally's head a quick peck. As he did so, they both ducked, grinning as they avoided his hand and kiss.

Shirley came to the door to say goodbye, leaving the kids at the table munching their tiny oat donuts. Alex enveloped her in his arms as she buried her head in his shoulder. He gave her a quick kiss on the top of her head and pulled back, looking into her eyes.

"Are you seeing Sirikit this morning?" Shirley asked.

"Yes, before I go to work. Lamai's meeting me at their home."

"Give her my condolences. He was such a gentle soul," she said, shaking her head as the wetness welled in her eyes.

Alex knew she was thinking that less than a week ago she'd seen Sakchai, Sirikit, and Niran for their annual Thanksgiving dinner.

"I will. Yes, he was. And a tremendous agent."

"Take care, Alex." Shirley kissed him again, then laid her right hand on his chest.

"Yes." Alex turned and left. Shirley held the front door open and watched her husband until he disappeared around the corner in search of a taxi.

Alex, Lamai, and Sirikit were in the small living room of Sakchai's house. Sirikit sat with Niran on the couch, holding her groggy child in her arms. Lamai and Alex faced her, seated in upholstered chairs. Sirikit had served them each a glass of chilled tea, which they had sipped, then placed on the coffee table between them. Sirikit sat erect. Niran began to stir and wiggle, but she held him tight.

"You have news for me about Sakchai?" Sirikit asked, and Lamai translated.

"Yes. I regret to inform you that Sakchai died last night in the line of duty." Alex sat upright, his shoulders squared, facing Sirikit, conveying sympathy. "He was on a mission to stop lethal drugs from being distributed. The operation was totally successful, but tragically Sakchai paid the ultimate price to make it succeed. Please accept the condolences of myself, my wife, and all my staff." Alex watched Sirikit's face while Lamai translated his compassionate monologue.

Sirikit betrayed no emotion, but Niran wailed and kicked to free himself from her. She gazed at the window behind Alex and Lamai. Alex resisted the urge to turn so he could see what she was staring at. Niran, still trapped in his mother's arms, twisted and squirmed, seeking to escape. His cries pierced the cloud of silence enclosing the three adults as he arched his back and wailed. A full three minutes passed—Sirikit staring, Niran bawling, and Alex resisting plugging his ears to blunt the child's howls.

"Thank you for informing me in person, Mr. Butler," Sirikit said, and Lamai translated. Niran quieted, exhausted from his efforts, his sniffling broken by an occasional sob.

"Of course. Let me reassure you that our agency will provide you with a full pension. This is something we do for our agents who die in the line of duty, regardless of their length of service. Also, our office will take care of any funeral arrangements."

Sirikit's head bobbed down and back.

"Lamai will be in touch with you next week with the details." Again, a quick nod from Sirikit.

"Please let us know if there is anything else we can do for you."

With a final dip of her head, Sirikit rose, letting Niran escape onto the sofa where he curled up into a ball, sucking his thumb. She gave a deep *wai* first to Alex and then to Lamai. They both returned the gesture and left.

Later that day, Alex had his elbows on his desk, head slumped, hands pounding his temples. Robert sagged into one of the conference-table chairs, his gaze lowered to the floor. But Andrea stood tall and erect, square in front of Alex.

Alex spoke without looking up. "So, it was as we feared. This was a police-aided trap. We didn't fool them with our 'we can only do it on Thursday' ruse. How did Fon know it was a set-up, and how did she know we were doing it on Tuesday?" Alex scowled at Robert.

"She must have deduced it. She said area police patrols had been called off for that week…," Robert faltered, talking to the floor. "… her boss had told her I wouldn't be around next week. And then she didn't see me come home last night."

"Her boss?" Alex asked, his voice squeaking.

"She worked for Police Internal Affairs," Robert mumbled, barely audible.

"But that means the police have been spying on us through you, Robert."

"Yes, but she came to the alley last night to help us! She fired at the Dragon gang while I crossed the street." Robert's head flew up, looking at Alex as he spat out the words.

"A change of heart?"

"I suppose," Robert said, choking up. "I only learned about her police work last week, and I wasn't sure if it was correct. I confronted her about it on Sunday, and she confirmed it. She said she was on my side. She didn't understand why she was assigned to me."

"You don't think this might have been something we'd like to have heard about?" Alex said, restraining his anger.

"I thought I could handle it," Robert said. "I thought I *was* handling it."

Alex clutched his head in his hands, took a deep breath, looked up and said, "I suppose they could have planned to watch for us all week, starting yesterday. It would make sense. Again, a failure of our ploy. Still, it's unacceptable that you withheld information from us."

"You're right. I should have said something as soon as I knew anything," Robert said glumly. "But she warned us!" he said, spitting again, fire in his eyes.

Alex sighed. "Worst of all, we lost Sakchai," he said, as if speaking to himself.

"That was my fault," Andrea said. "I should have gotten to him sooner."

"I'm not blaming anyone for anything. It was a total fuckup operation, which I authorized. Why did I trust the police to believe we'd do a raid on Thursday?" Alex lifted his head. "What kind of arrogance does that show on my part?" Alex bent his head again and pounded his fists on his desk. *Thud. Thud.* "Two agents in the last year." Alex thought of Colson and Sakchai and their capabilities but couldn't stomach the pain. *Pull yourself together!*

Alex stood and moved around to the side of his desk. "Robert, come here."

Robert stood, took a deep breath, and walked over to stand in front of Alex.

Alex grabbed him and gave him a bear hug, thumping him on the back three times. Robert was drooping, his hands at his sides, his head bent. Then Alex pushed him away, holding him at arm's length, his fists still clutching Robert's shoulders. "You did a great job protecting Andrea. You should be proud of yourself. The first kill is never easy. And you're new to the field. You now know how dangerous it is to get too close to the locals. You must always suspect everyone except the people in this room. We'll have your back, and we know you'll have ours. We'll get through this.

"Andrea, take this battle-hardened agent to the gym and make sure he gets a thorough workout. I don't want to see any more moping in the office. Understood?"

"Understood, sir," Andrea said, pulling herself even more upright. "Agent Jordan, you're coming with me."

Andrea cuffed him on his shoulder with her left arm, rocking him onto his back foot. She turned, walked to the door, and held it open for Robert to leave. Then she faced Alex and saluted with her right hand and swung out the door after Robert.

Robert felt Andrea's firm grasp at his elbow. She shoved him into her office and closed the door. He walked to the front of her desk, waiting for her to sit, dreading what she would say. But she came up behind him, spun him around, and grasped him by the shoulders in much the same way Alex had held him earlier. Now he gazed into her gray irises as she stared at him, his mouth pursed, brow furrowed.

"You need to get over these deaths: Sakchai, Fon, and the Thai thug. *And* your misstep about informing us of what you knew about Fon. You did some amazing things last night, and you need to focus on that. You helped us get out of there undetected; you provided cover when we needed to retreat; you saved my life. In short, you did a great job. Sometimes—too often lately..." Andrea sighed. "...a mission takes an ugly turn. Put that shit behind you." Then she leaned in close to Robert, within six inches.

Robert pulled his head back; a cloud of anxiety stormed across his face.

She held him for several seconds like that, with her eyes flitting back and forth across his face. Then she leaned back, released her grip, and slapped him hard across the face.

"Ouch! What was that for?"

"Don't you dare go PTSD on me!"

"Couldn't you have just told me that? You didn't have to whack me." Robert's cheek turned bright red. He rubbed it and moaned. "I may need some time to absorb this. I keep kicking myself over Fon and Sakchai's deaths."

"You didn't kill either of them."

"Yeah, but…"

"No buts! Shit happens." She slapped him on both shoulders. "Let's go to the gym."

Alone in his office, Alex rose and went to his cabinet, removed a glass and the whiskey bottle, and poured himself a heavy one. He walked to his window and stared out at the street scene below him. *What a fucking awful day! Sakchai died. I gave the news to his wife—never fun, and my new agent is freaked that he fucked up. What a crew. And you, what about you? You've lost three agents since coming to Thailand—what kind of station chief are you? Incompetent! Thank God for Andrea; she's like a rock. But what—or who—is next?*

CHAPTER 27

On Friday, Alex arranged for his staff to have a brief ceremony at a small Buddhist *wat* near their office. Lamai made the arrangements, so the monks at the temple were supportive of their event. They placed a photo of Sakchai on the steps of the temple and lit sticks of incense to help carry his spirit safely home. While one monk chanted, they each spoke a remembrance of Sakchai. Lamai spoke of his character—his respect for others and his devout Buddhism. Robert talked of his sense of humor and optimistic spirit. Andrea told of his bravery until the end and his generosity toward his colleagues, always putting them first. Then it was Alex's turn.

"Sakchai came to us after the tragic death of his sister from an overdose. Disillusioned with the police, he sought a job where he could be more effective at reducing the menace of narcotics. We are grateful to him for his dedication to our cause and for, on a couple of occasions, saving Andrea's life." Alex paused and looked at Andrea, who nodded. Alex knew his words were inadequate at expressing the sorrow he—and the team—felt about losing Sakchai, but he couldn't think of anything more meaningful to say.

"I remember the time he came into the office after Niran's birth. He exuded pride and joy. He was devoted to Sirikit and his son. I'm sure they miss him deeply. We pray they will thrive in life despite their loss. We thank him for his dedication to our cause of fighting narcotic trafficking and for his service to his country and the rule of law. I personally would like to thank him for teaching me to be a humbler person. He was a gracious, modest, self-effacing man, and we will miss him dearly. We wish him peace and joy on his final journey."

Only Alex attended Sakchai's funeral in Chang Mai that weekend. He forbade the rest of his team to go. Sirikit and Niran had traveled north with Sakchai's body to have the ceremony near his family's village. Alex arrived only for the last day—the cremation—with an envelope of cash, rather than a wreath, to show respect to Sakchai and his family. Separately, he'd approved the bill for the funeral's cost. Sirikit accepted the money with a deep *wai*, which Alex returned. Along with others, he circled the coffin at the crematorium three times counterclockwise and placed a shaved-wood flower near it. Once the flames began, he ate some food at the generous banquet, honoring the hospitality of the family. He also managed some small talk with Sakchai's parents, assisted by their other son, Tao, who spoke excellent English. A hollow ache filled his torso, but he wasn't sure he could be helpful in any other way.

Tao, a police officer, asked about the work Sakchai had been doing in Bangkok. He startled Alex with his knowledge of his brother's undercover work for the Orson Group; Sakchai had trusted Tao. Alex mentioned a few of Sakchai's accomplishments, but Tao knew all but one of them. Tao surprised and pleased him by showing interest in replacing Sakchai on the Orson team, saying he would be proud to carry on his brother's important work. They exchanged contact information.

Walking home from the office the following Thursday, Robert scanned the newsstands. The Bhopal disaster still featured in the headlines—the gas leak in India had slain thousands. That tragedy turned his thoughts to Fon and Sakchai. Was there any way he could have prevented their deaths? He agonized especially over Fon—she'd covered his race across the alley when he checked on Andrea. Why hadn't Fon yelled for them to protect her? Had she panicked also? Why did they take so long to see Sakchai struggling with Tianhao? And why hadn't he shouted for help? It was an overwhelming disaster—two people he cared about slain, and he'd killed others. That upset him also, but he lifted his spirits by focusing on the positive aspects. He'd dispatched or wounded people who were shooting at them. He'd saved Andrea. His actions benefited the team; he willed himself to embrace it.

As he approached home, Robert saw a woman standing in front of his apartment complex. She rushed toward him, excited to see him and speaking rapidly in Thai as she held up a box for him.

Robert feigned shock and perplexity as he listened to her, understanding everything.

"You must be Robert. Fon told me to give this to the *farang*—Robert—who lives here." Seeing his puzzled look, she pointed at him. "Robert?" Lifting the package with his name on it, she said, "Fon." Robert nodded, allowing some comprehension to break through his sham bafflement.

She continued to explain that she was Fon's roommate and that Fon had written her a note on the previous Tuesday that if anything happened to her, she should deliver this parcel to Robert and send the other to her brother in Surat Thani. She had not seen Fon for a week but had only just learned of her death. Holding the bundle out, she bowed her head. Robert took it, put it under his left arm, brought his hands together in front of his face and gave a respectful *wai*. The woman thanked him and darted away.

Robert sighed as he opened the door to his apartment block and ascended the stairs to his flat. After entering, he poured himself a whiskey and opened the posthumous gift which contained a letter. Robert took a swig of his drink and began reading.

My Dearest Robert,

If you are reading this, I am dead, but I was able to save you.

I hope you can forgive me. Our relationship meant a lot to me, but I was always working for the police's internal affairs unit. I wanted to help stop the corruption from drug money because my brother is suffering from his life as an addict. I couldn't understand why you—not a police officer—were the target of my investigation, and I became suspicious. When I learned you would not be my assignment after this week, I found out that my colleagues had helped set a trap for you.

I never expected to fall in love with you, but I did. I hope you can believe that.

All my love,

Fon

Robert read the note twice. He ran his fingers through his hair, drank more whiskey, and flopped back on his couch.

"Fuck!"

Rising minutes later, he set his empty glass on the coffee table. He thought about Fon. She'd been spying on him and then she'd saved him, paying the ultimate price to do so. His remorse tormented him. The events that led to so many deaths—Fon, Sakchai, the man he killed, and the one Andrea crushed—agitated him. Even though he knew he had to eliminate the Thai before he shot Andrea, it still didn't sit well. Perhaps he had a family? Small children at home? Where had he grown up? Why had he chosen a life of crime working for a notorious narcotics dealer? Robert did not believe people were born evil; something in their lives pushed them toward wickedness. Sakchai? What a tragedy with a wife and a small child at home.

Wang's gang had snuffed out the life of an exceptionally honorable man too early. He commended Andrea's slaying of his assailant. And Fon? Why had she died? She had a job that linked her to him, and she tried to get him and his colleagues out of a trap set for them. She had been naïve about the police but noble in wanting to stop the drug epidemic.

His thoughts turned to Wang. The drug lord was the person responsible for Fon's and Sakchai's deaths. What could or would he do about it?

Thoughts of revenge racked his soul. Sitting on his couch, he brought his head to his knees and rocked in place. Then he sat up straight and did something he hadn't done in a long time. He meditated.

On the Monday before the Christmas holiday week, Robert followed Andrea into Alex's office after Lamai told them he wanted to see them. A Thai man stood in front of Alex's desk, right up next to it. He turned as they entered and gave them a short, quick bow, then twisted again to face Alex.

"Andrea, Robert, meet Tao, Sakchai's brother. He'll be replacing Sakchai as your new partner. Tao was a police officer in Chiang Mai. He got in touch with me shortly after Sakchai's death, and I have now officially hired him, starting today."

Robert and Andrea welcomed Tao to the team and expressed their condolences for the loss of his brother. Tao gave a short, shallow nod to acknowledge their sympathies but turned toward Alex, saying nothing.

"I hope your parents are comfortable with you coming to Bangkok, where, tragically, both your sister and brother have died," Robert blurted, shocked that their new team member was Sakchai's brother.

"Thank you for your kindness, Agent Jordan," Tao said. "They both strongly believe this is my karma, my destiny," Tao said. "They are proud to see me replace Sakchai."

Alex continued, "I'm sorry I didn't consult you two on this, but it was a no-brainer to me, especially after I reviewed Tao's record. The CIA vetted him thoroughly. He's one of the good guys and a first-class cop, highly motivated in the fight against the drug trade, especially the Dragon gang. And he's arrived in time to help us with the large shipment due in mid-February."

Tao looked nothing like his brother Sakchai. While Sakchai had been slim, Tao looked like a rugby player, stocky and muscular with a thick neck. Whereas Sakchai demurred and stood back, Tao placed himself forward, projecting a physical presence, like someone ready to charge into action. Sakchai's face had been narrow; Tao's was round but had the same warm, brown skin. Unlike Sakchai, Tao shaved his head.

"Have you heard anything from headquarters about sending us more agents?" Andrea asked with her usual gruff bluntness.

"No, I'm still waiting to hear from them. I checked, and they are evaluating the request. You should make plans to do it with them and without them."

"How is the effort going with getting the Dragons worried about a Scorpion raid on their other large warehouse?" Andrea asked Robert. "The three of us could never take on Wang's full team."

Robert waited as Alex told Tao, who looked puzzled, about their plan for the February raid. Tao said nothing as he listened.

"After Sakchai's death, the police are convinced we are behind the mysterious operations that have happened in the past few months," Robert said. "We lost an agent on the very night they laid a trap for us. But despite that, from monitoring the police files, I know they are expecting the Scorpion raid," Robert said. "Since the police work so closely with the Dragons, this should also mean Wang expects it. The police have no insight into the Scorpion gang. None. They believe the information Sakchai fed them through his network of stooges. However, the buzz over the Scorpion's raid has dried up in Sakchai's absence."

"I can help with that," Tao said. Everyone looked at him. "I visited Sirikit to pay my respects and comfort her. She gave me a box of materials that Sakchai had hidden in the house. Inside were the informants' names and how to contact them."

"I like this new guy," Andrea said to Alex, arching an eyebrow and smiling.

"Good," Alex said. "We still have nearly two months. You'll need to make contact, establish relationships, and then sow seeds of suspicion about a Scorpion attack on the day we raid the Dragon's other warehouse."

"I can get on that right away," Tao said. "But I'll need some cash."

"Lamai will help you with that. You'll need to document your expenses. It sounds like you know what to do, so I'll leave it to Andrea, you, and Robert to make a plan."

Moments later in Andrea's office, Robert faced his senior partner and Tao at her conference table.

"Welcome aboard, Tao," Andrea said. "We're delighted you can join our team. We need someone like you. Tell us about your background."

"Thank you, Agent Cannon. In Chiang Mai, I mostly worked on containing drug trafficking. We had some success in catching many of the lower-level operatives, but none of the big bosses, who all live in Bangkok."

Robert couldn't detect any nervousness or unease in Tao. He brimmed with confidence, and he spoke English exceptionally well.

"Did you manage informants there?"

"Yes. I usually had about ten people who provided me with information, though sometimes they fed me false information. When this happened, I always educated them."

"Oh? And how did you do that?" Andrea asked, concern slipping into her question.

"I would arrest them and keep them off drugs for a few days."

"OK. That would work, I'm sure. But no beatings or…"

"No. They suffered, but I think it improved their health and let them know lying to me was unacceptable." Tao nodded, confident of the appropriateness of his actions.

Robert couldn't imagine Sakchai doing such a thing; Tao was a tough nut. A beat cop, not a detective.

"Well, hopefully we won't need any of that here—we don't have cells." Andrea paused, then pressed on with their mission. "We'll need you to work as quickly as possible to reestablish relations with Sakchai's informants. Spreading the rumor about a Scorpion raid on Wang's other major warehouse is essential to the success of our mission."

"With more than a month, that should be feasible," Tao said, nodding and looking into the distance as if he were already rolling out the deception to the informants.

"Robert and I will monitor the security operations at the target warehouse and scout out any retreat positions. Much of that will be at night, but given our recent lack of success at evening raids, we'll also monitor their daytime defense measures."

"A daytime raid?" Robert asked. *Is she nuts?*

"Yes, it may be the best time to catch them off guard."

"That would mean the Scorpion's actions would also have to be rumored for daytime," Robert blustered.

"Yes, *obviously*. But there has been no designated day or time yet, as I understand it."

"Correct," Robert said, breathing out to calm himself. "So far, we've only spread the idea of an attack by the Scorpions in mid-February. We'll need to be careful about when we finalize the specific date and time. If we release that information too early, it may become suspect before we have time to act."

"My informants can keep watch on the warehouse," Tao said. "If the shipment arrives on the twelfth, we can raid it the next afternoon."

"Good," Andrea said. "We have a target date for the raid. Wednesday, the thirteenth. If everything looks good for a daytime raid, we'll go in at 2 p.m. when everyone is sluggish after lunch."

CHAPTER 28

Back in the office after the holidays, Robert learned of his colleagues' vacation adventures. Everyone but Tao had taken a break. He worked, developing relationships with his brother's informants. Lamai had gone to the outskirts of Bangkok to visit her parents and face the perennial question, "When are you getting married?" Alex, much to his consternation, had spent the time with his family and in-laws in Minnesota, self-medicating with alcohol to keep warm and "in the holiday spirit." Andrea had vacationed in Phuket, doing everything athletic at the beach—surfing, scuba diving, swimming, and kayaking. She was now tanned and radiant. And Robert had moped around his apartment, cleaning it, buying more decorations for it, meditating, and endeavoring to put his guilt behind him. Some vacation.

For the first couple of weeks in the new year, Robert assisted Andrea in monitoring the security operations at Wang's building in the port of Bangkok, the same one that they had entered to search the files for information about the February shipment.

The warehouse resided in a long row of similar structures off a feeder road. Andrea had found an abandoned office block with a rooftop view of the street leading to their target. They used it to watch the actions during the day and night, taking turns so they could get a comprehensive overview of the comings and goings of workers and their safety precautions. Wang had increased nighttime security, with two more men, and the schedule was unpredictable.

Instead of changes of staff at set times, the relief crew came at irregular hours each evening. Sometimes at midnight., sometimes at 1, or 2, or 3 a.m. There was no pattern—they must have been drawing the shifts randomly from a hat. However, in the daytime, the guards changed always at 8 a.m. and 5 p.m. No security personnel were stationed outside during the day—the weather prohibited it since the sun shone harshly on the front entrance. Wang himself came into the building each day at 9 a.m. and left usually around 6 p.m.

Meanwhile, Tao continued to build trust with Sakchai's informers by asking for small favors and paying a reasonable price for them. By mid-January, they had confidence in him, and he could feed them information as well. But he wasn't sure they always believed him.

In late January, Robert and his colleagues were called into Alex's office. Their boss wanted to assess the progress of their plan.

"Tao, how is it going with your stooges?" Alex asked.

"I have spoken to my informants in both gangs. The Dragon members are convinced there will be a raid on their Phra Khanong warehouse. They are storing some drugs there, but the bulk of the stash will be at the Bangkok Port storage." Tao delivered the information like a police report. "The Scorpions are upset. They can't understand why the Dragons would think they would do such a thing. When they communicate with their counterparts, saying they are not planning any such thing, it just makes their rivals more suspicious. Neither trusts the other, if they ever did."

"Good," Alex said.

"And there's something else, but I'm not sure if it is relevant," Tao said, unsure of himself for once.

"Go on."

"The street sellers are furious about an increase in overdoses in the last month. They are sure that the Dragons have contaminated the drugs with an additive. A powerful one. The high is tremendous, but often fatal."

"What do we make of it?" Alex asked, puzzled.

"It's been useful to us, creating additional distrust between the Dragons and the Scorpions. But everyone, including the Dragon's dealers, is upset and blames Wang."

"Interesting. Robert, what do we know from the law enforcement files?"

"They confirm the increase in overdoses and increased tension between these two gangs. More importantly, however, the police are planning on being at Phra Khanong at the appointed time, 2 p.m., with a large contingent. They will observe and contain the raid but not prevent it."

"Tao and I have visited Amonsak twice in the past three weeks and continue to plant the seed that this conflict will provide an opportunity to reduce the number of gang members and confiscate some drugs after the two sides have fought each other," said Alex, with a smug smile. "It's simply a matter of timing—step in after the fighting wanes, arrest the warring parties, seize the narcotics, and make a splash in the papers. I told him that my entire team would be there to provide any support they deemed necessary. My mission when I am with Pravat is to stop him from diverting any resources to the other warehouse if he hears of something happening. So, we're all set. Any questions?"

"Yes," Andrea said. "Any word on the extra help from headquarters?"

Alex nodded his head for a few moments before replying. "Yes, the response was definitive. There will be no support coming to help us. We'll have to do this with the resources we have. Meaning…us."

CHAPTER 29

Finally, the day of the raid arrived. This was the shipment Robert had been sent to Thailand specifically to help stop—a massive amount of heroin with a deadly additive. He hoped Wang would be in the warehouse and would perish with it. Robert couldn't stop thinking of Sakchai and Fon slain by Wang's thugs. His thoughts also raced back to his brother; this had to be the same stuff that killed him, the Bangkok Dragon.

Robert, Andrea, and Tao loaded their backpacks with flashlights, lighters, gasoline, and two sticks of fireworks each, a crude but effective way to set a building aflame. They strapped on their shoulder holsters and put on their jackets. While Tao sported casual clothes, Andrea and Robert wore business sports coats and slacks, looking dapper. They put on dark eyeglasses and sun-blocking Panama hats, transforming themselves into corporate visitors with Tao as a guide in the Bangkok port district.

Alex put on his usual clothes—a sports coat that complemented his slacks. He looked like the cop he was, wearing a cheap jacket and tie. But he needed to appear ready to help his team, so he also had his gun. Alex skipped the head garment and sunglasses—he wanted to be recognized when he arrived on the scene to ease getting near Pravat.

Everyone took their walkie-talkies. It would be the only way they could communicate.

In the early afternoon, after gearing up, they left with plenty of time to spare; they didn't want the Bangkok traffic to delay them.

Outside their building, they separated and departed for their different destinations. Alex left first, taking a *tuk-tuk* to Wang's Phra Khanong warehouse to join up with Colonel Pravat and the police gathered there. It was less than a mile away from the Bangkok Port facility, so within walkie-talkie range.

Andrea, Robert, and Tao took a taxi to the port, with its lengthy line of buildings, all built for the same function—storage for the harbor's goods. On the drive over, they opened the windows, preferring the traffic fumes to the heat. The sweltering, muggy day would provide no relief until after sunset. The sun streamed in through Robert's window, baking his shoulder. He focused on Wang and how he wished to find him unprotected in his office. Andrea and Tao, too, were quiet on the way over, absorbed with the upcoming mission.

Andrea asked the taxi driver to drop them off about five hundred yards from the warehouse. Alex hadn't sent them an abort message, so everything was still going to plan—a large contingent of Wang's gang along with the police were at the other warehouse awaiting the Scorpions. Andrea, Robert, and Tao crossed a couple of streets, wove their way through the freight containers arrayed along the road to the building, and approached the entrance. As they had expected, the door was unguarded—the security men would be inside. Andrea picked the lock soundlessly, and they rushed inside.

Alex extricated himself from the *tuk-tuk* when he saw a few plainclothes police officers on the street two blocks from the target building. Searching the area, he found Colonel Pravat sitting at a café, looking to the right and left as he watched Wang's Phra Khanong warehouse. Alex surveyed the scene, checking the area and the surrounding buildings. He counted six of Pravat's men. When Alex walked up behind Pravat and tapped his shoulder, the police chief jumped, then turned quickly, putting his hand on the gun holstered on his right hip.

"Alex! You startled me. Don't do that! Where's your team?"

"I thought you might know. They should be here by now."

"No, I haven't seen them." Pravat spoke into his walkie-talkie and listened to the response. "No, my team hasn't spotted them either."

"Shit! They must have gotten stuck in traffic. They're coming from the office while I came from home," Alex said. "Let me check in with Andrea." He stepped away from Pravat and spoke into his walkie-talkie, then pretended to listen to a response.

When he returned to Pravat's side, he said, "Yes, there is a traffic jam on the road they are using to come here. But you won't really need them, will you?"

"No, of course not. I have a large team here. We need it. Wang has many thugs—too many—inside the warehouse. My men saw them arrive early this morning. Everyone is in place, waiting for the Scorpion's gang. If our information is correct, they should be here at any moment."

After breathing a sigh of relief at the news that Wang's people had gathered in the warehouse, Alex pretended to inspect the details of the surrounding buildings and streets. "You've done a great job of keeping your officers out of sight. I can't see any of them," Alex said, stifling a smirk.

"Oh, they're here all right," Pravat said, with a wide satisfied grin. "I placed them myself, all thirty of them."

"Excellent planning. Now we can only wait for the bad guys to arrive. Let's hope there's no collateral damage."

"Oh, I have another team ready to come in and clear the area of civilians. They're standing by a few streets away so they won't attract attention."

"Good. You've thought of everything. As always." Scanning Pravat's face, Alex was grateful that Pravat didn't notice how much butter he lathered onto his comments.

"Thank you. Yes, I believe I have," Pravat said with pride as he looked at his watch. "I wonder what's keeping the Scorpions?"

Robert charged into the building behind Andrea, followed by Tao. A guard seated in front of them gasped and jumped to his feet. He reached for his gun, but Andrea knocked it out of his hand. After swiveling his head between the gun and Andrea, he dove for the gun next to the door. Andrea kicked his head, knocking him out, and he collapsed on top of his pistol. She scowled at him while Robert poked him, confirming he was unconscious.

The warehouse looked much the same as the last time they had visited—a sea of tables. But now each table hosted large and small bundles—heroin and the additive, ready to be mixed. On the right side of the warehouse, two red freight containers were open, revealing heaping mounds of bagged rice.

"Quick, help me start a fire," Andrea said, flipping off her backpack while Tao and Robert did the same.

"I'd like permission to find Wang," Robert said to Andrea, recalling Fon's blood-soaked body in the alley. "I don't want him to get away."

Andrea looked at Robert. And he knew she understood she couldn't stop him. "OK. Get him! Tao and I will set the fire. Leave your explosives. You have three minutes."

"I'll be right back."

Robert flipped off his backpack as Andrea lit the fuses and arrayed the fireworks across the floor a few feet apart, pointing at the far wall of the building.

The eighteen-inch fuses burned six inches every minute.

While Andrea and Tao sprinkled gasoline over the tables of drugs, Robert trotted to the stairs leading to Wang's office, then rushed up the steps, one at a time on his toes. On the upper landing, to the right of the office door, a tall Thai snoozed in a chair.

Robert grabbed the man's gun from his waist and pointed it at his nose, waking him. The Thai's eyes bulged wide, and his hands shot up. Robert leaned forward and whispered into the guard's face, using his best Thai, "Get out of here without making a sound, and you'll live. Jump to it! Take the back door!"

The guard scurried down the stairs, taking two steps at a time then jumped the last few and landed with his feet wide apart. He raced to the back of the warehouse, his long legs taking enormous strides, slid open the heavy metal door, and rushed into the daylight.

Robert listened at the wooden door but heard nothing inside. He could hear some rustling noises from his colleagues. He pulled out his gun, turned the knob, and eased the door open.

Pravat, his face stern, brow knitted, asked Alex, "Where's your team?"

Alex rose from the table where they were sitting and, mumbling a complaint about the signal being bad after a fake test of it, walked away. He pretended to speak again with his squad.

"They should be here soon," Alex said as he sat back down. "They've broken through the traffic jam. How's it going here?"

"Nothing is happening. None of my men see any Scorpions approaching. I have a man at their headquarters, and he says no one has left their hideout."

"That's strange. Do you suppose they've called it off?"

"This wasn't a trick, was it?" Pravat asked, glaring.

Shaking his head, Alex presented the perfect picture of innocent confusion—what could have possibly happened?

Pravat stood and paced. Alex sipped his lukewarm tea, pinky finger cocked in the air, still wagging his head. Pravat spoke into his walkie-talkie, checking in with his troops stationed in the area.

No sign of the Scorpions.

Andrea and Tao were leaning down near the fallen body of the guard and had just lit the gasoline with their lighters. The fuses on the six sticks of fireworks were already burning; less than three-minutes remained for them to get out of the building.

Suddenly, a massive man burst from behind a container and jumped at Andrea. She tumbled to the floor. Swirling, he kicked Tao's gun out of his hand. It clunked in a far corner of the cavernous building. As flames rose, illuminating the three figures, Andrea drew her gun from its holster. Tianhao! How could it be? He was dead. Tianhao batted the gun out of her hand, sending it flying to the middle of the warehouse. It skittered on the concrete floor underneath the tables laden with drugs for cutting. Tianhao pounced on Andrea, pinning her to the ground.

Tianhao's right hand choked Andrea's neck. Tao sprang onto Tianhao's back, attempting to pull him off Andrea. It helped, and Andrea rose to a kneeling position. But Tianhao's left arm was free to plant an elbow in Tao's sternum, sending him to the floor, breathless. Tianhao reached to get his other hand around Andrea's neck, but she grabbed it and used her elbow to go for a blow to his head. It landed below his chin and encountered hard plastic. A collar brace! She hadn't saved Sakchai, and she hadn't killed Tianhao. *Shit!* Fury flooded her eyes; guilt stabbed her stomach.

The strike on his brace hurt her elbow, but she fought through the pain. The punch had put Tianhao off balance. She staggered up, pulling his heavy body with her. He still held her neck, but she had his left hand. This time, the sharpest part of her bent arm jabbed his stomach, eliciting a loud *oof*. She grabbed his right thumb and bent it back sharply, freeing her neck from his grip.

An alarm went off, triggered by the smoke from the fire.

Tao sprang at Tianhao. But Tianhao twisted and kicked Tao's stomach, sending him reeling. Tao slipped, and his head crashed into a table, knocking him out. Tianhao didn't even glance at Tao after striking him; he looked only at Andrea.

Andrea squared off against Tianhao, and they revolved around each other. The acrid smell of burning gasoline filled their flared nostrils; the smoke burned their eyes. Andrea wheezed from the damage of Tianhao's grip on her neck. Her heart thumped in her ears even louder than the crackle of flames and the fizz of the fuses. Sweat cascaded down her body as they circled each other. She longed to rush at Tianhao, crush his head, and leave him for dead. But emotions bred weakness. *Stay calm. Stay focused. Wait for his next move.*

After another revolution, Andrea was next to Tao, so she faked a look at him, hoping Tianhao would attack. He did. He stepped closer, aiming a kick at her chest. She sidestepped it and caught his ankle with her left hand, then pushed his leg high into the air, thrusting it toward his head. Tianhao flipped onto his back, and Andrea moved in for a kick to his leg. But Tianhao had already rolled away, rendering her blow ineffective. He sprang to his feet. Andrea moved closer. She vaulted forward and retreated immediately, testing Tianhao's reaction speed. He let loose a volley of fists, which flew into the space between them. Andrea felt the pumped air push on her cheeks.

The fuses had burned six inches; a minute had passed.

The instant Tianhao began to lower his hands, Andrea leaped forward. She landed a one-two punch to his chest and head. Tianhao struck back, hitting Andrea's shoulder and chest. She lurched backward as his blows staggered her. Hers bounced off him. She kept her face blank. Pain wouldn't stop her. She thought of retrieving the guard's gun but knew it would take too much time to roll him over and grab it.

Now wary, Andrea began circling again. They traded punches, succeeding with body blows but missing with their strikes aimed at their opponent's head. Again, they pummeled each other. And again. Andrea's knees weakened; Tianhao's hits to her midriff debilitated her. Then Tianhao landed a punch on the upper-left side of her head, sending her spinning. Light flashes splashed before her eyes as she staggered back.

Twelve inches down on the fuses, one minute to go.

Alex kept looking at his watch and shaking his head, feigning bewilderment. "My crew should be here by now. I can't understand what's happened to them."

"They're not somewhere else by any chance?" Pravat asked through clenched teeth.

An officer came up to Pravat and spoke to him in an excited and rapid clip, his voice an octave higher than normal. Pravat turned to Alex and said, "There's been a fire reported at Wang's port warehouse. The fire engines will be there in five minutes."

Alex stared blankly in confused incomprehension. "OK. I'll check again on my team." He then spoke into his walkie-talkie, but this time he actually pressed the communication button. "Are you still stuck in traffic?" He shook his head, repeated the question, then turned to Pravat. "There's no response. I hope they're OK."

"Did you give us false information?" Pravat demanded, hissing. "Are we at the wrong warehouse?"

"My information said the Scorpions would come here to attack Wang's men. I thought your officers confirmed that." Alex backed away from Pravat, who alarmed him. Alex smelled the other man's sour breath as he approached.

"Hey, don't worry. How could it be a bad thing if one of Wang's warehouses burns?" They both knew the answer, but Alex knew Pravat wouldn't say why.

Pravat left in a hurry after calling his troops. Alex headed back to the office.

Andrea's movements were jittery. She flinched when Tianhao got close, retreating quickly. She couldn't hide her pain anymore. But she was still standing. Tianhao leered, puffed out his chest, and charged. Andrea sidestepped him and, using her extra height and long arms, landed a glancing blow. He turned and moved in close, throwing all his weight into a punch to her upper chest that knocked her to the ground. Tianhao leaped toward her to pin her down, but she pushed him away by flipping up on her shoulders and using both legs to kick him in the stomach. He backed up for a moment, then attacked again.

One firework went off near Andrea's head.

The blast sent the stick holding the flammable material flying backward. It hit the wall near the door behind Tianhao. Pyrotechnic flames flew across the warehouse, knocking over a table, hitting the opposite wall, and bursting into a bright red fireball. The flash momentarily stunned Tianhao.

Andrea, still prone, glanced to her right and grabbed one stick near her head, planted it on her shoulder and aimed it at Tianhao's face as he plunged toward her. As that stick exploded, the power of the rocket pushed Andrea backward, singeing her hair in the fire behind her. Tianhao took a direct hit to his face that knocked him off his feet. He landed on his back, blinded, screaming, and rolling in agony. He touched his face with his hands but quickly pulled them away. Colored smoke rose from his seared fingers.

Andrea grabbed her backpack. The final four explosives lit up the warehouse in flashes of bright white and blazes of emerald green. She pulled out her knife and stood over Tianhao's writhing body. She considered letting him die a slow, painful death. Relenting, she stabbed him in the heart, enjoying the satisfaction of his death as she twisted the blade; at this point, a mercy killing.

She rushed to Tao's side and slapped him awake. He shook his head; his cheeks reflected the red, white, and green flames behind them.

"We've got to get out of here!" Andrea shouted. "Where's Robert?" she asked, looking toward the office.

"I thought I saw him run out the back door," Tao said, his skull wobbling, his words slurred.

"That doesn't sound like Robert." Andrea lifted Tao up, threw his arm over her shoulder, seized his waist, and dragged him toward the entrance.

"Maybe he was chasing Wang?"

Andrea shook her head. The inferno roared toward them, eating tables and drugs with its multicolored tongue. They coughed from the caustic smoke billowing in the air.

Andrea's walkie-talkie beeped. Still propping up Tao, she seized it. "That's Alex. The fire engines are coming. Shit!" She glanced back into the fiery warehouse. No time to go back. Into the flaming inferno, she shouted, "Robert! Get out! We're leaving!" She kicked the front door open and dragged Tao into the fresh air. Andrea's long strides distanced them from the flames. Tao jogged to keep up. Andrea wished, hoped, prayed that Robert had left the building.

Stooping low, Robert eased open the door to Wang's office. He pushed it inward, an inch at a time. Peering in, he saw the door to the second room. Closed. Then the safe with the dragon on it appeared. Finally, the desk and the filing cabinets emerged. But he couldn't see anyone or hear anything. He thought he might have heard the sounds of a struggle below, but he wasn't sure. His heart leaped in his chest, and his hands glistened with sweat. Could Wang be sleeping on the cot in the other room? Or simply not there? Growing more comfortable, Robert straightened up and stepped into the room, his gun held before him. A swift chop to his wrist sent his Beretta clattering to the floor. He rushed into the room, swinging his left fist into Wang's face, landing a solid blow. Wang dropped his pistol, and it clanked at their feet, while he lurched back. Robert didn't see his own pistol, so he dived to grab Wang's, but Wang kicked it under his desk and aimed a hit at Robert's neck with his fist. Using his shoulder, Robert deflected it, then he stood and threw punches at Wang.

It worked for a couple of seconds.

Wang wheeled away from Robert and released a torrent of kicks and punches, sending Robert wobbling backward. Robert's wrist, chest, and head ached from the blows, slowing him down. Recalling his training sessions, he launched kicks and jabs. His long arms kept Wang's fists away, but not his feet.

The fire alarm blared through the warehouse. The sound startled them for less than a second. Their fight resumed.

Robert landed three punches with his long arms. Pop. Pop. Pop. Wang countered with roundhouse kicks to Robert's legs. A few landed, staggering Robert. Then Robert turned left and push-kicked with his right leg, knocking Wang back. Wang responded with a jump kick to Robert's chest. A spear of agony spiraled through his torso as he stumbled back. Then stepping closer, he sent a flurry of punches at Wang's head. Several landed. But Wang recovered and kicked Robert's left leg out from under him. Robert stumbled into a chair, then fell on his buttocks with a thud.

Wang jumped, poised to throw kicks and punches. Robert grabbed the legs of the chair and swung it at Wang's knees. Wang fell, slamming his shoulder into the floor. Both sprang up. Wang moved more cautiously now. They faced off, eyes locked on each other. The image of Fon's lifeless body in the alley slammed into Robert's brain. He inched forward with his fists up. How to attack Wang? Time was running out. Out of the corner of his eye, Robert saw two Siamese cats huddled near the filing cabinets, cowering. They both were emitting a low, guttural mew, more in fear than anger.

Wang attacked with confident kicks. First with the left, then the right leg. Robert countered with a solid right to Wang's head. Shaking his bruised knuckles, he stepped into Wang. Wang wheeled to face Robert. With his left hand, Robert landed a sharp jab to Wang's face, tottering him back. Recovering quickly, Wang leaped in, throwing a volley of punches and kicks. Robert crashed to the floor. Something hard gouged his back, sending stinging bolts along his spine.

Wang stood over him, grinning. Just then, they heard fireworks go off in the warehouse. One. Two. Three. Four. Five. Six. A second between each whoosh. Wang panicked, looking left and right, and Robert rolled over to get the gun under him. Fumbled it. Then grabbed it. Wang dived behind his desk, seizing his own gun.

Robert had his gun pointed at Wang. He heard Andrea's shout, muffled by the door.

"Ah, but Amonsak told me you have trouble pulling the trigger," Wang said as a sneer slashed across his face. He aimed at Robert.

And a shot rang out.

CHAPTER 30

When Andrea and Tao arrived at their arranged meeting point a mile from the warehouse, the sirens of the fire trucks ceased, and they knew the engines had arrived at the blazing building.

"Are you sure Robert ran out the back of the warehouse?" Andrea asked for the third time.

"It looked like him. It was dark and smoky," Tao replied, his voice muted with uncertainty.

They waited five minutes.

"We can't wait any longer. We've got to get out of this area."

They strode to a main road, hailed a taxi, and returned to their headquarters.

Andrea and Tao stood before Alex in his office. "Where's Robert?" Alex asked, looking back and forth between the two of them. "Wow. You guys stink of smoke and fireworks. No offense."

"None taken. We were hoping he'd be here," Andrea said, her face sagging.

"I thought I saw him leave before we did," Tao said. "He could have been chasing someone. I saw a tall person leaving. But it was hard to see with the flames and smoke." Andrea shook her head, hoping Robert had gotten out.

Alex dialed Robert's home phone number but got no answer.

"Damn." Alex looked at the agents standing wearily in front of him and said, "Our mission was a complete success; you destroyed the entire place. The fire department put the fire out so that it didn't spread—the adjacent warehouses only suffered minor smoke damage. They found a couple of charred bodies in the ashes." Alex took a breath and whispered, "Let's pray Robert wasn't one of them."

"Only two bodies?" Andrea asked, her voice lifting a register.

"Yes, why?"

"Tianhao and a guard were on the floor when we left. But what about Wang and Robert?"

"What are you saying, Andrea?" Alex asked.

"I gave Robert permission to get Wang. Tao's intelligence shows he is the key person pushing this additive—I thought it best to kill him. And Robert held him responsible for Fon and Sakchai's deaths."

Alex banged his fists on his desk. "You gave him permission to assassinate Wang? Didn't you think about how dangerous that would be?" With his nostrils flaring, Alex took a deep breath and collected himself. "Did you hear any gunfire?"

"No." Andrea shook her head.

"He had three minutes?"

"Yes." Andrea nodded.

"How's Robert been in the gym lately?"

"He's improved a lot, but I'm not sure how well he'd match up against an expert in kung fu."

"Great," Alex said with a mournful sigh, throwing himself back into his chair. "This sucks! That would be three agents we've lost in the last year." Alex phoned Robert's home again, even though it had only been a couple of minutes.

No answer. He slammed the phone down.

"I'll go check his apartment," Andrea said, walking to the door. "Maybe he hasn't been able to get to the phone."

"I hope he's OK," Tao said, almost to himself.

"Me too," Andrea said. Hearing a commotion in the hallway, she opened the door. Lamai was squealing with joy.

And there was Robert, reaching for the handle to come into Alex's office.

"Where have you been?" Andrea yelled at him. "We've been worried sick! You should have phoned!"

Alex jumped up from his chair, a large grin on his face. "Welcome back!"

Tao exhaled in relief and grabbed his head with both hands, then slipped them into a clasp and bowed deeply to Robert.

"My phone's out of order. I got here as fast as I could. But I had to take care of the cats."

"Cats?" Alex asked. Andrea looked at Robert, her forehead scrunched into a scowl of disbelief. Tao smiled like a Buddha as he straightened up, confident the cats were a reincarnation of someone.

Robert walked into the room. "Yes, the cats. Wang had two Siamese cats. They were very upset when I…uh, what is it you say, Andrea? Dispatch? Yes, when I dispatched him."

"Cats?" Alex asked, still showing bewilderment. "We're worried sick about you, and you couldn't get to a phone booth?"

"I couldn't leave them, could I? They were terrified. I opened their pet boxes. They jumped in. At the front door, the guard was still alive. The other man didn't have a face. It looked like Tianhao." Robert looked at Andrea, querying her. She nodded. "I put the cats outside. I dragged the guard through the door. Wow, that felt good. Fresh air. I barely made it out in time," Robert continued, the words tumbling out. "I heard the fire engines. I walked away."

Alex let out a long breath. Still perplexed, Andrea regarded Robert, her mouth slightly open. Tao grinned broadly.

"It's a male and a female. They've both been neutered," he added, apropos of nothing. Andrea thought he might be in shock.

"I had to buy them some food. A bed. A cat box. They need a home. They've been stressed."

"And what about you?" Andrea asked, baffled.

"I'm OK. The cats helped. They kept my mind off the killing. I really wanted to get rid of Wang. His thugs murdered Fon and Sakchai. Neither deserved to die." Robert's head nodded in thought. He looked into the distance, unseeing.

"We nearly died of worry," Alex began again. "Oh, never mind. It's good you're safe, Robert." Alex crossed the room to where Robert stood and shook his hand. "That was a job well done. Congratulations."

"Thank you. Tao and Andrea set the fire. I just eliminated Wang. He might have escaped. I couldn't let that happen," Robert said, his unseeing gaze still on the window.

"Here, come on in," Alex said, putting his arm around Robert's back and ushering him into the middle of the room. He stood before his three agents. "You performed magnificently. A totally successful mission. You destroyed a large shipment of heroin and that additive, killed Wang, put some bad guys out of commission, and torched some of the Dragon's infrastructure. I couldn't be more pleased with the three of you. I'll see what I can do in the way of compensation and perhaps even promotions. Thank you. Thank you. Thank you! Now, for a drink. I know I need one."

Andrea wondered if he was also thinking about a promotion for himself. Burning this quantity of drugs had to be close to a record.

Alex went to his cabinet, took out four glasses, and poured three whiskeys. He handed two drinks to Andrea and Robert and asked Tao if he was a teetotaler, like his brother. Tao shook his head, and Alex gave him a whiskey, then poured one for himself.

"Here's to a job well done!" Alex toasted, and he lifted his glass and drained it. The other three took a swallow, and the tension drained from their faces. Alex turned to pour himself another drink. Facing his bar, he murmured in a barely audible voice, "My guy saves the cats. Crazy!"

"Thanks, Alex," Andrea said, finishing her drink and preparing to go. "Robert, I'd like to see you in my office. Tao, you can take the rest of the day off—what little there is left of it." Robert walked into Andrea's office and turned toward her. Andrea closed the door and in two strides had her face right in front of Robert.

"I was scared shitless about you!"

"I got to the rendezvous point as fast as I could," Robert said in a monotone. "But I was exhausted from fighting Wang. No one was there. So, I went home to get the cats settled."

Andrea sat on her desk, her hands grabbing the edge, her anger deflated by Robert's fatigue. He rubbed his face, massaging the soft parts of it.

"You know, your job's done here now. This was the mission they sent you here for—the big shipment with its frigging additive. I expect Alex will let you leave in a week or so. You just need to do some paperwork, get a ticket, and fly home. I hate to admit it, but I'll miss you. If you ever want to return to the field, let me know. I'd be happy to work with you again."

"Thanks," Robert mumbled. "I enjoyed working with you. I'll keep your offer in mind. Now, I want some rest."

"Return to your cozy apartment?"

"Yes, I like it."

"Hmm. Will you come to Bangkok to visit us?" Andrea asked, musing.

"Probably not. Will you come to DC to visit me?" Robert responded, still looking dazed.

"Definitely not. But if I'm in the area, I'll look you up."

"Do that."

"OK. Well, I've got a couple of things to tidy up, so you can go now."

"OK. Thanks," Robert said, and he turned and tottered out without looking back.

Andrea continued to sit on her desk, drumming her fingers on the side of it, watching the closed door for any sign of movement. Then she turned and banged her fists down on the top of her blotter.

CHAPTER 31

Before his going-away dinner, Robert visited Sam one last time. Instead of buying street food, Robert took him to a restaurant.

Sam's eyes widened when he saw the prices on the menu. "You can get this for one-quarter the price on the street," he exclaimed.

"Yes, but you deserve a treat, and I can afford it."

"Thanks. You were helpful. We got away from those goons in the alley." Sam paused, looking thoughtful. "Maybe my math skills are better." He shrugged.

"I disagree."

"Oh?" Sam said, challenging Robert with his chin.

"Not just 'maybe.' You calculated accurately the cost of a curry here versus on the street."

"Yes. You helped about this much in math." Sam held up his index finger and thumb, pressed tight together. They both laughed.

Robert leaned back into the booth. As usual, the restaurant was busy. Sam had set the menu down and was squiggling in his seat. Robert leaned forward to encourage him to speak.

"I'm leaving the Orson center next month. It's time. I'm fifteen now. I'll go back to my school and help Mom with the store."

"Are you sure you wouldn't like to stay longer? I'm sure they'd let you, if you wanted."

"No, it's boring, and I want to live with my mom. I wasn't going to attend the AA meetings, but they convinced me I could help others, so I'll do that."

"Good for you." Robert could see that Sam was determined and confident. "I have a present for your birthday. It's a year of Muay Thai training at this boxing school." Robert shoved a brochure across the table with a receipt stapled to it. "We'll go by after we finish eating so I can introduce you."

Sam stared at the brochure, wide eyed, then up at Robert. "Cool. Thanks!" He beamed.

Sam looked at the brochure, turned pages, glanced up at Robert, turned more pages, and looked again. He was suddenly shy. Robert figured Sam rarely got gifts.

"I'm not much for writing, but I like Thailand, and I'll come back a year from now and see how you're doing. Would you like that?" Robert was thinking he could buy another year of lessons if Sam was still enjoying it.

"Oh, yeah! That would be great!"

"Good. Remember to give the Orson Group your address and contact info if you move, OK?"

"I will. But we won't move."

Sam was like a kid again, no longer putting on his mature front. Robert smiled. When they said their goodbyes at the martial arts studio, Sam bowed deeply, and Robert acknowledged it with the *wai* a teacher would give to his favorite student.

"What the hell is this?" Andrea asked as she stormed into Alex's office with a stapled report held aloft. She shook it at Alex and flung it onto his desk. "That's the lamest request for backup I've ever seen. It almost screams, 'Don't send any help!' What were you thinking? Oh yes, and congratulations on your promotion. These things couldn't be related, could they?"

"Why were you reading this?" Alex said as he gingerly picked up the document, opened a drawer, and put it inside.

"Hiding it again from us, are you?"

"No. Just putting it away for safekeeping. How'd you hear about it?"

"Lamai mentioned to me she thought it was oddly worded. She didn't understand it. So, I requested to see it."

"Yes, I may not have been as forceful as I could have been in the requisition. But I had total faith in my team. And that was prescient. The mission was completely effective. We did everything we set out to do."

"I love your royal 'we,'" Andrea said, striving to make her words impale Alex, as she paced in front of his desk, her eyes fixed on his face.

"I kept Pravat away from your raid and delayed the police at the other warehouse. And since the three of you escaped unharmed, I must have impeded them enough."

"You almost got us killed! And by the way, *you* were never in danger."

"You all returned to base without injury. Robert even had time to save two cats." Alex rose to face Andrea. "You three did a magnificent job. An immense service to your country by reducing the supply of drugs into the US, saving many lives. You should be proud of your accomplishment."

Andrea continued to pace in front of his desk, while Alex stood grim-faced behind it, unyielding.

"I've put in a request for you to replace me. My family and I will be returning to Washington in a couple of months. I have every expectation that the DEA will approve your promotion. You have always been an outstanding agent and an inspiring leader."

Andrea continued to stride back and forth, then stopped. She sneered at Alex, turned, and strode out the door, leaving it open behind her.

"See you at the dinner tonight!" Alex called after her.

Andrea stepped into her office, where she found Robert fiddling at her computer terminal.

"What are you doing?" she asked, still cross from her encounter with Alex.

"I've just sent you a note on this university messaging system. We're set up now to communicate with each other without sending letters. Wild, huh?"

"I don't like writing."

"I know. That's why I set up this method for you. Here, I'll show you." He explained the system to her, and they exchanged messages as a test.

"Pretty neat, huh? We can stay in touch without mailing letters."

"OK," Andrea said, doubting that it would work once Robert was on the other side of the world. She saw Robert's deflation after he failed to impress her with his new software trick, but she didn't care. She was still fuming about Alex's treachery.

"I'll pick you up tonight at your apartment at 6:30. Be ready."

Robert was tying his tie when Andrea pulled up to his apartment block and honked the horn. He then heard her signal through his open window with an ear-piercing finger whistle. Robert poked his head out and shouted, "Down in a second!" Then he stuck his head out again, leaning far out to get a better view of Andrea. She was now perched against the car, tapping her foot, her arms folded across her chest, surveying her surroundings.

She was wearing a dress.

Robert shook his head, wondering if he was hallucinating. Then he pulled himself back into his flat and petted his cats goodbye. They ignored him. Both were eating the food he had just given them.

"Whoa!" Robert said as he emerged from his building. "Who do we have here? You are looking absolutely fantastic this evening, Ms. Cannon. To what do we owe this honor?" Andrea was wearing a black cotton sheath dress with a single shoulder strap slashing across her chest, the other shoulder bare. She accompanied this with black pumps, a pair of drip pearl earrings, a matching necklace, and a black leather clutch bag with a gold clasp. A stylist had tamed her hair into a choppy pixie cut. No makeup.

"It's your going-away dinner, Agent Jordan," Andrea said in a clipped tone as Robert bussed her on each cheek, Parisian-style, while lightly touching her hips. He smelled her perfume. Jasmine. The same as Fon's. She couldn't have known. Robert's stomach clenched as he told himself simply to enjoy the fragrance.

Andrea opened the door for him. Robert nodded his thanks and climbed in. She walked to the other side of the car, fired up the engine, and pulled away from the curb, wheels squealing. Robert buckled up, held one hand on the dashboard, and braced his legs against the floorboard. He didn't chat during the ride, for fear of distracting Andrea from her driving. They arrived at the restaurant— the fancy one at the Royal Mandarin—in record time.

While they waited for the others to arrive, Robert got the distinct feeling people were looking at them and wondering why Andrea was with a disheveled guy in a tweed jacket and wrinkled slacks. Robert couldn't understand the concept of ironing clothes—it took time, and the garments didn't get any cleaner. What was the point? Standing next to her, even his tie seemed tawdry, a greenish affair with dancing elephants he'd bought at the Jim Thompson House. His face flushed. Maybe this was why people pressed their clothes? Andrea was the picture of serenity.

Soon, Tao, Lamai, and Alex arrived, and they sat down at their table, much to Robert's relief.

"Here's to Robert," Alex said, offering a toast after the server had poured their wine. "Thank you for your support over the past several months. We couldn't have done it without you."

"You're welcome. Thanks for teaching me everything I know about operational work. I couldn't have worked with a better team or for a better senior officer." Robert looked Alex in the eye, then Andrea, then Tao, and finally Lamai. Everyone lifted their glasses a second time and took a sip.

They had a booth in the far corner of the restaurant. Two small floral arrangements—red carnations—livened the center of the table. Tao and Lamai examined the table settings with great interest. For them, being at an international hotel restaurant was an exceptional evening out.

"What are you going to do with the cats?" Tao asked.

"I'm taking them with me. Alex expedited the proper permits for me through the embassy," Robert answered. He was still getting used to the idea of returning to the US. What would it be like? Who would he be?

"It was the least I could do," Alex said.

"What's the first thing you'll do when you get back to the US?" Lamai asked.

"After I get my cats settled, I'll hook up with my friend Jermaine." Robert knew that seeing his best friend would be the highlight of his return. But he also realized his feline friends would facilitate his re-adjustment to living in DC. Taking care of them would shift his focus away from his darker days in Bangkok.

"Did you always have cats?" Lamai asked.

"When I was a kid, we did—a series of Siamese coincidentally— but I haven't had one since I left home for college."

"Children next?" Andrea asked, arching her eyebrow. Robert scowled at her, shaking his head.

"How are Amonsak and Pravat faring?" Robert asked after looking around to make sure no one was within earshot.

"They took credit for the warehouse fire, of course, and basked in the glory of their successful operation. But I doubt if they're thrilled with the outcome. A lot of potential 'revenue' went up in smoke." Alex chuckled.

Their food arrived family-style. The air burst with the smell of curried shrimp, spiced beef, basil, cilantro, and ginger. A plate of drunken noodles, one of Robert's favorite Thai dishes, landed in front of him. The servers placed in the center of the table a multicolored salad of carrots, red cabbage, green mango, onions, sweet green and red peppers matched by green and red chilis. They shared everything and feasted while they chatted.

"How are the Scorpions and the Dragons getting along, Tao?" Alex asked while serving himself a generous portion of red chili curry on rice.

"There appears to be an unspoken truce between them. No one wants a turf war, especially when their coffers need refilling. The Dragons already have a new kingpin—Wang's son, Arthit. He was running their supply operations in Chiang Mai, so I am familiar with him. He is much like his father, ruthless and efficient. The good news, if you can call it that, is the Dragon's heroin no longer contains an additive. The Dragon's US connection banned it. Also, I heard Dr. Golovanov is looking for a job with the Scorpions, but so far, they don't want him."

"Only the faces change, not the operations," Alex said. "I'm glad to leave it in your capable hands, Andrea. I don't expect anything to get easier."

"It would be easier if Robert stuck around," Andrea said, putting a green chili in her mouth and munching it—without batting an eye.

"Nope. Not going to happen. I've had enough adventure to last me a lifetime. I'm looking forward to getting back to doing research. It's a tad bit safer than your work here."

"Pity. You're a natural field agent," Andrea said, causing Robert to choke on the water he was sipping. After a few coughs, he recovered.

"Natural agent. That's rich. I like that. You weren't so impressed with me in the gym when I first arrived." Robert scooped up some drunken noodles and beef.

"You grew into the role." Andrea beamed at Robert, a smile of abundant pride.

The banter continued. Robert, weary after the long evening, looked forward to returning to the US. He counted himself as extremely lucky to have survived the five clandestine missions, only two of which were successful. He didn't want to stay and take more chances. Before they finished eating, he silently lifted his glass in remembrance of his brother. *Best I could do, Russ.*

Andrea drove him home. They were mostly quiet in the car, which—for once—Andrea drove within the speed limit and without rapid lane changes. At his apartment block, Andrea leaned across the compact car and opened the door for Robert. He caught another whiff of her scent, bittersweet to him, as she punched him, urging him to get out. "Take care of yourself, Andrea." He gave her a kiss on the cheek.

"Ugh. What was that for?" She said, rubbing off the wetness.

"I always give my sister a peck when I say goodbye," Robert said, puzzled by her reaction.

"Of course you do," Andrea said, her voice suddenly thick. She nodded once as her hand leaped over to squeeze, then pat his thigh. She stared straight ahead.

"I'll send you a message when I get home."

Another nod.

"You'll stay in touch?" Robert asked. Was that a welling of tears in her eyes?

Andrea continued to gaze over the steering wheel. She gave a final nod and, without looking at Robert, shoved him out the door.

Robert climbed out, closed the door, and leaned over to wave farewell. Andrea's hand shot up and waggled. Then she used it to put the car in gear. She eased out from the curb and drove away, never looking back.

CHAPTER 32

Thomas's plane arrived on time, and he grinned when he saw Jermaine at the airport. He had two bags and the cat carriers—an awkward combination for one person to lug.

On first meeting, they hugged—a long one with slaps on their backs. Afterward, Jermaine held Thomas at arm's length, patted his shoulders, and said, "Dude, you feel much stronger than when I last saw you!"

"Thanks. I've had lots of physical training since leaving DC. And I'm not bad at Muay Thai now." Thomas smiled, allowing himself some satisfaction.

Thomas took his baggage, while Jermaine toted the cats. Now that he was back in the US, Thomas repeated a simple mantra to himself. *Thomas, Thomas, Thomas. Not Robert. Thomas, Thomas, Thomas.* It reduced the shock when people addressed him by his first name.

"When did you get the kittens?" Jermaine asked, baffled, as they struggled to exit Dulles International.

"Just before I left. They're full grown," Thomas said as they neared the taxi stand.

"That's nice. But where will you put them?"

"They're indoor cats. I'll get a litter box and food. They like to sleep separately, so I'll get a basket for each of them," Thomas said.

"How did it go in Thailand?"

"Everything was fine. There were a few hairy times, but nothing I want to talk about."

Jermaine looked at Thomas and nodded.

"It was tough, huh?"

"Yeah. Much worse than I expected, but I survived, and that's all that matters for now. It's great to see you." Thomas looked over at his friend and grinned.

Thomas, delighted to be home and back on familiar turf, radiated optimism about everything. *I survived!*

At the apartment, Thomas set his suitcases down to unpack later. He fussed over his cats and let them explore their new surroundings. Satisfied they were settling in, he left to pick up their accoutrements at the local pet store.

He named them Fon and Sakchai. Weird. He knew that. But he liked to think their spirits were still with him. It comforted him.

After taking a cab back to his apartment, he familiarized his pets with their new possessions. While he spooned the kibble into their cat bowls, Fon and Sakchai wrestled on the kitchen floor.

Before going to his desk on Monday, Thomas met with Stan to debrief in their usual interview room. Thomas shook Stan's hand and looked him in the eye before sitting down. Stan's eyes stayed focused on the wall behind Thomas.

"I've heard only great things about your work in Bangkok," Stan said, still looking beyond him.

"I survived. No help from *you*." Thomas discharged the words like bullets. Stan bobbed his head, his mouth ajar, his gaze now directed at Thomas's hairline. "You could have told me how dangerous this mission would be!" He flung the words at Stan.

"Alex Butler gave you a fabulous commendation and recommended you get a bonus for your work. He termed your performance there 'outstanding.'" Stan kept nodding his head and folding and unfolding his hands. He couldn't keep still. "My boss was extremely happy I hired you. They were desperate to get someone there to help. I got a nice pay raise this year, partially because of my recruitment skills."

"That's because you're an outstanding HR person," Thomas said, laying on the sarcasm as thick as he could, knowing it would elude Stan.

"Thank you. I appreciate that," Stan said, continuing to jiggle.

Thomas softened. Stan was only doing his job. A rather shitty job of coloring the truth to recruit agents who would put their lives on the line. But Thomas acknowledged he had gained much—and lost much. "And I appreciate you giving me the opportunity to go to Bangkok and experience a different line of work."

Stan sensed the change in mood. He sat more erect, stopped fidgeting, and cracked a smile. "You do? Good. We in HR always strive to do our best to please."

"Sure. I know."

"I'm recruiting for two full-time positions in Bangkok. Ms. Cannon will replace Alex as head of the unit, creating an opening, and I still haven't filled Colson's position. Andrea said she would be thrilled if you came to work for her. Any interest?"

"Sorry, Stan. I can't help you this time."

"No? But you'll keep the offer in mind?"

"Sure, Stan. You'll be the first to know."

At work, Thomas found his cubicle much the same as he had left it. He went around the office greeting everyone, spending some time with each of his colleagues. They welcomed him back with enthusiasm—the work had not diminished while he'd been away.

He presented himself first to Theo, his boss. His manager shook Thomas's hand for a full minute, a wide grin on his face. He told Thomas it was good to have him back—three times—while pumping his arm up and down. Finally, he ordered Thomas to get back to work.

Bryce greeted him especially warmly, making Thomas wonder how he'd been getting along with Wade. But Bryce made no complaints. As promised, he had a gift waiting for Thomas—a bottle of single malt whiskey. Thomas thanked him and then retrieved a couple of paper cups from the coffee room so they could taste it. They stood up and surveyed their cubicle area for any visitors before Thomas poured a small shot into each cup and they toasted his return to DC. They marveled at the smooth, smoky flavor. Thomas then stuffed the bottle into his backpack for later consumption.

Jane was subdued when she explained to Thomas that Wade had been getting Bryce to help him while he was in Thailand. They agreed that they would have to put a stop to it and, if needed, tell their boss they were tired of fixing Wade's reports.

Of course, Wade had other plans.

"I was really hoping you could help me with my Czechoslovakia report," Wade said. "It's a bit late, and you have a fabulous way with words."

"No. I can't help you, and don't bother Bryce about it, either," Thomas snapped.

Wade leaned close and kept his voice low so Bryce wouldn't hear. "Bryce has been very helpful to me while you were away, but his writing skills aren't nearly as good as yours."

"No, I won't help you. And don't bother Bryce anymore…or…" Thomas said, his voice growing hard, without looking at Wade.

"Or what?" Wade asked, confused.

Thomas stood and faced Wade, leaning in. The images of the deaths he had seen in the past six months flashed before his eyes like one of those motion-picture flip books. The last frame was Wang's face with a look of fading disbelief as his gun slipped from his hand and the blood poured out of his chest.

Thomas continued to glare, tilting his head closer to Wade's.

Wade paled and stepped back. He looked at Thomas, taking in his stance and his muscular physique under his button-down shirt. "OK," he said, turning and scrambling back to his cubicle, his hand waving a shaky goodbye from his hip.

On Tuesday, Thomas showed up at the Thai language class unannounced. The teacher clapped at his appearance and gave him a *wai*, which he returned. Jermaine slapped him on the back, and the other class members nodded their welcome.

After class, Jermaine and he retired to their favorite pub, ordered beers, and settled into their booth at the back.

Thomas lifted his glass to Jermaine and tilted his chin up. "Cheers."

"Cheers, my friend. It's good to have you home."

"Thanks. How's everything for you?"

"Great. I met someone. She's a computer programmer in Treasury."

"Cool! Congratulations!" And they clinked glasses. But then Thomas remembered Fon, and he choked on his next sip of beer.

"You OK?"

"Yeah, I'll be all right. I met someone in Bangkok, but she died saving my life." His throat was so thick he could barely say the words.

They were quiet for a time.

Then they switched to sports. After losing their first two games, the Redskins had a decent season.

As he finished his pale ale, Thomas asked about Jermaine's friend Chloe.

"As a matter of fact, she's available. She had a brief fling with someone, but it didn't work out. Are you interested in meeting her?"

"Yes," Thomas said, nodding.

Thomas exited his Metro stop and stepped around a couple of homeless people. Were they the same ones from last summer before he left for Thailand? He couldn't tell. One of them, sprawled out against a cement wall, had a needle near his arm. Thomas couldn't see any movement; his stomach tensed, and he held his breath. My problem? Not my problem? He got closer to see if the man was alive. He was. Thomas released the air he'd been holding in. When he got to his apartment, he phoned the social services agency and watched from the window as they came to gather up the guy who still hadn't moved.

Were his efforts worthwhile? He'd gone to Thailand to help stop the flow of drugs into the US, but not much had changed. Reagan had tightened the drug laws during the past year, even on cannabis, and his wife, Nancy, continued to tell everyone to "Just Say No." Fat lot of good that would do. They had finally identified the additive as fentanyl, whatever that was. Something lethal. He'd phoned the DEA in New Orleans, and they told him the supply of Bangkok Dragon had dried up. No one had seen it for weeks. Maybe with Wang out of the way, the Russian mafia against it, and the supplies disrupted, fentanyl wouldn't come back to the US for a while? They'd only know when it returned.

His cats wolfed down their food. After it disappeared, they became playful, batting each other and racing around the kitchen. Then, Sakchai chased Fon into the bedroom, leaving Thomas alone. He made dinner. A TV dinner. He didn't feel like shopping for food. Or dining alone at a café. Mostly, he felt nothing. Just drained. He found a bottle of wine in the pantry, opened it, and poured himself a glass.

Thomas filled the next few months mostly with work, Sakchai and Fon, and beer-fueled meals with Jermaine after the Thai classes. But he had new pursuits compared to his old DC routine. After Jermaine introduced him to Chloe, they went on double dates with Jermaine and his girlfriend. He also resumed his Thai boxing lessons at a local gym.

He sent messages to Andrea through the messaging application he had set up. She surprised him by replying to all of them. She said little, but it was nice to hear from her, and she reiterated he could work for her if he wanted.

One night, Sakchai woke Thomas with a loud, guttural meow. The cat was standing near his bed. Thomas buried his head in the pillow. Then, he rolled away and pulled the covers over his head, but Sakchai persisted. Still groggy, Thomas leaned over to see why he was making such a commotion.

The feline had killed a mouse and neatly displayed it on the floor in front of him.

Thomas congratulated Sakchai and praised him, stroking him repeatedly as he spoke. Then he picked up the small carcass by the tail and held it away from his body until he could put it in a plastic bag and dump it in the trash. He washed his hands, gave Sakchai a couple of cat treats and then one to Fon, who appeared as soon as she smelled the special morsels.

For now, Thomas was enjoying the monotony of his daily schedule, but he knew something was missing. His mind flooded with images of Bangkok: Andrea's crazy driving, his Muay Thai training, the team's exploits in attacking gangsters and destroying drugs, his accurate shooting and effective fighting in deadly alleys, and the look on Wang's face as life slipped from his body.

It was then that Thomas realized he had become Robert.

Acknowledgements

I am enormously grateful to Tembisa Aborn, Sandra Herner, and Alison Imbriaco for their editorial support. Without their help, *Chasing the Bangkok Dragon* would be a shadow of its current state. Thank you also to Tembisa Aborn and Julia Conover, who helped improve early drafts of many of the chapters in this novel. Finally, thanks to my sister, Kay Payne, who provided numerous useful comments on the book's nearly final version. Any remaining errors in facts, editing, and proofreading remain the author's sole responsibility.

About the author

K. E. Karl's first book, *Our Man in Mbabane,* is a novel based on his years in Swaziland (1977-80) when he was a gunrunner supporting Nelson Mandela's African National Congress. His second book, *The Red Door and Other Stories,* is a collection of quirky, eclectic stories. His fiction has appeared in the *Pennsylvania Literary Journal, Lowestoft Chronicle,* the *Evening Street Review,* and the *Gumshoe Review.* He has lived and worked in Oregon, London, Mbabane, Philadelphia, Maputo, Bangkok, New York, and Zurich. See kekarl.com for more information. Karl currently lives in Philadelphia.

www.ingramcontent.com/pod-product-compliance
Lightning Source LLC
Chambersburg PA
CBHW021045310726
48969CB00006B/1813